P9-CEL-637

Walk the Wild with Me

Rachel Atwood

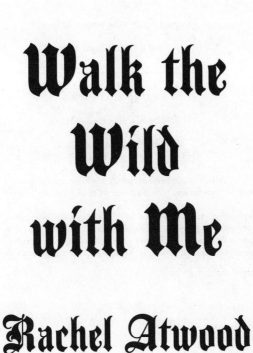

DAW BOOKS, INC.

DONALD A. WOLLHEIM FOUNDER

1745 Broadway, New York, NY 10019

ELIZABETH R. WOLLHEIM

SHEILA E. GILBERT

PUBLISHERS

www.dawbooks.com

Copyright © 2019 by Rachel Atwood.

All Rights Reserved.

Jacket design by Leo Nickolls.

Edited by Sheila E. Gilbert.

DAW Book Collectors No. 1841.

Published by DAW Books, Inc.
1745 Broadway, New York, NY 10019.

All characters and events in this book are fictitious.
Any resemblance to persons living or dead is strictly coincidental.

The scanning, uploading, and distribution of this book via the Internet or any other means without the permission of the publisher is illegal, and punishable by law. Please purchase only authorized electronic editions, and do not participate in or encourage the electronic piracy of copyrighted materials. Your support of the author's rights is appreciated.

First Printing, December 2019
1 2 3 4 5 6 7 8 9

DAW TRADEMARK REGISTERED
U.S. PAT. AND TM. OFF. AND FOREIGN COUNTRIES
—MARCA REGISTRADA
HECHO EN U.S.A.

PRINTED IN THE U.S.A.

*This book is dedicated to the original cast of
"The Adventures of Robin Hood" (1955-1960), who gave me
my first glorious introduction to the British folklore in its highly
romanticized form.*

Richard Greene: Robin

Alexander Gauge: Friar Tuck

Alan Wheatley: Sheriff of Nottingham

Paul Eddington: Will Scarlett

Bernadette O'Farrell: Maid Marian

Acknowledgments

here do I begin to acknowledge all the people who helped me write the book that has simmered in my lizard brain and sizzled in my blood since I first became aware that I wanted to write all the other stories in my head?

First off, much love and thanks have to go to my beloved husband Tim who wanders the wild with me and first introduced me to the wonder of camping. He also puts up with a lot of my fanciful meanderings in the mind where I carry on conversations in other worlds and times.

Then there is Big Brother Ed who introduced me to the struggle and the joy of archery. Under his guidance I actually hit the target. Once.

I can't forget my other brother Jim, the poli sci professor. When I asked his interpretation of the Magna Carta he told me to "Read the damn thing and form your own opinion." I did.

My beta readers, Leah, Joyce, Lizzy, Sara, Gregg, and Bob. But mostly to Sara for prodding me to write more in "my period," because I knew so much about it.

Over the years I have found and explored more books than I can count on British history and folklore. They have all contributed to this book. All through public school and college I have had wonderful teachers who encouraged me to find my own path of study as far away from the curriculum as I needed to go. And so I dug further and deeper into folklore and present to you characters of the wildwood in close to their original form.

Prologue

 "ime runs different 'neath the Faery Mound than it does here in Sherwood Forest." Little John whispered the words so softly they had little more sound than the soft rustling of leaves from a spring breeze. Beside him, the boy Tuck crouched, peering with him through the bushes at the low Faery Mound. In his youth and innocence, the boy could find wonder as he looked at the round hill isolated on a flat plain, the patterned stones around the base and the poisonous toadstools that marked it for what it was.

Deep despair ran through Little John as his body sought to return to its natural form, to be able to feel the solidity of a branched trunk, his toes becoming roots digging into the nourishing soil, and experience the air dancing among his leaves. It was times like this, so close to the old ways that he had difficulty holding his human form when his heart so longed to return to his tree, a three-hundred-year–old oak. A tree has patience, marking seasons but not years or decades.

"Aye," the boy replied. Only twelve and he had already experienced tragedy, disaster, and loss. The loss of his family to disease—one of the wasting fevers that periodically swept through a village—had led to his displacement from the forest to a human home. Even though his body, once only a shadow of his current self, thrived under the care he received in the Dominican monastery of Locksley Abbey, his soul sought more, driving him incessantly to seek the Wild Folk. He came by these needs honestly; his great-grandfather, Herne the Huntsman, cherished his mostly human offspring, teaching him the wisdom of the forest.

Little John rested a big hand on Tuck's head, not yet tonsured. He wondered briefly if any but the Wild Folk could see or feel the tiny horn buds beneath his thick bark-brown hair.

Tuck huddled in on himself, cradling the tiny silver cup hidden in the deep sleeves of his student robe. "I'm sorry," he whispered. "So, so sorry."

Little John heaved a sigh that ran all the way from the rootlets his toes wanted to dig deep, up to his mossy beard and hair.

"I love her, you know. Jane. My Jane," Little John said, as much to reassure himself as to inform the boy. "And she loves me, too. She was running away from her village to come to me. We are meant to be together."

The boy sniffed and nodded. He clenched his fist around the cup so fiercely that Little John feared he'd bend the metal that was the home of the gentle goddess Elena.

Little John felt her roll over and bask in the closeness between herself and the boy.

"But Elena's so new to me, I'm afraid if I let her go, she'll never come back."

Fear. Fear drove them all.

"Come, Tuck, the sun rises. The night of Midsummer has passed," Little John said sadly. "The portal to the Faery Mound will not open to us again for another fifty years when the moon phase of our time matches the moon of Faery on Midsummer Night's Eve. There is nothing we can do for poor Jane until then." He wiped away a tear. "She's not like the dryads who tempt me. Jane wants permanence. She wants only me. Not a mating and then stalking away to the next tree with pollen to spread."

Despite his soothing words, Little John's heart raged at the boy. He forced himself to remain calm and patient in demeanor. Elena was the key to opening that enchanted doorway. But now that she had found a companion to teach and share her wisdom with, she would only leave her cup upon the boy's request.

John could not ask him to free the goddess. He had to volunteer willingly. And the boy was afraid to be abandoned. Again.

"You and Robin Goodfellow should share a long tankard of beer," Tuck said, rousing from his shame that he'd let his fear govern his actions rather than the wisdom of the little goddess. "If you spend the next fifty years searching for the Cave Outside of Time where the Wizard of Locksley secreted the body of Robin's lady love, you won't hurt so much for your own lost sweetheart. That curse must be broken, and the dead wizard's spirit banished from the castle environs."

Little John snarled at the boy. He didn't want to share a drink with anyone. He wanted to crawl into his tree and sleep through the next fifty years.

Would his Jane notice the passage of years locked away beneath that hill? Fifty years at the beck and call of Queen Mab of the faeries would be vile. No one deserved that kind of enslavement. None of them. Especially not the girl he loved and had courted these many months. No dryad or water sprite or sylph tugged at his heart as did the sweet girl who sang as she gleaned nuts and berries from his forest. None of the others trusted him with their safety as Jane did. None of the others wanted to stay with him, talk to him, share their lives with him.

Next time, the goddess within the cup promised him, *I will make certain I am available when next you can free your lady love.*

One

ather Tuck threw back his cowl, baring his tonsured head to the morning breeze, and stretched
his legs into long, mile-eating strides. With
each new step he breathed deeply of the fresh
air. For a moment, he wished he'd worn his
wool shirt beneath his robe instead of spring linen. He'd huddled near the fire too often over the winter; he needed to
stretch all his senses again, including bringing fresh cool air
into his lungs instead of warm but stale interiors.

The sun peeked through thin clouds in a rare effort to
bring spring life to the land. He sniffed and found traces of
new greenery trying to burst forth on the roadside verge. The
equinox was not far away.

Very soon the landowners would direct their freeholders
and serfs to begin plowing.

In the meantime, he could escape the musty and crowded

Benedictine abbey near Locksley Downs, outside Nottingham. The abbot had been ill and dying for months, leaving Tuck to handle the details of keeping the abbey running and following the Order as laid down by their patron saint.

The twenty monks, three priests, and ten orphan boys demanded his attention continuously. He had grown weary of tiny details and confinement. Escape to the land was finally his to claim. Outlying villages needed him to say funeral masses for those who had died over the winter and perform marriages for couples who could not wait for spring to wed as their first child would pop out before then. Perhaps he could also share the joy of baptizing babies born a bit early. He loved performing that sacrament more than any other.

But he feared he'd have to send more spirits beyond the grave than welcome new souls into the Church. The winter had not been overly harsh, but outlaws roamed at will. If only King Richard would come home and set this kingdom in order before finding another war to fight on the continent.

A nearly forgotten sensation tickled the back of his neck.

"Elena?" he whispered. "I put you back into your niche decades ago, on the night before I took my novitiate vows."

You are needed in Withybeck. Now. One of ours is in peril.

And then his head grew numb as the little goddess withdrew.

Withybeck. The village had grown up beside the Withy, a stream barely big enough to be classified as a river. Its importance lay in the drop in elevation, marked by a half mile of rapids. A century ago an enterprising builder had erected a mill; the wheel turned the grinding stones by the force of the flowing water. Even in high summer when the water levels lessened, the wheel turned raw grain into flour.

Tuck turned his steps south by southwest, cutting across fallow fields and jumping creeks and downed trees with the agility of a much younger man.

One of our own. Elena meant a child of mixed-blood from human and forest creature. Not many such children had been born in the last forty years. Elena must be getting desperate to find one to carry her when the moons of human time and faery time aligned once more on Midsummer's Night Eve.

At the crossroad, he turned his steps due south. Shadows from overhanging trees made the way look forgotten and ill-used. But the green hump in the center of the narrow road showed signs of recent trampling by many heavy feet.

Within a few steps the stink of wet smoke gagged him.

He choked back tears of despair while panic pumped speed into his limbs.

The reek grew stronger. His eyes burned from the pall that overlay his path.

"Heavenly Father, bless those who are innocent victims of whatever tragedy has visited them," he murmured. He didn't have time to pull his prayer beads from his inside sleeve pocket, so he called up the image of his green glass beads with silver filigree decade pieces and ran the texture of them through his memory.

By the time he saw the remnants of burned thatch through the thinning trees, he feared the worst. Wattle-and-daub house walls leaned inward, doors sagging upon broken or burned leather hinges. Chickens, goats, and sheep lay senselessly slaughtered in random clusters upon the green. Mutilated bodies of men, women, and children sprawled in awkward attitudes of flight cut off by arrows and axes.

The odor of spilled blood grabbed at his throat.

He had to stop and clutch his knees as he dragged in tainted air to replenish his laboring lungs. Before he'd managed to control his ragged breathing, he crossed himself and spoke prayers for the dead by rote, his mind too paralyzed by the horror of the massacre to remember what he said.

"NO!" A primal scream ripped from his body, pulling all of his strength with it. His knees wobbled, and he dropped to the ground, not in prayer. Not in awe or gratitude.

You need to hurry!

In that moment a whimper of distress overcame the sound of his heart pounding in his ears. Such a faint sound. He wasn't certain it hadn't come from his own throat.

One of ours.

There! It came again. Not a moan of pain, but an anguished sob. He followed the sound to his left, the north end of the little village, away from the ransacked storehouse and the burned cottages.

Tuck crawled to the edge of the fouled well and used it as a brace to haul himself to his feet. His knees held, and his back uncramped. Stiff and uncertain, careful not to step on any of the dead bodies, he followed the sound.

"Mama!" A toddler's cry for the first person it could think of for help.

"I'm coming," Tuck said quietly, careful not to alarm the only survivor. "Easy, child. I'm coming."

A heap of rubble blocked the path out of the village. The sodden thatch smoked. An overhanging oak tree had kept the soaking winter rains from drying out the bundled sheaves. And so the roof had been saved.

"Mama!" the toddler insisted.

Tuck threw off the mat of the house wall, the crumbling clay held together by woven wicker, split and disintegrated where it landed. There, in a pocket of space beside the fire ring sat a naked child. Tear streaks amongst the smoke and dirt that smudged its face told a story of its own.

The dead body of a woman stretched out beside the child, one arm reaching toward him. An ax protruded from her back. Bone and blood and guts lay exposed along her spine.

"Oh, you poor baby," Tuck knelt beside the boy, heedless of the broken bits of house that tore at his thick woolen robe. Without giving the child a chance to shy away from a stranger, he gathered him into his arms, rose to his feet, and backed away. Instinctively, he rubbed the boy child's back as he pressed the sorrowful face against his shoulder.

His gut clenched in sorrow and wonder. Tuck clutched the boy, digging his fingers into soft flesh.

"There, there, baby. Let's get you some clothes, and food, and water."

"No baby. Nick!" the child insisted, pounding his fist into Tuck, then with a trembling chin he buried his face into Tuck's shoulder again. His back rippled in a convulsive sob. "Mama?"

"Nick you be, then." Tuck fished a bit of bread from the scrip at his waist.

The boy gnawed at it hungrily. "Mama." Nick reached back toward the crumbling remnants of his home. His big leaf-green eyes spilled tears.

"Your mama can't come, Nick." Tuck choked back his own tears. "You'll have to come with me now. I'll take care of you. You're safe with me." He stroked the filthy hair which might be blond, maybe light brown.

"Mama," the boy sobbed again, as if he understood. "Mama."

In the back of his head, Tuck heard a sigh of relief from Elena.

Anno Domini 1208, the ninth year of King John's reign. Spring.

"Nicholas Withybeck, where be you, you miserable good-for-nothing-blasphemous nameless orphan?" Father Blaine shouted along the cloister of Locksley Abbey.

Nick winced at the tirade. He wasn't nameless. He'd known his name was Nicholas when Father Tuck had brought him to the abbey. He'd been but three at the time, perhaps as old as four, but undersized. Cold, hungry, missing his mum and da, he'd known his name but little else. Abbot Mæson had blessed him with the surname Withybeck because that was the village where he'd been found, digging through the burned-out ruins of his home, looking for his dead parents and something to eat.

Later he learned that soldiers returning to their lord after besieging the castle of another lord had roamed free, looting and pillaging at will, because King Richard had stayed in France and did nothing to stop his barons from warring against each other.

Now King John ruled. He hired mercenaries from all over Europe to fight his wars, turning them loose without paying them, and they roamed throughout England looting and pillaging as well.

Nick was glad he had the stout walls of the monastery to retreat within when marauders were about.

Most of the boys in the dormitory had similar stories. But Nick was the only one Father Blaine pursued, expecting him to err with every step.

Maybe because Nick was the one most likely to find trouble—or create it.

Nick had to smile at that thought. He was just trying to make life interesting. The never-varying routine of the monastery was comforting. Predictable. Safe.

Stifling.

And boring beyond measure.

He pressed himself tightly against the interior wall of the roofed colonnade, keeping to the deepest shadows. *Almost there*, he reassured himself. *Another foot's length.*

Father Blaine's leather sandals slapped against the paving stones. He kept to the open garden at the center of the cloister, in full sun. He cast his own shadow rather than hiding within those cast by the building. Shadows hid things Father Blaine didn't know how to explain.

Nick's fingers touched wood. Keeping his movements as small as possible, so as not to disturb his cloaking shadow and thus attract attention, he fumbled with the iron latch on the door.

Just yesterday he'd oiled the latch and the leather hinges on this door that he wasn't supposed to know about. But then he knew he'd be in trouble today, or tomorrow at the latest, and wanted to ensure his escape.

Nick still didn't understand why Father Blaine, the youngest and most recently ordained of the priests, found Nick's little drawings in the illuminated manuscripts in the scriptorium so offensive. All he did was embellish the trailing vines and flowers he was supposed to draw in the margins of sacred texts. With a few flicks and squiggles, the greenery revealed the hidden faces of fantastical creatures.

Nick saw those faces within the greenery every time he went into the copse on the abbey grounds to gather acorns or shoo the chickens back to their coop. Occasionally, he trapped a rabbit or downed a grouse with his sling, but he always asked permission of the faces first.

Ah, there, the latch in the door behind him clicked softly. Nick paused half a moment to make sure Father Blaine hadn't heard the telltale sound of metal against metal. The young priest had made his way around the garden to the far side, next to the entrance to the boys' dormitory.

Before Nick could think better of his plan, he eased his

slender body into the musty darkness and closed the door behind him. Again, he waited for sounds of pursuit with his ear pressed against the thick wooden panels. Nothing. He doubted he'd hear Father Blaine even if he paced and shouted right in front of that door.

With one hand trailing the damp stone wall and the other in front of him, he moved down the lightless, narrow spiral staircase that began less than a full pace inside the door. Father Blaine—too new and uncertain of his authority and his powers as a priest to venture into the unknown—would never follow him here.

Nick counted thirty-three steps and shifted his balance to meet the stone floor of the landing. Then another thirty-three steps downward into the crypt. His senses told him he was beneath the Lady Chapel, behind the high altar of the abbey church.

He had to be more quiet than usual. Noise might filter up through the small spaces between building stones. Since the Holy Father, Innocent III, had imposed an interdict upon all of England, no Masses could be sung at the high altar, or anywhere. And all the senior clergy, including his own Abbot Mæson, had to leave England for Paris or Rome. So the three remaining priests, twenty brothers, and the dozen orphans who lived here knelt in the Lady Chapel to offer prayers. People from the village did, too. The place was rarely empty these days.

Nick held his breath as he struck flint to rock, a particularly hard one placed conveniently on the stairwell just for this purpose. A spark glowed against a rush light. It found food and flared to cast a golden glow. When Nick knew that the flames would continue, he turned and surveyed the small circular cavern lined with narrow shelves where remains of the dead rested. He lowered his gaze, not willing to converse with ancient skulls and bones crumbling to dust.

No new bodies resided here now. Two generations ago, the then-abbot had declared this place full and began burying the dead in a cemetery in a secluded courtyard outside the main abbey buildings.

He shifted his attention away from the dead toward the low altar pressed into a niche against the far wall. Elaborate figures carved into the stone marched in an orderly row just beneath the top lip. A scrolled column supported each corner.

Nick didn't think the founding monks of Locksley Abbey had made those carvings to honor their dead fellows and patrons. A scroll in the scriptorium he'd read hinted that the founders had chosen this place to build an abbey because locals had worshipped here for as long as anyone could remember. The altar was here when Romans bricked around it. The altar was here when the walls were built above it. The altar was here honoring the dead before the first abbot was laid to rest in his niche on the bottom left.

Nick sat on the single low step leading up to the altar. A bracket on his left accepted the rushlight. He let his fingers trail down the Roman brickwork. Old bricks. Older than the stone walls and floor. He found the imperfections in the mortar and picked at them nervously, waiting until he was ready to face Father Blaine and his punishment. He knew that hiding only enraged the priest more and made the punishment worse. But . . . he needed the peace of this place while he gained the strength to accept his due.

Pick, pick, pick. He worked at the old mortar, feeling a measure of satisfaction in each crumb he loosened.

Pick, pick, pick. The brick wiggled under his fingers. He looked more closely. The rushes had burned down to embers. Time to return to daylight and Father Blaine.

Wiggle, wiggle, shift. The brick dropped onto his palm.

He looked at it, wondering if it had a life of its own trapped into the baked clay. If the brick wanted out, then. . . ? But the brick was inanimate. Then. . . .

He peered into the blank spot behind where the brick had lain. Something glinted back at him. He moved the remains of the rushlight. Another glint. Something metal.

He reached in, felt around, and found something solid but not smooth. He pinched it between two fingers and carefully drew it outward. A protrusion caught on the side bricks. Then, with a scrape and another wiggle, it burst free.

Nick brought the object up to his eyes to examine it in the fading light. A tiny figure of a woman, she had braided hair wound around her head into a crown, and she was seemingly draped in graceful folds of cloth made from the same metal that formed her body. Her back rested against a cup along with two other identical figures. Between each woman the cup formed a pouring lip. And each of the three women held forth a tiny candle lantern. They glowed faintly when exposed to the dark of the crypt.

The cold metal warmed under his touch and seemed to mold to fit his hand perfectly.

The rushlight flickered ominously. But the tiny lanterns continued to glow.

Nick hastened to the staircase, reminding himself to bring new rushes next time he sought refuge here. Absently, he thrust the tiny cup into the pocket hidden within his deep sleeves so that he'd have both hands free to clasp the railing and balance against the curving wall.

All will be well, a voice that might have been his own, but wasn't, whispered into the back of his mind. His feet bounced up the stairs with new vigor.

Nick opened the door a crack and peered through. Father Blaine was nowhere in his narrow field of vision. No misshapen shadows—though they were a lot longer than when he went down to the crypt.

He opened the door a bit farther, holding his breath. Still nothing.

Cautiously, he stepped into the open cloister and looked around again. Father Blaine stood behind the door. But his eyes remained fixed on the door as if waiting for it to open.

Nick froze in place, his heart pounding loudly in his ears and near bursting from his chest. The priest remained motionless, eyes focused on the door but not noticing that it had moved. If he had noticed, his short temper would have pushed him to grasp the edges and rip the door open wide.

Continuing to hold his breath, Nick tiptoed in the opposite direction. And he didn't stop until he reached the refectory where the delicious smells of chicken broth, roasted turnips, and fresh baked bread enticed him. He released his pent-up breath and replaced it with another deep intake. He released that and continued to breathe normally as he picked his way through the long room filled with tables that stretched from end to end. Boys and novitiates sat on benches. Chairs on a dais were reserved for the abbot and priests. No one sat there tonight.

Abbot Mæson had fled into exile by royal decree. Father Blaine still searched for Nick outside. And Prefect Andrew presided over the cauldron of broth and greens for the abbey supper.

Nick bowed his head reverently and walked slowly to his place near the far end of the table farthest from the arched entry to the kitchen, with the youngest of the boys. Their food was always nearly cold by the time it got to them. He sat and clasped his hands before him, as did everyone else while they waited for someone to begin reading the lessons for the day.

A few benches away, Brother Theo from the scriptorium nodded briefly to Nick, acknowledging his lateness with a tiny curved smile.

Father Blaine burst into the refectory with a scowl on his face, searching right and left. When his gaze lighted upon Nick, he looked startled, amazed that the boy was where he was supposed to be, as if he hadn't been hiding for half the day.

Two

"**T**onight," Dominick whispered to Nick. He kept his auburn head bowed in an attitude of prayer.

"Huh?" Nick grunted, also keeping his head down. He risked lifting his eyes to survey the frowning visage of the novitiate who read the lessons for the evening.

"It has to be tonight. My sister will look for us at midnight."

"If anyone can figure out a way to rescue Hilde from that odious convent, it's Nick," Henry said.

Nick's stomach bounced nervously. "May Day is only a few days off. If we get caught . . ."

"We won't get caught." Dom's voice rose in agitation. "We can't afford to get caught. Hilde's depending upon us."

Across the long refectory, Prefect Andrew twitched his rod of discipline.

Nick knew from experience that another word and they'd all feel that shaft of hard polished oak across their knuckles.

"I'll cover for you," Henry whispered from the other side of Nick. "They think I'm slow and unthinking. I can divert and misdirect as well as you can."

Nick dug his elbow into Henry's ribs. "You'll do anything to get out of work."

Henry flashed him his big grin, pursing his mouth while he stared at the end of his nose rather than look him directly in the eye.

"You look stupid when you do that," Dom grunted.

"That's the idea," Henry admitted, returning his attention to his folded hands.

Nick hid his laughter behind his folded hands. "One of these days, the priests will figure out just how smart you really are and won't let you hide anymore."

Then their turn came for food. Each of the boys on their long bench grabbed their wooden bowls and filed toward the door to the kitchen where Prefect Andrew presided over a cauldron filled with broth and a few precious chunks of chicken meat and vegetables. Likely, the priest had made certain the ladle dug deep to capture those treasured mouthfuls. As the eldest among the boys, Nick, Dom, and Henry stood at the end of the line, the last of any to get their supper. The nine-year-old assisting Prefect Andrew lifted his half-full ladle and poured only a little of it into the bowl of the five-year-old directly in front of Nick.

The little boy's face screwed up, his mouth ready to loose a mournful wail.

Nick cleared his throat noisily.

Prefect Andrew scowled and nudged his helper. "You'll not steal more for yourself by shorting those in need," he said.

Reluctantly, the boy dipped the ladle again and this time filled the small boy's bowl almost to overflowing.

"Less fer you," he muttered as Nick presented his bowl.

"I don't think so." Prefect Andrew tapped his rod against the rim of the cauldron and handed Nick his half round of bread.

The boys continued their meal in silence.

"I'm still hungry," Nick complained quietly when he'd sopped up the last of his broth with the new bread.

"Not ours to claim," Dom replied. "Though I'd like a bit of cheese to take with us tonight. It's a long walk to visit my sister."

Dom watched as Prefect Andrew slid two poles through the handles of the soup cauldron.

Nick rose from his place and hurried to assist him with transporting it to the postern where the poorest of the poor from the village lined up for any leftover food.

"I thank you for your help, young Nicholas," Prefect Andrew said. "I'll see that you get an extra portion for it." The middle-aged priest tucked his rod of discipline in his belt rope and shouldered the poles. Nick took up the other end and crouched beneath them. Then he stood, easily taking the weight of the heavy iron pot. To his surprise, he stood tall enough to keep the burden level with the prefect's shoulders.

"When did I grow so tall?" he asked himself.

"Over the winter, boy. I had to find you a larger and

longer robe after the last snowstorm. Your sandals will need replacing by May Day. You're like a puppy. Your feet grow too big for your body, so you stumble over everything. Then you grow into them and are fine for a while."

"The line of petitioners looks longer than last time I brought out food," Nick mused.

"Sir Philip Marc has raised their taxes again. He purchased his office as Sheriff of Nottingham from the king. He figures the people need to reimburse him. If they've no coins, then he takes the taxes in whatever food they have left in their stores. They've nothing left to barter with the miller for flour and end up trading skills and services for an egg."

If Nick had a free hand, he'd cross himself. The villagers who lived closer to Nottingham than the abbey deserved every blessing they could beg for.

When the last of the petitioners had left the gate, barely a drop of broth remained. Nick looked askance at the emptiness at the same moment his stomach growled for more sustenance.

"Don't worry, my boy." Prefect Andrew chuckled and clapped a reassuring hand on Nick's shoulder. "I'll see that you get something more before you retire. A goodly chunk of cheese, I think. Big enough to share with your friends, who are also growing faster than the berry vines along the back wall."

Father Tuck suppressed a yawn as he waited within the branches of an apple tree in the orchard behind the abbey. A half-moon rose above the thin layers of clouds as the time approached

midnight. His boys should be returning to their beds after
Matins. A low glimmer of candlelight flickered, highlighting
the glorious reds and blues of the rose window behind the
altar of the Lady Chapel, turning the colored glass into brilliant jewels.

Silently, he recited the words of the Mass. The beauty of
the Latin words rolled across his mind, reminding him of why
he had chosen the regulated life of a priest over the freedom
of living with the Forest Folk.

Only now that King John warred with the Holy Father,
Tuck was back in the forest ministering to those whom the
Church had forgotten.

The branches of an adjacent tree bounced, the new leaves
rustling and stray, white flower petals drifting down.

He sat up straighter in the junction of a stout branch that
angled to the tree trunk. He could see the shadows of two
lithe young men scrambling from the wall of the herb garden
to an overhanging branch and down again on the other side
of the wall. He'd used that unofficial exit from the protection
of the abbey when he was the same age as Nick and Dom.
When he lived within those walls, he'd watched many boys
discover the same path to adventure.

But Nick was special and needed closer observation.

Once on the ground, the boys walked cautiously among
the apple trees, feeling their way toward the road that would
lead them north.

Tuck waited until they'd broken free of the orchard and
walked in the dim moonlight before descending from his
perch more slowly and with less agility than the boys. He

cursed his aging bones and dimming eyes. His forest blood might extend his life beyond normal humans, but he still aged.

"Did you hear that?" Nick whispered to his companion.

Tuck froze in place and cursed silently. He thought he'd forgotten most of those phrases that he'd learned at an early age while living wild. Of course, Nick heard him tiptoe through the lush grass. He had to have forest blood in him, or Elena would not have chosen the boy for rescue.

He also would have better night vision than his human friend.

"Just the wind in the trees," Dom replied. "We have to hurry if we want to be back by Lauds at dawn." He set a faster pace.

Tuck held back. He knew their destination and needn't fear losing them in the darkness. He'd walked to the Convent of Our Lady of Sorrows many times over the years as an itinerant priest.

"No, Dom. I'm sure we are being followed," Nick insisted.

"If Father Blaine is following us, he'd have cried out and stopped us before we left the orchard. It's just your imagination."

"But . . . there are still raiders and outlaws roaming the forest."

"Not this close to the city or the abbey. Now come on. We've only got a few hours to get there and back."

"There are as many hazards on the road as in the forest," Tuck reminded himself.

Tuck slid into the shadow of a tree and contemplated his options. He needed to follow the boys and find out the true situation at Sorrows. The sisters there wouldn't reveal much to him during the day. The orphans in their custody would reveal much, much more without knowing what he discerned.

Once he considered the boys out of earshot, he whistled the call of a common night bird.

"You don't need to shout," Little John growled in his ear. The big man emerged from the depths of the tree where Tuck paused.

"I need to reach the Convent of Our Lady of Sorrows before those boys. May I ask your assistance?"

"Of course." Little John bent and scooped up Tuck's much shorter and frailer body and settled him on a shoulder.

"They need to arrive and return safely. I'm no match for wild animals and wilder men."

Little John mumbled agreement. "Watch your head." They ducked beneath a thick branch and he started off with the long strides of one used to traversing vast distances within the space of a few hours.

Tuck clutched the big man's mossy hair tightly, feeling like a child again, carried by his father.

Hilde lay in her cot silently, listening to her friends breathe. The older girls had carried the youngest ones back to bed after Matins. They all slept now.

She watched the moon rise through the narrow slit of a window that looked east over the kitchen garden.

Soon, she told herself. Dom would be here soon. Maybe tonight he'd figure out a way to release her.

She flopped over onto her side, restless, but knowing safety lay in feigning sleep until Sister Marie Josef gave up waiting for her to slip from her bed. The tall, gaunt woman rarely slept.

At last, the quiet flap of sandals on the flagstone flooring ceased. The moon rose higher. An hour had passed since Hilde had returned to her bed. Sleep tugged her eyes closed. She drifted asleep—then woke with a start at the sound of a step on the gravel path that circled the walls of the convent.

Dom! Hilde's heart rejoiced that her twin had come at last, as he always came on the night of the waxing half-moon.

The flagstones burned her bare feet with cold. She gritted her teeth and endured the discomfort. No worse than Sister Marie Josef's rod across her knuckles or her backside. Sandals made noise.

At the door to the girls' dormitory she paused, listening. No sound, not even Sister Marie Josef's measured breathing. A quick look confirmed that the nun was not lying in wait for Hilde to break the rules.

She tiptoed to the back stairwell and descended blindly to the postern gate. Her feet found the dip in the stone stairs made by hundreds of feet over the years. Her hand glided along the perpetually damp wall. She paused again at the tiny landing and listened. Still no reaction to her movements.

Taking a deep breath, she lifted the stout crossbar and set it aside. The door swung outward freely. Then she ran across the open space between the building and the wall with the postern gate.

"Dom? Dom? Are you there?"

"Yes, Hilde. It's me."

"Oh, Dom, I am so happy to see you." She gripped the bars of the window to the outside world.

"I brought my friend Nick," Dom said. "I told you about him."

"Yes, Nick. He's the one who finds hiding places and hidden doors."

"Hello, Hilde," came a strange voice that cracked between words. "I don't see any locks on this door. What's on the other side?"

"No latch or lock here either," Hilde moaned.

"Why have a door if no one can open it?" Dom asked. He shook the window bars.

Nothing moved or rattled.

"I don't know," Nick said. He sounded thoughtful, almost as if he'd drifted away. But he couldn't move without crunching on some gravel. "This place is built like a fortress. The only way in is by the front gate. No overhanging trees to climb, no other way out unless . . . Are there any tunnels?"

"Where would I find a tunnel?" Hilde whispered, hope lighting blossoms inside her heart.

"You'll have to explore crypts and storerooms," Nick replied.

"I'm afraid." She turned her face away from the grille. "If only Da hadn't died, Mum would have kept us all together." The last words came out as a sigh.

Dom's fingers encircled hers where she gripped the iron bars across the viewing window. "Da was deaf. He knew how to get along with people when they took the time to face him directly and speak slowly. He could understand what they said. But the sheriff didn't know that."

"The sheriff didn't care!" Hilde's voice rose in volume. She'd relived that horrible day in her mind too often to find forgiveness. "He and his huntsmen ran Da down with their mighty horses as if he were no more than a squirrel. Da couldn't get out of the way because he didn't hear them coming!"

"We can't change that, Hilde," Dom said. "We have to make the best of our lives now. Mum found a new husband who was willing to take on the three little ones because they are young enough to apprentice with him as a cobbler. Mum had no choice but to send us to the abbey and the convent where we have food and shelter, and maybe a vocation."

"Mum doesn't know about the beatings and the missing meals for disobedience." Hilde couldn't help the hot bile in the back of her throat. Dom's life was easy compared to having Sister Marie Josef always looming over her with her stick. The nun took pleasure in wielding the stout oak branch indiscriminately.

"Hilde, close your eyes and feel along the door where you think a lock might be," Nick instructed her, breaking the flow of her regret and anger.

Reluctantly, she released Dom's warm fingers and slid her hands down the stout planks of the portal on each side. Something felt . . . odd. She tried again. "There, on my right, your left. There's an imperfection flush with the wood but . . . different from the wood."

"Is it metal?" Dom asked, excitement making his voice rise to match her own girlish tones.

"I can't tell. It's warm like the wood but smooth like metal."

"I feel it, too," Nick said. "But we can't see it. That means it's hidden by sorcery. Someone inside your convent really doesn't want anyone to enter or leave by this door."

Hilde's stomach clenched. "I think I know who." The back of her neck itched. She looked around for any shadow in the moonlight that might reveal a watcher.

"It's getting late," Nick said. "I think I know some scrolls I can consult. We'll be back next month and maybe then we can get you out."

"Promise?" Hilde asked, not liking the way her voice shook.

"Promise," Dom affirmed. He touched her fingers on the iron bars one more time, then backed away.

She waited until she no longer heard their footsteps, then waited a few heartbeats longer in case they turned back to say one more thing.

They didn't come back, so she trudged up to bed, not daring to hope that Nick would figure a way out of this . . . this prison.

Three

"as Elena chosen a new companion?" Little John asked Tuck. They crept toward the postern gate at Sorrows as soon as they knew Nick and Dom were out of sight and out of earshot. "Time grows short before the moon aligns with Faery and we can rescue my Jane." His heart ached that his lady love must endure slavery at the hands of the faeries.

"Elena has not told me if she has," Tuck replied. "I thought she'd choose Nick. He is of mixed-blood, and he is bright and adventuresome."

"So were you. Fifty years ago," Little John taunted. He ran his fingers along the stout wooden panels of the door in the wall. Good workmanship by a smith who knew his trade. Possibly one of his own sons who had chosen a life among humans rather than the Forest Folk. He concentrated his search on the left side where the children had looked for a lock.

"I do not like this talk of locks hidden by sorcery," Tuck

mumbled, ignoring Little John's statement. He used his own, more sensitive fingers to look for evidence of a lock.

Little John found it first. His senses were more attuned to the disruptions in the wood grain from the presence of a metal fixture. "It is here. A simple mechanism if you have a key and know how to find the lock."

"But, without a key, one would need sorcery to open it." Tuck crossed his arms and clamped his hands into his armpits, as if protecting them or applying pressure to ease an ache or a burn.

"Who would do such a thing? I thought sorcery was forbidden by your Church." Little John stepped back to inspect the entire wall surrounding the gate. Even he was not tall enough to climb the wall without assistance. No trees grew nearby to hang a branch over the top to aid someone in leaving or entering the convent. There were no chinks in the mortar either. The place looked impregnable. He could not help but harken back to the Faery Mound. It, too, had an unbreachable entrance protected by magic that only the goddess Elena could open.

"Sorcery is forbidden. But if someone merely willed the lock invisible without knowing what she was doing, then the act could be forgiven under the seal of confession."

"I ask again: Who?"

"I think I know, but I no longer have the influence or authority I once had. I cannot present myself and ask questions."

"Not as the Abbot Mæson in exile, no. But as Father Tuck the wandering priest ministering to those in need?" Little John looked at his friend. Tonight, he wore the long shirt and breeks of a common peasant. The long skirts of his heavy woolen robe, while giving warmth, would hinder his steps during a long trek through the forest at night.

"That is what I must try if I can get past the good sisters who are very wary of strangers, as they should be during these troubled times. I anxiously await the end of the war between King John and the Holy Father, Innocent, the third of that name."

"But that war has halted the influence of the Church on the daily lives of most people, noble and common. Without being told that the Forest Folk cannot exist, people can see us now, work with us. We can help each other through the long winters and protect each other when King John's mercenaries roam and pillage freely." Little John sighed. He had longed for a time when this could happen. In his father's lifetime, the old gods and goddesses and the Forest Folk had been free to roam and interact with mortals. Then the Church had become powerful enough to banish them to the darkest shadows of the forest—there, still alive, but unseen and ignored.

"The moon sets. We should return home and prepare for May Day. I will come back here during daylight, when the sisters are more likely to open their doors to me. Nick and Dom will not return here for another moon cycle to rescue the girl. I hope by then to be able to open that door, with or without Elena's magic."

"I heard that Father Blaine isn't going to let us go to the village tomorrow for May Day," Dom whispered to Nick as the novitiate reading the daily lessons raised his voice to emphasize, but not shout, dire warnings of the punishments in purgatory for errant boys.

Nick did not raise his head from his feigned meditation of his sins while he slurped thin gruel for breakfast. "Abbot Mæson always gave us a free day for May Day," Nick whispered. His voice rose high into childish tones on the last words. He swallowed deeply to relieve the dryness in his throat. Thankfully, his friends didn't notice.

"But the abbot isn't here. He fled to Rome when King John . . ." Henry said a bit too loudly.

"I heard Brother Theo arguing with Father Blaine about May Day," Dom continued. "Father Blaine said that since Abbot Mæson left without instructions, we need to follow the Rule of our Order. Isolation and prayer are our only approved activities. Then Brother Theo countered that we need to continue as if Abbot Mæson is still here until King John makes peace with the Holy Father and he's able to return to us."

"Brother Theo, of course. Sometimes I think he's the only one who understands what it means to be a boy," Henry said.

"Brother Theo isn't afraid of Father Blaine," Dom said. "He's only afraid of you, Nick." Dom jostled them with his elbow.

"Brother Theo isn't afraid of anyone," Nick scoffed. Though, he knew, ghosts and the faces of Wild Folk frightened the tall scholar, as thin as the rod he carried. He pointed out errors in copying and translation and occasionally rapped knuckles for inattention.

"He doesn't like you because you are too curious, always reading scrolls he thinks are dangerous or you are too young to understand. Why do you want to read all that stuff anyway?" Henry asked.

"I'd rather dig turnips or tend sheep than read," Dom admitted.

"We know the way out of the abbey," Nick said quietly. "We could go to the May Day celebrations on our own."

"And, of course, you know how to evade watchful eyes." Henry said, rolling his own eyes.

"How do you think I found the exit when I visit my sister? I followed you over the wall." He jabbed Nick with his elbow.

"But if we're caught?" Henry gasped.

"What can Father Blaine do to us that he hasn't already?" His friends didn't look convinced.

"Are we agreed?" Little John bellowed to all the Forest Folk gathered around him—including three of his sons, by three different dryads, who seemed interested in learning how to rule the forest. They did not need to see how short his temper grew. He needed more time in his tree to relearn patience.

The ancient standing stones surrounding them showed the patience of the ages. Little John didn't feel up to bonding with them or learning anything from their long silence. Stones didn't whisper into his dreams as trees did.

"Yes, m'lord," Herne the Huntsman replied, glaring defiantly at Ardenia, the water sprite.

"Agreed," Ardenia said, not willing to grant authority or dominance to anyone, even though the Green Man had always

ruled the forest. Verne, the youngest of the three sons, straightened his shoulders and peered closely at the faces of the dispu-
tants, looking for signs of deceit. Good boy.

"Agreed to what?" Little John demanded. He had no
sympathy for these two. They fought as often as they loved,
and his son had pointed him toward ways these two might try
to twist out of the agreement.

A pang in his heart reminded him that he'd had no lover
to fight with for nigh on fifty years. Dryads tended to mate
and drift away, never committing, rarely returning. Every
time he thought to make the time pass more swiftly by drows-
ing in his tree, these two, and all the others forced him to
wake up and deal with their petty issues. Even the stones did
not invite him to rest among them. They had their own
agenda that had little in sympathy for the short lives of those
who considered this ground sacred.

"I agree that I will not hunt the creatures of the wood who
come to Ardenia's spring to drink. That is a sacred place, a
healing place, sanctuary to all, second only in sanctity to these
stones. Even the humans come to the spring to pray, while the
stones remain secret from all who do not dwell within their
shadow. Ardenia, your pond is the center of the world, an
extension of these stones," Herne said formally and bowed to
both his lady love and Little John. His twelve-point antlers
brushed Ardenia's flowing gown, almost tearing the shimmering fabric that looked more waterfall than cloth.

"And I agree not to drown this disrespectful beast when he
hunts along the creek that flows from my sacred pool."

"Then you shall kiss and be at peace," Little John blessed their treaty. "The stones observe. As long as they stand, your treaty must last or forever live beyond their peace."

Herne tilted his head as Ardenia closed the distance between them. They kept their hands clenched at their sides as they brushed lips on each other's cheeks. Right and left. Then they formally bowed their heads to each other and to Little John.

This was the proper time to settle disputes. May Day, a time of bonding. Midsummer's Eve approached, as did the alignment of Little John's moon with the one that shone within the Faery Mound.

If only the ancients had granted him dominion over the faeries as well as the Wild Folk! The Faery Mound lay within the bounds of his forest, but outside his authority.

The faeries were a law unto themselves, ignoring the rest of the worlds within and without. Law to them was whatever they wanted that instant. Traditions and treaties meant nothing to them.

But soon. Soon he'd be able to rescue poor Jane, free her from enslavement to the faeries, and love her for an eternity.

"This be May Day," Father Tuck announced. "This be a time of joy, of courtship, and of bonding. Herne, kiss your lady as if you mean it!" he thundered.

Ardenia threw back her head, laughing and sounding much like the chuckle of a stream running free over a tumble of rocks. When she righted herself, Herne wrapped his arms around her and pulled her tight against his chest. He paused a moment, contemplating just how best to kiss her.

She took the decision away from him, placing his face between her palms and initiating a deep kiss that spoke of long familiarity. And they kissed and kissed, holding their embrace long past the time one of them must breathe.

"And so I bless this union once again." Tuck made the sign of the cross—crossroads coming together rather than the Roman instrument of torture the humans revered—in the air above them, then held up both hands, two fingers on each hand stood up straight above the two outer curled digits, and thumb tucked close against the palm in the universal sign of peace and blessing.

Little John noted, not for the first time, that the old man could not completely close his fist. The joint disease twisted his knuckles painfully. And he walked more hesitantly, favoring both knees. He had indeed aged as any human would. His horn buds had retreated when he took Church vows of obedience, chastity, and poverty, though they were still visible as dark spots on his skull to those who knew what to look for. He had not enough of the Huntsman's blood in him to fight off the inevitable aging and death. He'd already lived longer and disease-free than most of his human kin.

Then Herne, a different and younger Huntsman than Tuck's grandsire, scooped up his mate and carried her off to his hidden bower.

Satisfied that life continued on a balanced path, Little John led Tuck toward a small clearing where he knew they'd have at least an illusion of privacy.

"The time is coming when the moon aligns properly," he

whispered. "Have you heard from Elena? Will she be able to help open the door to Faery?"

"Yes. Elena chuckled a greeting to me only yesterday when I passed through the apple orchard. She chose the best time to be found. I believe we will observe the one who carries her later today at the village festival."

Four

ick roused at dawn out of long habit. Even though the bells no longer rang the changes of the day, his body knew that the sun crept toward the horizon. Time to put on his robe and sandals and trudge to the Lady Chapel for Lauds. Along with silencing the bells that ordered the day, the Holy Father had silenced the Mass.

Nick missed singing the plainsong Mass more than the bells.

Dom joined him and Henry in line to proceed into the chapel. The boy's eyes drooped with fatigue, black shadows encircled them, and he frowned.

"You did not sleep after we returned from Our Lady of Sorrows?" Nick whispered.

"My sister is not happy in her convent," Dom replied, his frown deepening. "How can I rest comfortably now that I know she is entrapped by sorcery?"

"I don't know how to help," Nick said, mind racing to find a new plan for opening that door or getting over the wall. "Sorcery is beyond my ken. I can read about it, but that won't give me a way to break the seal on the postern."

"First I have to find a place for her. Perhaps with the Woodwose?"

A stern look from Brother Theo silenced them both.

More than one drowsy boy fell asleep during the long silent meditation that replaced the joyous hymns to greet the day. Nick ran the Latin words through his head just to keep himself awake.

Within minutes of filing into the Lady Chapel and dropping to their knees, Henry breathed deeply, evenly. His head nodded. Nick had to shrug his shoulders high, twice, to dislodge Henry's head before he began snoring. Just then, Father Blaine stepped up behind the altar. Thin as a willow switch, the youngest of the priests—Abbot Mæson had hastened his ordination by two years to perform the sacrament mere hours before the interdict forbade such things—the young man cleared his throat and looked apologetically toward Prefect Andrew.

"Today is May Day. By long tradition, each of you has a free day to visit the village. We encourage you to mingle with the locals, get to know them so that you may minister to their needs when the time comes that we may do such things again. Return here by Compline."

"How're we supposed to know when it's Compline?" Dom whispered. He'd only come here a year ago and hadn't lived with the orderly routine long enough for it to become a part

of the natural rhythm of the day. "At home, the chickens ordered the day for us."

"Compline is sunset. You'll know to come home before
the sun dips to the horizon," Nick whispered back. His voice
started to waver into higher notes, but he closed his mouth
before it did.

Dom nodded. "Why can't they call it sunset?" he muttered
as the boys walked a little too eagerly toward the refectory
and their early breakfast of yesterday's bread, hard cheese, a
withered apple, and a pint of morning brew.

Barely satisfied, Nick and his chums folded their hands in
reverence as Father Blaine recited the final prayers of thanks-
giving for the meal. Then, as one, all the boys, novitiates,
monks, and priests pushed back their benches and stood.
Hands still clasped before them, they filed out in order of their
rank within the community.

The moment Nick stepped free of the refectory into the
cloister, he aimed his steps toward the exit to the courtyard
and outer buildings. He led all the boys, from the oldest—
himself and Dom—down to the newest entrants at the age of
six. Each step grew faster until Nick hit a good run through
the outermost gate set into the surrounding protective wall.

And then he was free. An entire day of freedom!

He walked rapidly, with long strides, over the arched stone
bridge spanning the wandering creek that fed the fishponds
and irrigated the orchards and gardens. A quick right turn put
him on the path that skirted the oak copse and stretched along
the sheep pasture to the miller's pond and spillway that turned
the waterwheel and thence the giant stones that crushed grain

into flour. A ford across the scattered stones of an ancient collapsed bridge put him on the same side of the river as the
monastery, but above the bog. The new bridge stretched before him, spanning both the creek and the water meadow on
the other side. The main road came from the north, leaving
the abbey mostly isolated to all but foot traffic. He crossed the
creek eagerly on the wider span meant for wagons, and into
the ring of thatched cottages partially encircled by the edge
of the Royal Forest.

The baker sang as he set out a table filled with mince pas-
ties, buns, and—best of all—honey tarts. Nick snatched a pas-
try filled with dried apples and walnuts. He paused to wipe a
drip of wild honey from the corner of his mouth, savoring all
of the special flavors as they burst upon his tongue. Along the
way, the weaver twirled and snapped lengths of linen and
wool dyed with woad or oak tannin or dandelion.

The abbey's brewer banged his wooden spurtle against a
copper pot. "Cider! Last of the autumn's brew," he called to
one and all. The common folk would have to trade something
for the refreshment. To the abbey boys it was free. "Fresh
small beer brewed yesterday."

Dom and Henry stopped before him, each holding out
their wooden cups tied to their rope belts. The thick amber
liquid frothed as it settled into the cups.

Nick passed by, attracted by the sound of the loud bong of
a stout branch against a hollow stump.

"Races! Line up for the races," an old man with a bald pate
and an astonishingly clear voice pronounced. He hadn't performed that chore last year, the blacksmith had.

A dozen young men and boys formed a straight line be-hind the marks in the turf. Nick and the other boys from the abbey kilted up their long robes, tucking the tails into their rope belts.

"From here to the millrace and back. First one to cross this line on the return will get a loaf of fresh bread and a kiss from the Queen of the May!" the old man continued. "Ready, set your mark . . ." He paused as if searching for the right words, but licked his lips with teasing relish.

The expression reminded Nick of someone. Someone he ought to remember but couldn't. Maybe he'd seen him before he came to the Abbey in the arms of the itinerant monk who had rescued him from the burned-out village.

The racers shuffled their feet anxiously. "Get on with it, Tuck," someone called from the far end of the line.

"Tuck?" Nick whispered in astonishment that the man no longer wore the robes of his vocation.

"Go!"

The runners took off. People pushed and jostled Nick from behind, keeping him from gaining ground. At last he had open space. He didn't waste any more time, setting his feet to moving as fast as he could lift and replant them. Right, left, right, left. He caught his rhythm, his breathing evened, and he surged forward.

In a few long strides he passed the littlest boys. He stretched his legs and matched Henry step for step. Then his friend be-gan to flag, and Nick matched shoulders with Dom. He, too, fell behind.

Nick's thighs grew hot and heavy. His breaths came short and sharp, piercing all the way to his side. He should give up, as had so many of the younger runners. He still lagged behind the pack of young men with longer legs. He'd turned twelve last winter and had a growth spurt soon after. Those men weren't so very much taller than he.

The millrace up ahead sounded muffled beneath the pounding of his heart in his ears.

A tall man dressed in expensive Lincoln green came up behind him. He had a bow and quiver slung across his back.

"What's keeping you, lad?" he asked, not breathing hard at all. Then he surged ahead of Nick, and quickly outpaced the pack of locals.

Nick felt the challenge deep in his gut. Something about the man's tone taunted him. A lot like Father Blaine's disapproval challenged him to create more little faces in greenery drawings.

He gulped air and plunged ahead.

He reached the turn at the millrace and pivoted on the toe of his left foot. Most of the others ran in wide circles, not nimble enough to control their turns. Nick moved ahead of them.

But the archer in green saw the homestretch and lengthened his stride.

Nick's chest hurt from trying to breathe. He couldn't let the stranger win. His vision narrowed, and bright sparks flashed before him.

He forced himself to keep running.

They left the watermill behind. The man stayed five paces ahead as every one of the others fell behind Nick. Did the archer's feet even touch the ground? Each stride stretched longer and longer.

Nick wanted to stop and puzzle out the bewildering man. But he'd been challenged.

He kept stumbling forward.

One. Foot. In front of the other. The village green came into view. Tuck, the bandy-legged old man in the floppy brown felted hat, bounced up and down at the finish line.

The archer practically danced across the line, raising his arms in triumph and prancing in a circle. Then he doffed his cocked hat as he bowed gallantly before a young woman with silvery blond hair.

For three heartbeats the archer appeared to elongate and grow short brown fur, while tall, strong antlers grew upward into twelve-points, each horn tipped in silver. Nick blinked, and the man returned.

A small gnome of a man, also in Lincoln green, pranced around them in an intricate dance, slapping his knees, tossing his cap in the air, and catching it on his head again. His nose looked like a twisted and knotted branch that nearly met his elongated, beardless chin.

Nick almost stumbled trying to slow down as he crossed the finish line. He had to bend forward, grasping his knees as he dragged gulps of air into his laboring lungs.

The archer clapped him on the back. Nick coughed and choked, but air moved easier in and out of him.

"Good race, boy. Your courage astounds me. Here's the loaf I was promised. You earned it, and I don't need it." He pressed the fresh bread wrapped in fresh leaves beneath Nick's arm.

Before Nick could gasp his thanks, the archer disappeared, along with the gnome, who could only be Robin Goodfellow according to descriptions of unnatural forest dwellers in the newest tome in the scriptorium. His words fell into the blank space where Robin Goodfellow had been and came out all breathy and uneven. He saw nothing of the pretty blond girl in a white gown and a circlet of tiny white daisies (or were they water drops glistening in the sun?) crowning her.

The remaining runners staggered in.

No one seemed to have seen the man in green. They all presumed Nick had won the race; he had the loaf of bread to prove it.

A procession of costumed people danced out of the nearest forest path. The sunshine caught the dew still lingering in the shadows and sent shimmers of light across the dancers. Their faces went all blurry and vague, taking on sharper ears and chins, their hair greening, and their eyes slanting up. Nick blinked, and the Green Man became a shepherd on stilts. The Huntsman with a stag's face and an antler crown returned to the look of an ordinary man—the tall archer. The troll and a lady tree spirit remained the same. And elven Puck, or Robin Goodfellow, took on the guise of a strong man with a noble face and an unstrung long bow slung over his shoulder— another archer, but not the Huntsman. Then he faded, becoming almost invisible before resolving into the shorter gnome.

The lovely woman wearing a shimmering gown that reminded Nick of a waterfall wavering in and out of view had been the blond girl with a crown of white daisies the Huntsman had kissed as his prize.

Nick blinked again, and all the dancers reverted to their fae forms. Another blink and they resumed their humanity.

A chuckle sounding in the back of his mind reassured him that he had nothing to fear.

"Those are the best costumes I've ever seen," Dom said, coming up beside Nick. He had refilled his cup with small beer. Nick frowned at him. On ordinary days they were only allowed the essential beverage of life at meals.

"I wonder who wove the silver into that lady's gown?" Henry asked. "Much too rich for the likes of this abbey village."

Silver? Maybe that was it. She could be a baron's lady or daughter taking a day away from her noble responsibilities to have some fun. All Nick could see was water, falling water, no pool above or below, just water rippling downward with a delightful chuckle, similar to the one he heard in the back of his mind.

And then he fingered the little cup in his pocket graced by three ladies, wondering if he dared fill it from the brewer's barrel. Suddenly, he knew why the dancers' forms wavered back and forth.

They weren't people dressed in costumes. These were the actual Wild Folk of the forest. The fae. With the Pope's interdict, the Church could not preach to deny their existence, they were now free to wander the real world and enchant normal humans. Or would they lead people astray into the ways of sin as the Church insisted?

What is sin but another way of looking at life?

"You met with a boy the other night," one of the convent girls taunted Hilde. Then she turned serious and looked all around as if making certain no one listened and whispered, "Is he nice? Are you going to run away with him?"

The others called her Nan. Of all the girls, Nan seemed the most destined to take her vows as soon as allowed and then rise to running the convent. She spent hours every day and night on her knees. But occasionally she stepped down from her pedestal of piety and acted like she wanted to be Hilde's friend.

Sister Marie Josef did not approve of friendship. She urged all the girls, ungently, to learn to endure the aches of solitary inactivity for longer and longer periods each day. The older woman frequently stated her goal of being able to pray to God for mercy and redemption for a full day and night, then go about her daily chores joyfully.

Some days Nan joined her. Most days she behaved normally.

Hilde decided to not answer, lest she be overheard. Just talking to Dom about life in the outside world, about their mother and their three younger siblings, remembering when life was happy and secure, was enough to allow her to endure life within the convent.

Sister Marie Josef came up behind Hilde and pinched her

hard upon her upper arm. Even through the thick gray wool of her habit, she knew she'd have a bruise tomorrow when they had to remove all of their clothing for their weekly cold bath. Would the sisters who supervised the ritual cleansing inquire about its source?

"Who is he?" the sister demanded.

Hilde said nothing. Any excuse she made, good or bad, would result in more strikes with the oak cudgel.

"Where were you that you'd notice if I wasn't sleeping deeply in my bed?" Hilde turned the question back on her inquisitor. Nan had scurried ahead with the other girls.

"Where I was and what I was doing was not the question," Sister Marie Josef sneered. "You wandering the gardens after midnight is."

"Is it? I thought you might immerse yourself in deep prayer in the Lady Chapel. If that was your reason for defying the Rule, then you should be punished. But if you accuse another of wandering the gardens after midnight, when it was you, then perhaps I should tell Sister Mary Margaret of your whereabouts and your lies and your sin of meeting one of the local village men making plans for May Day."

Hilde lifted her chin and set her feet to taking her place in line with the other girls.

"You will pay for this," the nun hissed, then dropped her head in feigned humility as she folded her hands into the sleeves of her habit.

Five

ick crossed himself out of habit, a brief prayer of protection that Brother Theo had taught him passing his lips. Then his curiosity won out over his lessons. He stared agape in wonder and awe at the dance of the newcomers.

"By the grace of God, what is this?" he added to his prayer. "What am I seeing and why?"

Robin Goodfellow bounced up and down, knees level with his chest, and slapped each in turn. The bells tied to the points of his green jerkin jingled in lovely counterpoint, or invitation, to the sound of gentle water rushing to meet . . .

Nick shook his head to clear it of these strange thoughts.

He released the little cup in his pocket.

Nothing changed, except that Herne the Huntsman danced up to the water lady, or lady in the water, and held out his hand to her. "Ardenia, my dear, join me?" He turned a circle in place, jingling as he clapped his hands over his head.

She curtsied and circled him.

A lady clad in fabric leaves over a brown tunic touched the Green Man's arm with fingers that looked like twigs. She stood nearly as tall and strong as he. He jerked out of his thoughtful stare at shadowed figures within the forest and smiled at the tree woman. Then he slapped his knees enthusiastically. If he'd truly been an ordinary man on stilts, he'd have fallen off them. They danced off together, feet lifting high and hands clapping—hers against his—in light counterpoint to the bells and drums.

A pair of massive trolls—who truly resembled the abbey blacksmith and his wife—broke into enthusiastic stomps and hops. The ground shook with each step, and they laughed loud and long. Their joy sounded like thunder.

"Hey, Nick, look over here!" Henry said, pulling anxiously at Nick's sleeve. "They're starting a game of mad football."

Nick looked over to the village green. Men and boys lined up on either side while the old man who'd officiated the race stood in the middle of the field juggling an inflated pig's bladder. Tuck had a fringe of gray hair beneath his floppy hat to match his sagging hose and stained leather jerkin. The hat shadowed his face, and he moved so constantly Nick had trouble focusing on his exact height and form. He still thought the old man might be the wandering friar who'd rescued him ten years before.

Whooping joyously, Nick and his friends ran to the line on the far side that seemed short of players. Local boys, near their own age, slapped their backs and welcomed them into their ranks. The villagers seemed to have separated themselves in youth and maturity, ten to a side.

"All set?" the old man yelled while twisting his neck right and left.

Something about his voice triggered a memory in Nick, a different memory from the wandering priest. He didn't have time to puzzle it out. His eyes focused on the ball.

Then Tuck tossed the ball straight up and backed away. All the players rushed forward, each eager to be the first to kick the ball to his own mates.

A rough and tumble game followed. No rules to this game, except they could not touch the ball with their hands. An elbow to the nose, a kick to the shins, followed by a wrestling roll in the mud they churned up in the damp grass and sheep droppings. Nick gloried in the game and his renewed strength kicking the ball. Most of the time his kicks sent the ball wild, but that didn't matter.

Eventually, they all fell together in one huge shoving match. Laughing uncontrollably, Nick grabbed Henry and Dom and dragged them backward before they were crushed under twenty stout bodies. He felt the tingling numbness, and sharp ache of a bruise forming around his left eye.

"I'm hungry," Nick said. He barely remembered when he'd shared a small loaf of bread with his friends. He aimed for the baker's booth and the dairymaid's cheeses spread out on a worn blanket.

"We've got no coins for the vendors from outside the abbey village," Henry protested. "And the abbey people have nearly run out of the goods they may give us. Maybe we should return home . . ."

"If we go back now, we'll have to stay there," Nick replied, his voice rising in anger. A heavy knot formed in his belly at the thought of losing this one day of freedom. In years past, Abbot Mæson had given each boy a few coppers for extra food at May Day. The elderly priest had left, fled for his life. Therefore, no coins.

"I have an idea," Dom said. He bowed his head reverently and drew up his wide cowl. Then he folded his hands before him in an attitude of prayer. "Honored sir," he said quietly to the baker. "I offer you prayers for your well-being and pros- perity in exchange for a few crumbs of bread."

"One of the abbey boys, eh?" The baker looked Dom up and down, noting his lack of stature and maturity. "Since the interdict, you can't really offer prayers anymore, or sing Masses for my soul, but by the rood, you're a boy and growing boys are hungry. Fair bargain, the prayers of an innocent . . ." He raised his eyebrows at Nick and Henry appearing on either side of Dom. "The prayers of three innocents are worth a small loaf." Chuckling, he wrapped said loaf in a ragged cloth and turned it over to Dom.

Smiling broadly, Nick approached the dairymaid. She didn't look to be much older than himself. "How old are you?" she asked with a sneer.

"Twelve years, my lady."

She threw her head back laughing loudly. "Old enough to take your first vows, but you can't do that while the church bells hang silent and Masses unsung. Will you stay a boy until the king and the Holy Father make peace? Or will you grow into manhood with no calling and no skills to market except your worthless prayers?"

"I'm a fair shot with a sling, my lady. I am always the one sent to bring in a grouse for the stew or a rabbit for the abbot's dinner. But that is a skill that will not benefit you. My prayers, the prayers of an innocent, are the only thing of value I have today."

"If you have such skill with the rock and a twist of leather, will you kill the sheriff for me?"

Nick reared back appalled at such an idea.

"I can see you are too much a coward to do what needs doing. Here, take this round of cheese and come back when you're grown enough to see the right and wrong of the man who rules us in the king's name without the king's knowledge of how he punishes us for his own amusement." She threw a round of white cheese at him.

Nick caught the treasure in both hands and bowed to her. "Many thanks and blessings to you, my lady. May the Lord God look kindly on you." He ran with his friends to the shade beneath the tree that towered over the blacksmith's forge.

From their nest among the spreading roots, they watched the villagers clear the hay barn's outside walls of obstacles, and pin sheepskin targets to the sides. Archers took their places behind a line marked in the dirt. Robin Goodfellow, once more looking tall and strong with a noble's grace and strength, helped.

Off to the side, in the flattest portion of the village green, three men and three women leveraged the Maypole already strung with garlands of ivy and fresh flowers into place.

Other figures danced a weaving pattern around them. Nick couldn't bring them into focus and didn't know if they were fae or human.

Before Nick could decide which activity demanded his

attention first, the loud pounding of heavy horses along the
road from the north caused everyone in the village to pause
and stare, then scurry away from the muddy track that ran
beside the green.

Sir Philip Marc, who had recently purchased the office,
rights, and privileges of Sheriff of Nottingham, galloped to
the edge of the green and reined his horse into a rearing halt.
When the horse settled after a sharp curbing pull, Sir Philip
dismounted and tossed the horse's restraints to his groom. He
smiled at one and all, his gaze lingering too long on the dairymaid. She cringed and hastily packed her wares into a basket.
Then she scuttled away without looking toward her overlord.

Sir Philip threw his head back and laughed, sounding a lot
like his snorting horse.

Nick had overheard a quiet conversation behind a closed
door about men who enjoyed inflicting pain on others. Sir
Philip Marc, reputedly, was one of them.

Something silvery glinted in the green shadows. Sir Philip
cut short his braying laughter. His gaze homed in on the water lady. He shifted direction in mid-stride, sword bouncing
against his hip menacingly, spurs clanking with each step to
remind everyone of his rank and authority.

Then Robin Goodfellow, now firmly in his human form,
stepped between the sheriff and the lady.

"Come for the archery contests, my lord?" he asked in a
cultured voice and fully visible to everyone. He sounded much
too well-educated for a simple peasant, or one of the Wild Folk.
"I hear the grand prize is a kiss from the lady of St. Anne's Well.
I'll gladly challenge you to better my shots at each distance."

The sheriff narrowed his gaze, making him look almost as fae as the wild ones. "Well met, my lord, late of Locksley. I'll best you shot for shot, and then I'll dance 'round the Maypole with the lady yonder." He shifted his gaze back to the water lady.

"And if you lose the match?" Robin asked, keeping himself between the sheriff and the lady.

"Then I might consider petitioning the king to grant you your rightful patrimony."

"I accept the challenge." Robin bowed low.

The water lady had disappeared into the woods.

Nick wondered at the tale that must explain how Robin Goodfellow had become a baron with a patrimony that had been stolen from him. And the Sheriff had named him Locksley. The name of the abbey, and of the abandoned tower fortress on the next ridge overlooking the forest and the vale. A forbidding place. Haunted? Enchanted?

Jane stumbled over the hem of her dress, landing on her hands and knees. The rough forest path scraped and stung everywhere she made contact. Sharp stabs of burning pain jarred her teeth and joints. Nothing new.

"Thunder and storm!" she cursed, borrowing frightful words from her captors. She really wanted to damn them all to hell and back again, but they had no fear of human punishments, or the God humans worshipped.

Queen Mab giggled as Jane tripped again trying to right herself. Royal handmaidens joined their leader in laughter.

They sounded like a bunch of jackdaws squabbling over a piece of carrion.

Jane found little comfort knowing that the ladies of Faery had no choice but to mimic the queen's moods.

"Hurry up, Jonquil," Queen Mab called dismissively, as if Jane's clumsiness was her own fault. "We do not want to be late for the May Day dances. Such fun to see how the patterns around the Maypole pair up different couples."

Taking a deep breath for calm—she hated the flowery name the Fae had given her when they captured her—Jane hiked her skirts to an immodest level and tried to get her feet beneath her. A green hand reached down in front of her, palm out in peace.

Jane looked up to find the queen's current favorite, Bracken, a green male the same shade as his name. He placed a finger across his mouth, signaling silence, and winked at her.

Jane breathed deeply for the first time all day. She placed her own small palm in his and allowed him to guide and support her until she stood on the firm ground. He floated half a foot above the leaf litter, his fern-frond wings fluttering lightly.

"Trust me, please. We are not all cut from the same mold as Her Majesty."

The restrictions binding Jane's chest unwound and she smiled. Only then did she realize that the green faery had lifted her more than a foot's length above the forest floor to his level. He kissed her fingertips and fluttered them both back down.

The pretty gown still dragged on the ground, the cut and fit suited the illusion of Jonquil, tall, slender and graceful. But it, like most Faery magic, was illusion only. Jane remained short and sturdy and the dress trailed along the ground, ready to trip her again.

If Queen Mab had but given her an hour's notice, she could have hemmed the garment to the proper length and embroidered some flowers, or just a sinuous vine to disguise the alteration.

Faery traps and tricks. They found her most amusing.

Jane kilted up the skirts, tucking the hem into her girdle of braided strands of fabric. Her knees and feet moved freely. As she righted herself she checked the position of the sun, as she was wont to when she lived in the village. Through the lush green of the tree canopy, she caught a bright glimmer halfway between the horizon and the height of the sun's path. Nearly Prime.

Her entire body stilled in anticipation. Any moment now the church bells should sound the call to Mass. If only she could hear the bells, be within range of their influence, she had a chance of breaking the Faery entanglement that kept her within a few feet of Queen Mab.

If only . . .

She waited and heard only the normal sounds of the forest: birds chirping, squirrels chattering, foxes stealing among the ground cover, and wild pigs rooting in the dirt. Then the un-natural giggling among Queen Mab and her ladies overrode the animal sounds. Even the breeze in the treetops stilled for their passage.

Then, off in the distance, not so very far now, came the shouts and drunken laughter as the villagers and the Woodwose—those who lived in the forest outside the law— dominated the other sounds around her.

Why hadn't she heard the church bells?

Her eyes focused only on her feet, and she barely avoided tripping again. Her bruised hands still stung, and her knees ached.

Queen Mab couldn't humiliate her much more, so she dared ask the question burning in her mind. "Why can I not hear the church bells?"

"Silly child," Mab smiled, full of delight as well as malice. "Didn't you know? The mortal king of England is at war with the mortal king of the Church. The Church no longer has power in this land. No bells ring, no rituals are performed. Without their governance, we are free to walk among the mortals once more. We are finally allowed to celebrate the coming of May as we should." She laughed long and loud. Then her attention shifted toward the village. "Ah they have remembered to hoist the Maypole in our honor. Let us dance!"

Something tugged at Jane's awareness. Something familiar, safe, and sane. Could anything be familiar, safe, and sane without the Church, without the bells ordering the day and reminding people of the times to pray, to eat, to bring the cows and chickens into the byre, and to sleep?

She looked up and found a tall man, dressed in browns and greens peering through the trees toward her. His eyes drooped with sadness and his mouth opened slightly in silent questions.

John! Her John had come for her.

But no, though his hands might reach for her, he could not break through Mab's hold on her.

Six

"**S**ir?" Nick stepped in front of Locksley, the archer. Could he truly be the younger son of the last baron? Village lore said that he had fallen in love. But without land and honors of his own to entice the girl's guardians, he had gone off to the Crusades with King Richard—no, before that, on the second Crusade some fifty or sixty years before and never returned, presumed dead in one of the grand battles against the heathen Muslims. Both his father and older brother had died. So the title, lands, and castle had forfeited to the king and never been awarded to another.

What had happened to the girl he loved? Probably married off to another and dead many a long year since.

But that tale couldn't belong to the tall archer in expensive Lincoln green. This man looked too young, mid-twenties at a guess. Perhaps he was grandson to the lost heir.

Locksley dropped his gaze to Nick from where the sheriff strung his bow and tested the string. "Yes."

Nick swallowed deeply to make sure his voice didn't falter and betray him when he had something important to impart.

"Do you know that Sir Philip Marc does not miss a single target? He practices endless hours at the butts and then turns his aim on game in the forest—with and without the king's permission. He can take down a boar with a single shot from fifty paces. When he runs out of game, he goes after poachers and the Woodwose."

"I know, young one. But I thank you for your concern. I have dedicated my life since before the death of King Henry and the loss of my patrimony to protecting those who are hungry and must seek food in the protected royal preserves, and to those who dwell hidden in the forest, outside the law." He turned his attention to selecting his best arrows with the freshest fletching. "Best you turn your concern to those who dance around the Maypole. They do not belong here."

Nick looked in the direction the archer tipped his head. Sure enough, a dozen tall folk, dressed in the finest silk and softest linen, adorned with bright jewels and pearls and lifelike embroidered flowers and small creatures—similar to the ones he drew in the illuminated manuscripts–jumped high, clapping their hands and landing gently without disturbing the grass at their elegantly shod feet.

Nobles did not come to village May Day celebrations except to disrupt and cause pain. True nobles would have arrived with showy horses and litters. There would have been trumpets and heralds and well-armed guardsmen.

As he watched, the creatures flickered in and out of his vision much as the Forest Folk had. At the moment of reappearance, gossamer wings in bright jewel colors, to match their fine clothes held them aloft, half a finger's length above the grass. Could it be? Faeries had come to the celebration.

He crossed himself in silent supplication for protection.

The voice in the back of his head chuckled. *They only have as much power as you are willing to give them. Stand firm in your beliefs, and they are but fluttery butterflies on the morning mist.*

One ageless male, half a head taller than an average man, with unnaturally long arms and legs, touched down a little harder than the rest, forgetting that this village green was normally used as pasturage for sheep during the long winter. Not all of the droppings had soaked into the earth with early spring rains, replenishing the soil.

The faery's red-and-white slippers offered no protection for his feet against mundane manure.

Nick smothered a laugh, thankful for the sturdy leather sole of his sandals.

The ruby-and-pearl faery sputtered and protested the soiling of his dainty feet. Head hanging and pointed ears drooping, he slunk off into the forest, bowing low at a woman who glittered in gold and white. She had pale clear skin stretched over high cheekbones, a dainty nose, and golden eyes slitted vertically. The most beautiful woman he could imagine, more beautiful than the stained-glass window of the Madonna in the narthex of the abbey church.

Those eyes. They compelled Nick to watch her, follow her every gesture. And yet they repelled him with their strangeness.

More than strange. *Alien*. More alien than the Moorish prince who'd visited the abbey once.

Mab. Queen of the Faeries.

She lifted a corner of her upper lip in disdain for the male with the soiled feet. In that moment, her face became lined and misshapen, her nose twisted, knotted, and elongated. Her chin sprouted bristly hairs and grew a black-and-red wart, marring her once flawless skin.

He blinked. The beautiful, ageless woman returned.

Illusion.

He fingered the little silver pitcher in his sleeve, thanking the figure that looked three ways at once for the gift of true sight.

The figures at the edge of the Maypole shifted and re-aligned their dance as the male passed them. The females twitched their skirts away from his noisome presence. All except one stepped away, putting more distance between themselves and the soiled one.

A young human female hid within the shadows in a simpler version of the elaborate gowns of the faery women. It stretched tightly across her full bosom—the faery women had none—and trailed loosely on the ground, too long for her. And her wings sagged rather than fluttering wide to catch any breeze. A human woman, not much older than himself, enslaved by the fae. He'd heard tales of people who wandered too deeply into the forest becoming ensnared by faery traps and never seen again by humankind.

He shivered in fear. Was he doomed to fall into such traps now that he saw the otherworldly creatures in their true form?

Shouts of triumph behind him drew his attention back to the archery contests.

Little John shook his fist at Queen Mab.

She laughed, throwing her head back and rising two body lengths into the air, barely flapping her shimmering gold-and-white wings.

He wished one of Robin Goodfellow's arrows would go astray and pierce those wings, shatter her illusions, and allow him to grab Jane away from her control.

She hadn't aged a day since the day she ran away from her father and found faery traps instead of John's loving arms.

"Soon, my love. I will come for you soon."

She buried her face in her hands and turned away from him, her back rippling with deep sobs.

He took one last lingering look at his beloved and turned back to the events and people he *could* help.

By narrowing his eyes, he discerned the fine grain of the arrows both the sheriff and Robin used. The wood spoke to him. Robin's, of course; the grain of the wood was straight and true, barely needing smoothing to turn fallen branches into hunting tools. Perfect. The Green Man made certain his companion and friend received only the best materials. Robin's points were flint, knapped precisely with no flaws.

The sheriff, on the other hand, didn't have those choices. The grain in the arrows twisted. He'd taken larger branches and lathed them down to the proper diameter, but he paid no attention to the way the wood had flowed in different directions as the seasons changed. His aim might be exact, his fletching flashy, and his iron points tooled by an expert, but his arrows could not fly true because of the imperfections in the wood.

Robin didn't need Little John's interference to win this contest. But the villagers needed to believe that other agencies toyed with the sheriff's aim.

What would winning gain him? Sir Philip hadn't truly promised to petition King John for the return of Robin's patrimony. And if he did return to his honors and his castle, would he be able to break the wizard's curse on himself and his lady love? That must happen at the same time. Breaking one curse without the other would age them both to their normal human years and kill them both of old age in moments. Would Robin, once he broke the double curse, be able to remember his mother's folk in the forest and his vow to honor and protect them?

Little John thought on that curse, which put Robin in much the same position as himself. Little John had to rescue Jane, but he had to find a way into the Faery Mound to do it. The only way Robin could break the curse that condemned him to live within his gnomish body at least half of each day, and awaken Marian, was to break both evil spells at the same time. But first, he had to find the Cave Outside of Time where Marian slept. At least Little John knew where Jane was held captive.

Even Little John, who was master of every plant, rock, and stream in the forest, did not know where to begin looking for the cave.

As Sir Philip Marc drew his bowstring back to his ear, John inhaled a deep breath, enough to fill a cauldron with air. At the instant Sir Philip loosed his arrow, Little John released his breath and allowed it to find its own natural path. The arrow wobbled but still flew long. The villagers held their breaths, half of them watching only the target. The others warily marked the sheriff's reaction.

The arrow thudded into the barn wall. By Little John's estimate, it vibrated two fingers wide of the bull's eye painted on the sheepskin target. The strike sounded loud to Little John's ears. Louder than the smattering of applause from Sir Philip's entourage.

Then Robin stepped up to the line drawn in the turf, his bow already strung, and an arrow nocked.

With all of his forest powers, Little John whispered to the arrow, giving it words of advice on how to fly long and true, to honor the tree from which it sprang.

Faster than a mortal eye could follow, the arrow surged toward the target. Little John held his breath lest the slightest stirring of the air disrupt the arrow's mission.

With a gentle thwapping sound, the arrow pieced the center of the painted eye. If it had indeed been a bull, the animal would be blinded or dead.

Robin smiled and bowed to the gathered villagers.

Sir Philip scowled and crossed himself as did his guardsmen.

"Step back ten paces," Tuck called.

Men scrambled to retrieve the arrows and return them to the archers.

Sir Philip inspected his closely and cast it away. His upper lip lifted in disgust. All the while he kept his gaze fixed upon Robin.

Robin ran his fingers along the length of the retrieved arrow, whispering to it lovingly, knowing it to be his partner more than a tool. Then he smiled and stepped backward to the new line in the turf.

One of the abbey boys, the one who had warned Robin of the sheriff's prowess with a bow, ran to the barn with a lump of charcoal in his fist. With a few deft strokes, he revitalized the eye drawing.

Little John marked the boy's height and stance as one to keep an eye on. He had the spunk, and the initiative to be the one to help save Jane. But was he the one Elena had selected as her student?

⁂

Nick hastened away from the restored target. The sheriff was already drawing back his bowstring, heedless of who might stand between him and the barn at the edge of the village green.

Instinctively, Nick sought the location of each of the twelve boys from the abbey and counted. Ten familiar heads spread throughout the crowd. All of the boys were out of the path and range of the archery contest. Counting himself as number eleven, he realized one boy was missing.

Ah, Dom lingered by the dairymaid who had moved her cheeses to the far side, away from the sheriff's prancing horses. The way they tilted their heads toward each other spoke volumes of a close friendship beginning.

Dom had never wanted a life in the Church. Perhaps he'd found an alternative. Perhaps not. So many folk were bound to the land, incapable of moving away from their homes to find a better life. Only the Church offered the opportunity for young men to escape serfdom. Without a land tie, Dom had little chance to find a life within the law.

Nick turned his attention back toward the two men who tested their bowstrings.

Without a word of warning or prompt from Tuck, Sir Philip nocked an arrow and let it fly. With a zinging *thwap*, the boar point on the arrow pierced the planed planks of the barn wall dead center of the drawn eye.

A gasp rippled around the crowd. Locksley could not possibly best that shot.

The sheriff stepped away, smiling. His compatriots slapped his back in congratulations. They all laughed loudly and turned back in mute challenge of his opponent.

The man in Lincoln green stepped up to the line in the turf. His eyes focused only on the target. He raised the bow, slowly and deliberately drawing the string back to his ear. His knuckles showed white. His cheek muscle throbbed. The cords and muscles in his neck bulged with strain. The string came back another inch. Then another.

Just when Nick thought the string would snap, Locksley released the arrow. It flew straight. It flew true. And it . . . it split the sheriff's arrow down the center, shattered the brittle iron arrowhead, and embedded into the wall.

The crowd gasped, then burst into cheers.

Locksley sagged in relief. His illusion of humanity slipped

a bit as he shrank in stature to about Nick's height and his nose elongated. Then he drew in a deep breath and straightened, tall and handsome once more.

The sheriff called for his horse.

"My Lord Sheriff, you promised to petition King John for the return of my honors and lands if I won," Locksley called.

"I promised nothing. I call this a draw. We will meet again when I will claim the Lady Ardenia as my own." He shoved his foot into the stirrup.

"I am not yours, nor any man's to claim!" The lady's voice rang out from the depth of the forest, sounding more like the laughter of a wandering creek than human words.

An answering chuckle came into Nick's mind from the three-faced pitcher in his sleeve.

Now that was an interesting way of thinking! Nick sauntered back to the brewer's stand, whistling a jaunty tune that had not been born in the Church.

Seven

Deep shadows lay across the village green. The faeries had flown away, dragging Jane with them. Little John let his gaze linger on their fleeing flickers of light and dark.

He allowed his memories to go back to the laughing girl just ripening into womanhood who gleaned nuts and roots at the boundary of the forest. Each day she pushed her boundaries a bit farther into the woods, testing her courage.

Little John awaited her there, watching over her to make certain that no creature of the wood, human or otherwise, endangered her. They met. They snatched a few kisses. Made promises to each other. And always Little John made certain that she hastened back to her home before the shadows grew too long. The same time of day as now, betwixt and between light and dark, this world and the next. The time of day when faery magic was strongest, their illusions the most compelling.

Then came the day when Jane's father made good on his

threats to give Jane in marriage to the older man who owned the grist mill. He owed heavy tribute and taxes to the sheriff, but he owned the mill that served those outside the abbey's protection. The land did not capture him into a life of serfdom. The miller had already buried three wives and sired children ranging from ten to thirty. Village rumor claimed the only way one of his wives would survive his beatings was to give him sons to help him run the mill and one day inherit it.

Jane ran away to the forest before she could recite her vows on the porch of the abbey church. She ran long and fast. She tripped and raised herself up. She cried and called to John to come for her.

But Little John had been far away, in the center of the stone circle, dealing with yet another dispute between Herne and Ardenia. Outside sounds and awareness deserted Little John while within the influence of the stones. The sun dropped to the horizon and still she ran. Once Little John became aware of her plight, he had raced toward her with mile-eating steps.

Then just as he reached out his arms for her, she ran toward him and tripped once more. This time, though, she stumbled not over a protruding root but over a cobweb-fine rope set by the faeries. The silky bonds slid around and around and around her body, holding her fast and beyond Little John's grasp.

He shook off the memory and his tears. "Soon, Jane. Soon I will come for you." Unable to cope with his anger and his pain, he stepped into a tree. Not *his* tree, but an old and sturdy willow that would restore his mind, body, and soul for a time. With a deep sigh, he thrust his fingers and arms along stout branches and allowed his hair and beard to blend with the inner pith of the wood.

The ache in his feet and his heart eased as he blended with the forest, sending his roots deep to converse with the soil and all the creatures that dwelt there. Tingling vibrations told him how a squirrel scurried toward her nest, how a sparrow flew high, singing a few notes of satisfaction, how a fox lurked within the underbrush waiting for a rabbit to cross his path . . . how a young boy pressed himself against the trunk of this tree, watching and waiting as the Woodwose and the Wild Folk danced along a secret path toward their own homes.

Little John caressed the boy's back with smooth bark, shaping itself to fit him, and felt him lean into the comforting support. He whispered a welcome to the boy by rattling leaves.

"Hello," a female voice whispered into his mind. "I brought him, as I promised. Introduce yourself. His name is Nick."

Shocked that the goddess Elena spoke to him so clearly, Little John lost contact with the forest and with the boy.

In that moment, Nick removed himself from the tree's embrace and ran back through the village to the abbey. Little John had promised to watch for signs that this boy carried a tiny silver pitcher formed of three women looking out into the world, carrying lanterns that lit without aid of a wick or fuel. Elena, the key to opening the Faery Mound on the night of Midsummer when the moons aligned, infused him with hope.

Elena's laughter marked every step of the boy's retreat, and her lanterns glowed faintly, showing Nick the way.

Eight

autiously, Nick approached the portal beside the broad, gated entrance to the abbey. Father Blaine stood firmly beside the brother who had drawn portal duty. The young priest counted heads as boys and monks returned from the May Day festivities.

Nick counted, too. The younger boys were his responsibility.

Dom and Henry stood before the partially open wooden door. The slide across the barred viewing window was firmly closed. No one would enter once this pedestrian entrance closed for the night. It was only wide enough to admit one at a time. And the window was big enough that the monitor could assess the worth or the danger of admitting whoever knocked.

The sun had only half dropped below the horizon. The door should not be locked yet.

The last three youngsters ran across the green, holding hands, and gasping for breath. Almost too late. Only a few rays of the sun shone above the horizon. They bobbed in deference to the priest and the monk before racing toward the refectory and their supper.

"We don't know where Nick is," Henry whined to Father Blaine.

"I know you three. You do nothing without the other two. You may not enter until the last of you arrives, and you will all receive the same punishment for being late. No supper." Father Blaine opened the door a bit to peer along the road approaching the abbey.

"He left us right after the archery contests," Dom said.

"Why would he do that?" Brother Theo asked, his voice booming into the evening like the big bass bell in the abbey church tower. He approached the portal, a frown on his face and worry lines making deep furrows across his brow and from the corners of his mouth to his chin.

Dom and Henry looked at each other and then turned back to their inquisitor. "We think he had a rendezvous with the dairymaid," Dom lied.

Nick pressed his back against the abbey wall, wishing he could blend in with the stones.

Hold your breath.

Brother Theo opened the door wide and stomped out onto the road, leaving the door ajar. Dom and Henry scuttled inside. Nick started to follow.

Stupid boy, hold your breath!

Nick obeyed and slid inward, making certain he did not

touch either of his friends. They ignored him, watching Brother Theo as he scanned the open approach to the abbey.

"He's never been this late before." Was that a note of concern in Brother Theo's voice?

Nick stepped into the darkest shadow between the wall and the guesthouse. Then, gratefully, he released his breath and inhaled long and deeply.

Only when the sound of his breathing alerted them did Henry and Dom turn toward him. He stepped out of the shadow into the pool of light around the door.

"How long have you been hiding there?" Dom whispered.

"Long enough." Nick leaned on the open portal door. "Brother Theo, I came home long ago. Why are you looking for me out there?" he called, trying hard to smother his laughter.

Deep in his sleeve pocket the goddess of the silver pitcher laughed for him.

"I did not see you come in. You were not with the other boys in the refectory. Where have you been hiding?" Brother Theo demanded as he stomped back inside and firmly closed the portal, making certain the latch clicked before he dropped the heavy crossbar into place to prevent intrusion from the outside.

"Asleep," Nick lied. He kept his eyes cast downward, feigning shame. "There's a very comfortable branch in the apple orchard that overhangs the wall. I crawled up there to sit a bit in the notch. Before I knew it, the sun had dropped almost to the horizon. I think the quiet that comes when the birds seek their nests must have alerted me." He hadn't done that today. But he had many times in the past. So it wasn't totally a lie. He'd say three extra *pater nostras* with his prayers tonight in penance for the half-truth.

You'll say five, the goddess told him, as sternly as Brother Theo.

"Yes, m'lady."

Call me Elena. That is the name given to me by the first peoples to inhabit this isle. Before that . . . Never mind.

An emptiness opened at the base of Nick's neck. The lady . . . Elena had withdrawn. He thought she slept.

By dawn, Nick resolved to remain in the abbey, obedient, as he was supposed to be. Trees caressing him, a pagan goddess advising him, watching faeries and other forest creatures slip from one guise to another and back again—it all seemed too *wrong*. The Holy Father might have put all of England under interdict, but that didn't mean Nick should risk his soul by consorting with the godless creatures of the wood.

Except he'd really like to know more about all of it. He imagined himself defending his actions to Abbot Mæson. "How can I defend my soul against the uncanny events of yesterday if I don't know how the Wild Folk live and what their relationship with the Woodwose is?"

The abbot used to listen to the boys. He taught them to think through the logic of their actions.

Nick's resolve to stay home and concentrate on his studies and his work lasted only long enough for him to break his fast with some thin oat gruel and secrete some extra bread, cheese, and a raw turnip in his scrip. The moment he was alone in the orchard, sent to rake up fallen branches for kindling, he abandoned his tools and followed the tree shadows across the brook and through the copse of oaks, pausing to gather handfuls of old acorns to supplement his bread and cheese, and thence to the footpaths into the wildwood beyond the village.

Once out of sight of the last roofline he had to stop and reassess his position. The trail withered into nothing. He had no landmarks. This was as far as he'd ever explored on his own.

Stop thinking with your eyes, Elena admonished him with a giggle.

"How. . . ?"

Silly boy, she answered him with another laugh.

"I am not silly." His voice cracked, and he lost the last syllable. He was starting to resent that endearment.

You are silly if you do not listen to me, Elena, goddess of crossroads, cemeteries, and sorcery. Close your eyes and absorb the forest. The path will open to your other senses.

A vacancy gaped wide at his nape. Elena was done with him for now.

Nick sighed and, reluctantly, obeyed. He closed his eyes. How could he find a path if he couldn't see it?

He heard the rustle of leaves and scrapes on bark. A red bird landed on a mid-level branch and began singing joyfully. If Nick didn't know the mating season of birds had passed, he'd swear that Red celebrated a mating. Maybe he celebrated the successful hatching of a nest full of eggs.

How did he know the bird was red if his eyes remained closed?

Another of Elena's mysteries.

Red Bird. Will Scarlett of the Wild Folk wore a red feather in his cocked hat and shifted from human to bird and back again.

Nick smiled in recollection of the sprightly dance tunes the man sang with the lyrical quality of a songbird.

Then Nick smelled fresh, moist dirt disturbed by a burrowing creature. He breathed deeply, relishing the scent of new life ready to sprout inherent in freshly-turned soil this time of year.

Another odor, muskier, overlay the cleanness of the dirt. Then another rustling of leaves, closer to the ground, not leaves, more like . . . like fern fronds. A larger animal moved almost silently across a clearing left when a larger tree, probably ancient and diseased, had fallen in a windstorm several winters ago. Bracken ferns grew thick in the open space.

Deer tended to follow the same pathways over and over, making a trail. People used game trails to mask their own passage, and because the animals instinctively avoided boggy spots and tricky, thorned plants.

He opened his eyes and sought the faint depression among the ground cover.

Dew still sparkled on the tips of the ferns and grasses. A fine spider's line shimmered in the rising sunlight. Nick froze with one step over the line. In his experience spiders were smart enough to string connections to their web higher, where they wouldn't be broken by passing game or unwary humans.

He knelt to examine it closer, tracking it from a tiny knot on one plant across the path to a new branch on a sapling. The line was more substantial than spider silk. More like a fine weaving thread.

A trap for the unwary. He'd read folklore and heard tales from some of the older novitiates at the abbey about people caught in faery traps, never to be seen again. Stories tended to grow with each telling. But they had to begin somewhere. He didn't think this one was completely made up to keep people out of the forest. It had the ring of truth at its core.

Carefully, he skirted the silken line and continued along the faint depression of the game trail.

The red bird chirruped from an overhanging branch at Nick's shoulder. The vocalization sounded more like a greeting than any beak had a right to emit.

"You talk sweeter than I sing," he said quietly, so as not to disturb the wild creature.

"Of course I do." The words came from a human throat more used to singing a fair tenor than chirping like a bird.

"What!" Nick jumped to the side, startled. His heart pounded so loudly his ears throbbed.

"You are a long way from home, abbey boy," Will Scarlett, the bard from the May Day celebration, said. His hose and jerkin were dyed with berries to give them a rusty red hue. Only the bright feather in his cap retained the brightness of his bird garb.

"I . . . um . . . I . . ." Nick couldn't think of a lie to explain his thirst to explore the forest.

"You are curious," Will said flatly. "A dangerous trait in mere humans. Perils beyond your imagination lurk within."

He gestured broadly toward the towering trees beyond the clearing.

"How can I defend myself from those perils if I do not know what they are?" Nick replied. "Some Wild Ones might retreat from a prayer and making the sign of the cross— invoking our God's protection."

"Others can only be pierced by an enchanted spear wielded by one of the Forest Lords."

"Like Little John," Nick affirmed. "Or Robin Goodfellow."

Will threw back his head and laughed, the ripples of sound imitating the raucous calls of a full murder of crows. Gone was the songbird sweetness. "And the enchantment has to come from a long dead wizard or an ancient goddess who presides over crossroads and cemeteries."

Nick's chest clenched, and his breath caught in his throat. He reached into his sleeve to ensure that Elena was still there. He felt her chuckle in his nape, a calming tickle.

"Thank you for the advice," Nick said, without a bit of a quaver, wondering how to get past the man in order to find the Woodwose and the Wild Folk.

"As soon as you stepped off the Royal Road, Little John asked me to find you and bring you to him." Will Scarlett gestured Nick to follow him along the path that Nick had already decided was the right one. Except for the faery trap.

"Little John. He's the very tall man who dressed as the Green Man at May Day. And you are the bard who sang so sweetly, both for the dancing and victories."

"Yes." Will Scarlett paused, twisting his neck all around,

listening and peering deeply into the woods. "Come, quickly. We have unwanted company. You shouldn't be seen by the sheriff's men."

"Oh." At a fierce glare from the bard, Nick clamped his mouth shut and rose up on his tiptoes to tread the path more softly.

They continued silently for another half hour, doubling back and crossing and recrossing the road. In the distance, Nick heard galloping horses, their shod hooves pounding and reverberating against the packed dirt. He felt their presence against the soles of his sandals more than heard them. Once he spotted far ahead of them the sway of draperies for a litter. Someone important. A lady? Most men would ride astride unless very ill.

Eventually, Nick followed Will Scarlett into yet another clearing. This one was larger and more clearly defined than the one where he'd seen the faery trap. A dozen or more rough lean-tos were scattered around a central fire pit. Easily dismantled, the shelters could disappear in moments and the inhabitants scatter before a raid by the sheriff's men, or the king's mercenaries. One or two permanent houses with four walls and thatched roofs dominated the group—likely once owned by charcoal burners or licensed trappers. Those who dwelt there could not erase evidence of their lives so easily.

Except for the chickens. The semi-wild birds stalked the ground everywhere, clucking and pecking at seeds in the grass and bugs hiding in the shadows. One fat beetle basked in the bits of sunshine and soon found itself gobbled. The rooster set up a proud crow of triumph.

The presence of chickens would always betray any settlement.

A swoosh of sound like wind gusting through the upper canopy of leaves startled Nick out of his contemplation of how to move the village in a hurry if the king's men came calling. He tried to identify the creaks and cracks as if a dozen branches rubbed together and then snapped from that single gust of wind.

He spun around, scanning all the nearby trees.

But the villagers ignored the potential danger of broken limbs dropping on their heads.

His eyes focused on a giant oak, a monster that would need five fully grown men to link hands and stretch their arms widely to encircle the trunk. The bark shivered and rippled and the Green Man, bedecked in leaves and twigs, stepped forth.

Nick clutched his temples to keep his mind from exploding at this impossible vision.

Nine

"re you incredibly brave? Or the stupidest boy alive?" Little John roared. He shook his entire body, and his garb of leaves and mossy hair and beard slid into normal human appearance. Then he took one long stride to loom over the boy from the abbey.

His insides quivered with dread. The boy had to willingly give up possession of Elena at midnight on Midsummer Night in order to unlock the door into the Faery Mound. If anything happened to him before then, Elena would not have time to find another innocent to carry her. Little John did not understand why Elena had to have a human carry her about. She could roam freely if she needed to. But something about the bond between the goddess and her companion enhanced her magic and strength.

Nick searched the faces emerging from the shadows and the homes. Probably looking for Tuck, a friendly face among the strangers.

Not finding anyone to fix upon, Nick shrugged his shoulders, stretched his backbone, and firmed his chin.

"Neither, sir," he said, finally engaging Little John's gaze. "I am curious. I need to know if you all are a danger to the ordinary villagers. They live in the shadow of the abbey and are our responsibility. Now that the Church no longer ministers to England and the Wild Folk are visible, the people might need protection. Someone needs to know how to protect them. That cannot be learned from books. Only by experience."

"Huzzah!" Tuck chortled as he emerged from the tree line, righting his hose and straightening his tunic. "The boy has you there, Little John."

"He still needs to learn the hazards of the forest. This place is dangerous to the unwary. And even those familiar with the perils can succumb. . . ."

"I already know about the faery traps," Nick said, still standing proudly and facing Little John.

A smile tugged at Little John's face and laughter tickled his throat. Still, he needed to teach the boy the error of his ways.

"What would you do if you encounter a giant boar with tusks two feet long? Or worse, how would you counter Mammoch, the mother of all pigs in my forest? She is near immortal, and while her tusks are shorter than the boars', she is deadly, perpetually pregnant, and *very* protective of her young."

"I'd climb a tree and whistle for help." He pursed his lips and loosed a fair imitation of Will Scarlett's warning. Not many humans could mimic the bird's call so accurately.

"Why climb a tree? You might be stranded up there for days," Tuck asked, approaching the boy and eyeing him quizzically, as he might have before . . . before the current situation descended upon them all.

"Real pigs can't climb; they have cloven hooves and can't grasp a branch."

"And Mammoch?" Little John pushed Tuck aside to confront the boy.

"I presume that she can't climb either. I've never heard of her, so I suspect she is but a minor goddess and has few powers that endanger me."

Fire and flood! The boy was smart.

"You could get caught in a storm, take a chill, and die of a lung infection."

"That could happen in the abbey if I have the watch to protect the chickens and rabbits from a marauding fox."

"And if you stumbled in the dark and fell and broke your leg?" Will Scarlett asked, rubbing his own limb where he had broken it while in human guise about a hundred years ago.

Nick chewed his lip while he thought, looking down at his own feet that seemed a bit too long for his sandals.

"Well, I suspect I'd have to use that special whistle I heard Will Scarlett use to call for help." Then he looked up with a challenging gaze and grinned. "That is, as long as you do not order your people to ignore my calls."

Little John had to laugh at that. "You aren't safe in the woods, but then none of us are. We help each other, and we know the dangers to keep us wary. Now join us, help us gather some fresh roots and firewood. Then we'll eat well of the venison Robin brought in yesterday. Will, find your flute and play a lively tune to lighten our work." He slapped Nick on the back in comfortable camaraderie and nearly sent the boy stumbling across the clearing.

Little John felt a prescient pang. Something would happen to the boy, sooner rather than later. "You must promise me, young Nicholas, that you will not linger too long in the wildwood. You will *always* return to the abbey before sunset. Always."

The day after Nick's adventure in the wildwood, Dom whispered, "You're preoccupied this morning." He nudged Nick with his elbow as Father Blaine rerolled the scroll of inspirational thoughts he'd read from throughout the morning meal.

"Thinking about what you were really doing when you were late to supper?" Henry asked, keeping his eye on his spoon and his porridge rather than betray the fact that none of them truly listened to Father Blaine's droning voice. Prefect Andrew read with dynamic shifts of tone and volume.

"Trying to stay awake," Nick whispered. He, too, kept his gaze downcast so that his preoccupation didn't show.

Prefect Andrew took Father Blaine's place behind the podium. He peered closely at a piece of parchment. The middle-aged man didn't show his face in the scriptorium often. Reading, even in good light, was too hard on his rheumy eyes. "The tasks for today!" he announced.

Nick sat up straighter and listened closely. He hoped Brother Theo needed him in the scriptorium again. There he could contemplate his sins in quiet and plot ways to redeem himself.

"Nicholas Withybeck, the infirmary."

Nick groaned. "Is Brother Luke wandering again?" he asked his friends.

"He was quite docile when I sat with him four days ago," Henry admitted. "He talked a lot about working his garden and drying his herbs so that the essence of them remained vital when needed for cures. I remembered some of his plants from my mother's garden and always wondered what each was for. Wish I could remember what he said now."

"You should have written them down," Nick mused.

Dom made a face. "You write them down. I've got trap duty in the kitchen garden. Gotta keep the squirrels and rabbits from eating all our food. And make sure the crows don't make off with the newly planted seeds," he grumbled.

"Maybe I will write down the old man's mumblings. Might come in useful," Nick decided, already planning how to draw the plants with tiny animal faces hiding among them.

"Nicholas," Brother Theo stopped him as he aimed his steps for the scriptorium and writing materials. "I have spoken with the others. We all think you are the best of the boys to stay with Brother Luke."

"But you need me to transcribe . . ."

"We need you to write down all of Brother Luke's aimless mutterings. Even those that tell of his life before he took vows of obedience, chastity, and poverty. He remembers nothing of yesterday, but still can name every plant in his garden, what it looks like, and how to use it. Priceless information that should not be lost. You have the finest hand and the best memory."

"Yes, of course. My duty to the abbey and to all of the brothers must be fulfilled."

"Of course." A tiny smile touched the corner of Brother's Theo's mouth, vanishing almost before Nick noticed. "I've arranged for scraped and worn parchment, ink, and quills to be at Brother Luke's side at all times. You may have to write in dim light if the healing brothers forget to refill the oil lanterns, but I have faith in your abilities. I know you can draw the plants without looking at them."

"Thank you, sir. Um . . ."

"Spit it out, boy. We have no secrets here."

Nick doubted that. "Sir, the last time I sat with Brother Luke, he wanted to visit his garden and inspect his drying herbs. Should I allow him out of his bed?"

"The old man is feeble. I do not believe he can walk far. But if the garden helps him remember some of his healing knowledge, then perhaps helping him go there and then sitting with him will let the spring sunshine do him some good."

"Yes, sir." Nick's insides bounced with excitement. Something new to learn.

"After a trip to the garden, Brother Luke is likely to sleep. When Henry relieves you of duty, you have an afternoon to transcribe your notes. Take as much time as you need. I will not expect to see you in the scriptorium until after we convene in the refectory. Sunset comes late this close to the solstice. We will not waste the light."

Nick walked sedately along the cloister toward the infirmary, as he should. Then, when Brother Theo had disappeared into the scriptorium, he skipped a few steps.

I can teach you what the old man has forgotten.

"Thank you," he whispered to the goddess. "If I write it all down correctly, then I can spend the afternoon exploring."

You have much to learn.

"Just a few more steps, Brother Luke," Nick coaxed the old man while holding his arm and supporting him with the other hand at his waist.

"Did you know that in the Holy Land they grow olive trees?" Brother Luke said, almost as bright and clear as in his youth. "You can do marvelous things with the bark and sap and leaves, aside from the olives themselves. . . ." He trailed off as he lost the direction of his thoughts.

"Yes, Brother Luke. You told me that just yesterday." And the day before and the day before that. "Here we are, Brother Luke. Your garden. I've put a bench here beside the lavender. It's starting to bloom and smells wonderfully." Unlike the old man who had that sick, old smell about his unwashed body. The hospice workers had decided not to subject him to the cold water of a bath. It sent him into bone-racking chills for hours after. His skin was now as thin as old and scraped parchment . . . and the same color.

Carefully, Nick guided Brother Luke to sit on the stone bench that had warmed in the sun.

"Lavender. Heavenly flower. I remember when I first planted

this cutting, such a tiny slip of a thing. And now look at it. Bigger than the biggest cabbage. Nearly a full arm's length across. My people knew how to grow things in places they didn't want to take root. The Green Man can breathe on a cutting and make it eager to grow."

The lavender was now six plants, each a full arm's length across. The tiny slip of a cutting had had forty years or more to propagate, with or without assistance from the Green Man.

"Tell me about the St. John's wort, Brother Luke. Tell me how to make an unguent out of it." Nick sat at the old man's feet with a portable desk, parchment, ink, and quills stashed beneath the bench. He and his charge had sat here most every afternoon, after Terce prayers and readings. Most days he needed to prompt Brother Luke only once for the retired herbalist to ramble on about a single plant until Sext. Today Nick had asked five times about the delicate plant sheltered in a corner of the stone wall where it caught the sun and suffered no wind. He hoped that being outside with the wort in full view would trigger the proper memories.

"Ah, St. John's wort. I took my cutting it in Tuscany on my return from the Crusades. Such a lovely little plant. Did you know that you can crush a leaf and add it to the stewpot at the last moment and turn ordinary chicken broth into a marvelous delicacy?"

"Yes, you told me about that. What do I need to do to it to turn it into an unguent? You need an unguent to soothe your aching joints."

"Not as long as I sit in the sun. The sun in Tuscany is quite bright and soothing. It adds a gentle warmth to my swollen knuckles without blinding me with glare. I should wear a hat in the Tuscan sun, but it would block the light that warms my mind, and sparkles with ideas. . . ." Another breath and Brother Luke fell asleep, sitting up, head dropping to his chest.

Nick sighed and put away his writing tools. He pulled his knees up to his chest and crossed his arms across the top of them.

After only a few moments, his body twitched with inactivity and his mind wandered toward the copse and beyond that to the forest. "I wonder what you are doing today, Green Man, Robin Goodfellow, and Herne. I would join you and learn more of how you spend your days when you aren't dancing on the village green or besting the sheriff at butts."

Brother Luke snorted and roused. "Add some lavender to my bath. A warm bath in Acre . . ."

Nick grabbed the old man's arm and hoisted him upright, turning and guiding him toward the infirmary which, thankfully, opened directly into the garden. "Time to return to your bed, Brother. You need your rest."

"Rest. A beautiful thing is rest." He was asleep before he settled onto his bed.

Nick scuttled out of the infirmary and into the garden again. But he did not stay near the warm bench with the restful scent of lavender. At the base of the stone wall, he jumped as high as he could and grabbed the overhanging branch of an old and sturdy apple tree. From there, he pulled himself upward, not quite so difficult as it was only a few months ago.

When he knew that no one followed him or spied on his activities, he grasped the branch with both hands and lowered

himself to the ground on the other side of the wall. Then he
clung to the tree while he caught his breath and caressed the
bark with thanks for the assist. In the back of his mind, Elena
recited a prayer to the tree. Nick mouthed the words though
they seemed alien to what he'd been taught.

Moments later, he strode out across the orchard. His sandals slid a bit on the lush greenery that was still damp with
dew, never quite drying out in the shade until Midsummer or
later. He set his feet more carefully.

Just as he straightened, Father Blaine and Prefect Andrew
came through the gate from the courtyard, speaking softly as
they negotiated twisted pathways through the orderly rows of
fruit trees.

Hold your breath, Elena guided Nick. *Walk slowly, careful not
to make any noise.*

Nick drew in as much air as he could and held it, feeling
his chest swell and his stomach contract. Careful to stay out of
sight of the two men, he slipped from tree trunk to tree trunk.
Unfortunately, none of them were thick enough to hide behind while he replenished his breath. He had to move quickly.
From tree to tree, to bush, to the shadow of the laymen's
lodge, he hastened. Then he stepped quickly onto the flat
stones crossing the broad creek that watered the gardens and
orchards. On the third slick step, he teetered, windmilling his
arms for balance.

The world grew dark around the edges of his vision. His
head seemed to disconnect from his body. The sun glinting on
the burbling water brightened to starbursts, near blinding him.

He flailed for balance. Failed. Fell. . . .

Ten

ueen Mab tapped her dainty foot in disapproval.
Jane responded by applying more strength to her scrub brush. She hated marble floors. They showed every scrap of dirt tracked in on the boots of faeries. And Jane had to scrub them clean every day, before she attacked the piles and piles of mending. Queen Mab was never satisfied with the cleanliness of the tiles, nor with Jane's nearly invisible stitches.

How many times had she scrubbed this floor? Ten times, maybe a dozen? Her memory of the back-breaking chore grew fuzzier. The harder she thought about it, the less she remembered.

Back home, before she'd run away, the pounded earth floor didn't need scrubbing, just a sweep now and then.

She'd worked hard at home, caring for the wattle-and-daub hut and her father and four brothers. She worked harder for Queen Mab. And needlessly. At least for her family, she knew that her cooking, washing, mending, tending the chickens, and caring for the kitchen garden meant they all had food in their bellies and clothes on their backs.

Thoughts of her family took her mind back to the May Day festival. She had seen and recognized Little John right off. Hard to miss a man who stood a full head taller than most of the men she knew. He hadn't changed. But of her father and brothers, she'd seen none of them. Unusual. She'd never known any of them to miss the races and wrestling matches or flirting with the younger maids.

This year, she'd seen only boys from the abbey.

Where was her family?

Had the sheriff imprisoned or killed them for some small offense?

But then the sheriff she'd seen stringing his bow was not the same man who'd held the office two days before she ran away.

Her head spun with questions. She looked up at the openings in the ceiling that gave glimpses of the sky, sometimes bright with sunlight, sometimes dark with glints of stars.

Faeries rarely slept and barely noticed the state of the sky.

She had to stop and think. Had the wheel of stars ever changed since she came here?

"Your Majesty." Jane rose to her knees and placed her palms together in an attitude of begging.

She had never seen a king. But she knew that if ever young King Henry—the second of that name—should ride through the village, she must address him as Your Grace. He ruled by the Grace of God, not his own majesty. Apparently, Queen Mab ranked higher than the King of England.

"What now?" The Queen of the Faeries stopped in her
retreat from the hall to her clean bedroom. Not a bed for
sleeping in but for other sport.

"Your Majesty, how long have I had the honor of serv-
ing you?"

"Oh, I don't know. A while."

"But how long is a while? A few days? A week?"

"Longer than that, I'm certain. You came to us when the
leaves had turned bright yellow, orange, and red. So pretty.
And now we have celebrated May Day." She dismissed Jane
with a flick of her fingers.

"Three seasons, then," Jane mused.

"Oh, at least. Probably more than a year. Time runs differ-
ently here than out there."

"A full year and more?" Jane gasped. She didn't feel . . .
well, yes, she did feel older, wearier, with more aches in her
knees and her fingers. But . . .

"Is my family still alive?"

"Who cares? You'll never see them again." Mab turned
her back on Jane and proceeded into her private chamber.
"The passage of time and events matter not to us. We pay no
heed to changing kings or the death of mere mortals. Now I
must rest. Today has been most trying what with the festival
and all. Send Bracken to me. He has not visited me in a while."

"The festival was not today," Jane muttered, careful that
her words did not reach Mab's elongated ears. "I know I have
slept at least twice since we ventured out into the world."

We pay no heed to changing kings or the death of mere mortals.
Were any of her family still alive? She had feared her father

and older brothers, as well as the man they had sold her to—
the miller who had buried three wives already and had children older than she. She'd run away from them all. Did *she*
care if they still lived?

Her heart remained whole and free of ache at the thought.

Or did it? Maybe the carelessness of the faeries had infected
her, too.

She returned to scrubbing the same patch of floor she'd
scrubbed earlier, and the day before, and the day before,
and she'd lost track of the number of days, years, decades that
had passed.

"I will never be free of her. I will never be with my love
again."

Tears dripped down her cheeks to fall unchecked to the
floor.

Drip, drip, drip. Nick blinked away the moisture falling on
his face. He must still be in the creek.

Sunshine dazzled his eyes. Another drop on his cheek.
Rain then, not creek water flowing freely over his body.

If it was rain, then why was the sun so warm and bright?

His fingers flexed and grabbed grass and dirt.

Two more blinks and he was able to see a long shadow
above him to his left.

"About time you woke up," a gentle male voice said. "I
remember the first time I held my breath too long under Elena's tutelage. I don't believe I remained unconscious so long."

"Do I . . . know you?" Nick struggled to twist his head and see more than the long shadow. He hoped the speaker hadn't noticed how his voice broke between words.

The face of a wrinkled old man with a fringe of gray hair around a bald pate came into focus. He wore an ordinary brown jerkin over patched hose. A broad-brimmed straw hat lay on the ground beside his spotted hand. His other hand still held a leather skin filled with water—the moisture that had dripped on Nick's face, waking him.

"Tuck? The people of the village called you Tuck at the May Day festival. Before that you were an itinerant priest, the one who saved me from a burned-out village when I was tiny." Nick sat up, flexing and testing each muscle on his arms and shoulders and back as he moved.

The old man chuckled. "You have a good memory for faces, boy."

Look more closely, Elena instructed Nick.

He blinked rapidly.

Look beyond the clothes, beyond the present locations. See what few others can discern.

"You . . . Are those horn buds on your head?"

Tuck laughed loud and long, falling backward to sprawl on the grass. His mirth sounded like a ripple of wind through the tree canopy.

"Of course, Elena allows you to see beyond what others can perceive. I doubt any of your friends in the abbey or among the Woodwose can see those faint shadows."

Look deeper. Look into your past.

"I can't see into his past," Nick grumbled. "But I remember the man who pulled me from the burned ruins of my home."

"She said to look into your own past, Nicholas Withybeck," Tuck said, coming back to sit beside Nick. "After I pulled you from digging through charred timbers searching for your mother."

"Your voice . . ."

"Very good, boy."

"You speak as an educated man."

Tuck nodded.

"The only way to get an education is to be born noble or enter the church. Since you dress as a common laborer, I have to surmise that if you have noble blood, your politics do not align with King John's. That would explain your homespun. But if you took vows of obedience, poverty, and chastity before a sanctified altar, you would wear a cowled robe of a monk or priest . . . as you did so many years ago. If you are a senior member of the clergy who should have fled in exile to Paris or Rome but didn't, then you'd have to wear common garb to disguise yourself."

Tuck raised his eyebrows, almost in surprise. "Someone has trained you well, young Nicholas."

"Abbot Mæson." Nick bowed his head. Old as he was, the abbot looked younger and less careworn than he had a few months ago when he left the abbey in the middle of the night, in a hurry, taking with him only a small sack of personal belongings. No robes, no assistant, no scrolls. If he had any coins with him, he'd hidden them well.

"Very good, my boy. When all this turmoil between King John and the Holy Father dies down, and I can return to Locksley Abbey, I will make you my assistant. Now you must tell me all that transpires in my abbey. Has Father Blaine totally muddled everything yet? I doubt that I want to hear how badly he stumbles without proper tutelage."

"First, you must tell me of Tuck and those horn buds on your head. It does not reason that one of the Wild Folk would rise to become Abbot of Locksley Abbey."

Tuck laughed again. "No, there is little logic in how my parents died during the civil war between King Stephan and Empress Mathilda more than sixty years ago. Or how my great-grandsire, Herne the Huntsman, decided I needed to remain with my human relatives rather than run wild in the wood. I am more human than Wild, after all. But my human relations had too many children of their own. So they gave me to the Church, as so many do. I found more than a home there. Elena found me and educated me far above my station. Just as she is teaching you. As I approached my majority, I realized I could do more for the Wild Folk, the Woodwose, and the common villagers as a priest than I could living in the forest—though I escaped as often as possible to taste fresh air and freedom. Thus, I followed my calling and took my vows. With those sacred words my horn buds retreated, became nearly invisible to all but the most perceptive. Then Elena said farewell, and I returned her to the niche in the crypt where she waited for you to find her. But I am still aware of her, still hear her when she speaks, if she wants me to hear."

"Power flows from the pagan goddess. Power is a temptation

I should resist," Nick repeated one of Father Blaine's lessons—
admonishments.

"The fear of damnation blocks the timid from reaching for
more than their class entitles them or serfdom binds them. Those
who hold power fear having it taken from them. Think on that,
boy, before you reject the guidance of the gentle goddess." Tuck
stood up and brushed fresh greenery from his clothing.

"Sir?" Nick scrambled to his feet. "Sir, you have given me
much to ponder. Please, sir, I need to know where I am and
how I came to be here." Nick turned in a full circle, finally
noting a tall stone cross, with the circle of the eternal sunrise
connecting each of the arms, in the center of a grassy triangle.
Worn and faded knotwork carvings graced every inch of its
seven-foot height and five of breadth. Three roads joining
created the triangle of neutral ground.

"This is her crossroads."

Nick cocked his head, silently requesting more information.

"Come, look." Tuck beckoned Nick forward and pointed
to a place near the base of the cross.

Nick bent double to inspect what looked like a flaw in the
carvings. Even squinting, the details eluded him. So he
dropped to his knees and brought his face right up close.

"It's Elena," he breathed. Reverently, he traced the outline
of the three-faced goddess surrounding a pitcher, and each
figure carrying a lit lantern. His fingertips tingled with the
contact. His chest swelled with peace and balance.

"Aye. Crossroads are sacred. Have been since the beginning
of time, long before the Romans brought the true Church to
us and demoted the pagan gods to wild spirits with little power.

However, Elena is the guardian of all crossroads. The Church made her a saint rather than acknowledge her goddess status. This crossroad, more particularly than most, is her domain. Each time you hold your breath too long, while invisible to the rest of the world, when you lose touch with yourself, you will awaken here."

"The guardian spirit of crossroads. That's why she has three images each the same, each facing a new direction."

"You are not so far from Locksley Abbey. A quarter of a league down the road at most." Tuck pointed behind him on the right side. "The sun dips toward the horizon. You have just enough time to run home in time for your supper, boy."

The old man stepped across the road in the opposite direction from the abbey, still carrying his skin of water on a long thong across his shoulders and chest, and disappeared amongst the trees lining the path.

The abbey came into view when Nick had run only a short way and rounded one bend in the road. Of the three roads that met at Elena's Crossing, this one was the widest and most traveled—but nowhere near as developed as the Royal Road coming from the north. Deep ruts in the dried mud from wagon wheels made walking chancy at best. He kept to the verge, waving spritely to those returning home from the market, their carts carrying new lambs, cheeses, and produce they did not grow on their own plots in outlying villages.

Some of the weary faces he remembered from the games

and races on May Day. Most, he doubted he'd ever seen before. But all of them seemed to travel in family groups, multiple generations riding in the carts, gamboling about on the verge, or trudging beside the draft animal. One carter reached a hand to the woman walking beside him. They looked at each other for a moment with love and brief happiness. Their children came running up to them, gave each parent a quick hug and linked hands as well. They chattered brightly about the day's adventures, then fell silent, intent upon the long steps home.

Abbott Mæson's words, or rather Father Tuck's, about ministering to the villagers, the Woodwose, and the Wild Folk tickled his mind. A fine calling, indeed. But was it enough to make a lifelong commitment to the Church, taking vows of obedience, poverty, and chastity? He didn't remember his own family, didn't know he missed having one until now.

When the time comes, you will know what is right for you. For now, I am your family, and your mates in the dormitory are your brothers. Enjoy us, love us, while you can.

"When I'm eighteen, I can choose to leave the abbey and start my own family, or . . . or wander the world as I choose until I find my proper mate. I can read and write. There are always people in need of a scribe, noble people with coins to pay for my skills."

Or you can take your vows and wander the wild as you choose, ministering to those in need. You will know when the time comes.

Eleven

"ell, Elena, has the boy learned enough to tell him that he carries forest blood?" Tuck asked the goddess. He'd never given up the habit of talking to her, even when he outgrew the need for her answers.

Have you?

"What is that supposed to mean?" Leave it to the goddess of crossroads to answer a question with a question and leave him to figure out how the two connected.

Think back to the summer you turned fifteen.

"That was a long, long time ago. Only three years after I couldn't bear to part with you long enough to let you open the door to the Faery Mound. Because of me, Little John could not rescue his love. He's been a very lonely man since then." A pang of guilt twisted his gut and pressed against his chest, making it difficult to breathe and keep up his strides through the forest.

He sat on the stump to rest a bit while he thought. No. He

stood and began walking again. He always thought better when moving.

So long ago you do not remember that you considered giving up the Church to court a girl among the Woodwose?

Tuck stopped in his tracks, memories flittering ahead of him like a colorful butterfly. A smile brightened his blood, sending pleasant bubbles of excitement through him. How could he forget the long lazy days of that summer as he contemplated taking his novitiate vows to the Church. That was the first step toward becoming a priest. He could back away from those final vows any time up until the day he prostrated himself before the altar and promised his life, his honor, and his soul to Holy Mother Church.

"She was pretty, with auburn hair springing in curls around her face. A laugh twinkling behind her green eyes. Spritely steps that led me a merry chase."

It is good that you remember her so well.

"I thought she had a touch of the Wild Folk in her heritage. And I loved her for what I found in her."

More than a touch of forest blood in her.

He thought back to how easily she disappeared into the greenery when he chased her, always appearing farther ahead, leading him deeper and deeper into the shadows of the ancient forest, until she let him catch her.

The memory of them falling together into a thick nest of gathered grasses and moss that she had prepared for them heated his face and curled his toes.

He blushed at what had followed, young people thinking with their bodies rather than their minds.

You needed to know about that part of life before you took your vows.

"Yes, I think you are right. So how does this relate to Nick and his progress in learning about life?"

The girl was his great-grandmother.

Tuck choked on his own breath. "You mean . . ."

"Yes. The girl bore you a daughter."

"But she never told me."

You never saw her again.

"I was thinking of the best way to propose to her when I heard the abbey bells calling me home. Then I heard voices drifting on the wind, a plain chant extolling the beauty of the day as the sun set. I knew in that moment I couldn't leave the Church. It was—and is—my home, the place where my heart dwells."

He bowed his head as he reaffirmed his vows to himself and to God.

"My daughter must have thrived and borne children of her own." That amazed and startled him into a new awareness of Nick and why the boy seemed so special to him.

Your daughter, Lily by name, the same as her mother, wed the son of a dryad.

Tuck gulped again. "Was that man one of the Green Man's get?"

You must decide if Nicholas is ready to learn of his heritage. I do not know if he will ever be fully ready.

"Neither do I. I do not think he is ready yet. He is still getting used to you, my lady Elena. But I do know that it is time my good friend Little John learns of this. He spreads his seed far and wide as do the trees. Though he longs for a wife and lifelong companion, he must mate with dryads—women of the oaks—to continue the health of the forest. He monitors his children until they show some promise of succeeding him as king of the forest. If they drift to the human villages, then he turns them loose with love and understanding. He dismisses the descendants who are too human to understand his obligation to the forest."

Let that bit of knowledge rest a while until you become easy with it.

Little John heaved the cut end of a middle-aged ash tree onto his shoulder. A late autumnal windstorm had taken it down. Now the wood had dried, and the Woodwose needed it as a center roof support for a new hut. Every day villagers fled their homes and serfdom to take refuge from the sheriff's tax collectors here, deep in the forest. They needed shelter.

Soon he expected this nearly invisible settlement would become permanent rather than mobile. The sheriff and local barons became more and more fearful of straying from the Royal Road through the forest. Robin Goodfellow and his companions had made travel expensive, if not hazardous, in order to protect the Woodwose.

Little John was happy to assist in building these new homes. He needed to do something to fill his time before the summer solstice when the door to Faery, the only one humans and Wild Folk could access, would be opened again.

Step by careful step, he backed up toward the path where a cart awaited the ridge pole.

"I could just as easily drag this twig all the way to the village," he muttered at sight of the sagging two-wheeled wagon on the path and a placid ox in the yoke.

"You have to allow these people to do some of their own work, Little John," Tuck said. "They need to invest part of themselves in their new home in order to retain their self-respect." He rubbed his fingers where the joint disease plagued him.

"I could do it by myself in half the time," Little John muttered. He paused to adjust his position under the tree and his leverage.

"Easy now, sir. I don't like the feel of the axle," Dom, one of the abbey lads, said. He stroked the ox's nose and hummed a soothing tune, keeping the animal calm. He'd spent more of the last few weeks in the village than at his studies. He'd come once with Nick and returned on his own.

John expected him to take up residence here any day now. He had a way with animals. Any of the families would welcome him, either as a friend or a new son.

Sure enough, a quick glance behind Dom revealed Betsy, the dairymaid who had joined them after May Day, watching the work. A boy just reaching toward manhood seemed more to her liking in the illegal village than the sheriff's attentions at her lawful home.

Sir Philip Marc thought the serfs his own personal property that he could use and abuse at will. With no one else to enforce the laws upon him, he could ignore that a serf was bound to the land, not the landlord.

John eased the tree onto the bed of the cart. The ox shifted its feet. The cart swayed.

Before John could get his shoulder back under the tree trunk, Dom ran from the ox's nose to the side of the cart. He put his back against the solid wheel. It stood taller than he and weighed thrice what he did. At least.

The cart creaked and wobbled.

Little John dropped the tree, letting the top of it fall to the ground, relieving the axle of much of its weight. Not enough. Too late.

With an explosive sound, the axle snapped in half.

"Noooooo!" Little John wailed, grasping fruitlessly for the listing wheel.

Dom dug in his heels, pressing his back against the massive conveyance.

And slid downward on the muddy slope into the ditch below the road.

The wheel followed him, tilting dangerously for one long moment before succumbing to the pull of the earth.

A pale-faced boy lay beneath the wheel.

"Dom!" Betsy screamed as she knelt beside him.

Tuck grabbed his own chest and dropped to his knees on a gasp.

Quickly, Little John got his hands under the wheel and heaved upward, not caring how many ferns and ground cover plants it landed upon as long as it no longer pinned Dom beneath its weight.

He heaved the wheel aside and knew instantly he could do nothing to help the boy. He took one step toward his old friend.

Tuck waved him back toward the cart. "I'll live," he panted.

But his face was pale, and blue tinged his lips.

Little John hesitated.

"Do as I say, please," Tuck gasped once more. He made no move to stand.

Little John knelt beside Dom. The boy still breathed. Barely. His face had taken on the color of sun-bleached linen. The weight of the wheel had crushed something inside him. Only the tightness of his skin around his closed eyes suggested that life remained within.

But the boy did not draw a breath. His eyes shot open and he exhaled one last time.

"Dom, no. Dom, wake up. Dom, breathe!" Betsy pleaded. She lay herself across him, wailing. Her tears flowed freely as her body convulsed in grieving sobs.

Tuck crawled over to her and held her hand as he crossed himself and whispered prayers.

"Save your prayers!" Betsy snarled. She slapped Tuck's hand away from making the sign of the cross. "He never wanted the Church. He was never happy in your monastery. He wanted to live life, not hide from it."

"I'm sorry. So, so sorry. He didn't deserve to die. But what other chance at life did he have other than the Church?" Tuck moaned.

"He could have stayed with us. We loved him. Your eunuchs never loved anything but themselves."

"Is being an outlaw better than safety behind stout walls?" Tuck replied. "King John's dismissed mercenaries still maraud unhindered. Is a horrible and painful torture and death at their hands better than the safety the Church offers?"

"Sometimes."

WALK THE WILD WITH ME

"But he died here, with the outlaws," the Green Man muttered, as always confused by the arguments for where, when, and how mortals lived.

Sadness twisted Little John's heart. He lifted his head toward the sky and gulped back his own tears. These mortals were so vulnerable. So frail. And he could do nothing to save them. A tree or a bush would sprout new leaves from only a bit of root left alive. *He* could breathe new life into anything green except those totally uprooted. Not so with mortals. Only their God could bring the dead back to life.

He loved all his human friends fiercely, ever knowing they'd die too soon. But for one so young and so ready to embrace life, and love, to go so suddenly shocked him to his hardwood core.

"We'd best carry him back to Locksley Abbey," Tuck said sadly. "He has no place in the stone circle. He hadn't been among us enough to learn of their existence. At the abbey we can ensure he is buried in sacred ground. And I'll arrange for someone to tell his mum. She gave him up, knowing she couldn't feed him. But I know she still loved him."

"As did his twin sister," Betsy said on a sob. "I'll walk the league to the nunnery where she shelters and tell her. We can cry together."

"The sisters will not receive you." Tuck patted the girl's hand. "I hope they still respect my priestly status. That sorrowful chore belongs to me."

"I'll carry him to the abbey," John said, drawing a deep breath.

"Not your duty," Tuck protested.

"If not mine, then whose? You can't arrive on the doorstep with a . . . with a dead child. Too many there know you well even in your Woodwose guise."

Reverently, John bent to lift young Dom into his arms, cradling him as he would a newborn babe.

Betsy tucked Dom's abbey robes around him, neatly covering his legs and pulling the cowl over his head. Then she kissed his brow and backed away, tears sliding down her cheeks.

Tuck put his arm around her shoulders, a solid comfort to ease some of the pain.

They watched as, one by one, the Woodwose crept out of the forest shadows and placed a violet, a jonquil, a Johnny-jump-up, a daffy-down-dilly, and even a fern frond at the place where Dom had died. Tonight, while they slept, Little John knew he must return to the spot and breathe on these simple, heartfelt offerings to make certain they took root and remained as tribute to the boy's life.

Twelve

ick wondered how to hide a cat face within the trailing ivy vines he'd drawn to enhance a large C at the beginning of a text. The alarm bell startled him out of his deep contemplation. He looked up and around, listening. Five other scribes pushed back their benches and scurried out of the scriptorium at the first clang of the big bronze bell high up in the church tower.

Nick decided that he should join them. With three quick flicks of his pen, he anchored the cat face behind three leaves. Then he carefully set down the quill so the nib wouldn't break against something if jostled and scurried toward the big court-yard by the main gate.

Three paces beyond the smaller gate to the inner cloister he stopped short, mouth agape.

"What?" he asked one of the monks. The usually silent, middle-aged man shrugged his shoulders and pointed. Then he resumed his stately pace, hands clasped together within the voluminous folds of his sleeves, lips reciting silent prayers, and his head bowed deep within his cowl.

He might as well be a ghost.

Nick scuttled past him to the gathering throng of men and boys. One tall figure, clad in mottled moss green and bark brown, stood out among them. Nick picked out the afterimage of leaves woven into his hair and beard, twigs growing from his face. Little John.

The Green Man dipped his head as he gently placed his burden at the feet of Prefect Andrew. Then he backed out the main gate and disappeared from Nick's line of sight.

Nick ran to the gate and peered out, trying to pick out the man on the road or amongst the greenery on either side of the dirt cart track. Nothing. No movement, not even a rustle of a breeze along the crown of leaves.

There was one shadow out of place. The stooped figure of a wiry old man clung to the wall beneath the overhanging branches of yew tree. Nick squinted, and Elena let him see Father Tuck, slumped in grief. The old man touched his forehead, acknowledging Nick's presence and shuffled off, his steps unsteady and his back bent.

Nick gulped back his questions and turned back to the bundle on the ground. He froze in place, mouth twisting in sorrow.

Not an offering from the forest. A body. The corpse of his friend, Dom.

Not a single breath moved within his chest. No one could have skin so white and live, nor did his eyelids flutter in sleep.

A sharp pain pierced his chest.

Henry burst through the crowd. "No! Not Dom. He can't be dead. He can't."

Brother Theo grabbed him about the waist before Henry could fling himself across the body of his friend.

"How?" Nick asked around a dry throat and thick tongue. He struggled to accept the evidence before his eyes. "How did this happen?" He made his way over to Henry, needing to hold him close to keep himself from splitting in two.

"The . . . the villager said Dom was helping move a roof tree for a new hut. The cart axle broke, and the wheel fell upon Dominic and crushed him," Prefect Andrew said quietly, almost disbelieving. He crossed himself and whispered a prayer.

"Let this be a lesson to you all that life outside these walls is dangerous," Father Blaine intoned.

All of the gaping brothers and boys whispered "Amen," as they crossed themselves as well. Except Henry. He just stood there, shaking his head and mouthing "No, no, no, no," over and over.

Without thinking, Nick hugged his friend tightly. They weren't supposed to cry. Father Blaine said so. Death was God's will. They must thank Him for taking the boy to heaven.

Hot tears burned Nick's eyes, and he let them flow. He couldn't remember if he'd cried when his parents died. Didn't remember if he even realized they were dead until much later. He mourned for them now. He mourned for Dom's father, trampled by unthinking nobles. He mourned for everyone they'd lost over the years. And he mourned for himself and the family he never knew.

He cried until his knees sagged with weakness, and his

breath came in racking sobs and his chest hurt with the effort to breathe. Henry was the one who had to lead him to the infirmary where the duty of washing the body and preparing it for burial fell to them.

Tuck's feet felt as heavy as if he wore shackles weighing as much as his own body. He paused on the north road to rest, throwing his head back and letting the afternoon drizzle cool his heated emotions. He'd run out of prayers. "Dom died too young," he shouted to the heavens. Never before had he questioned God's plan for any of them. Never before had he considered throwing off his mantle of responsibility.

Responsibility. Archbishop Langdon had given him permission to stay in England when all the other bishops and abbots had fled to the continent. Someone needed to listen to politics and common concerns and know what needed doing when King John and Innocent III finally made peace. Tuck didn't think that would happen soon. Before that happened, he had responsibilities to those affected by Dom's death.

First, he had to find the boy's mother. He knew only that she had married a cobbler near Nottingham Castle. She'd taken her three youngest children into the marriage.

He turned east at the next crossroad and trudged onward, planning in his head what to say when he finally tracked down the woman.

The guards outside the city walls accepted his monk's robe easily. Two questions sent Tuck to a slate cottage snugged up against the castle wall. A cozy dwelling for a skilled craftsman. An ordinary-looking man with a week's worth of stubble and unremarkable brown hair brushing the shoulders of a leather jerkin and patched linen shirt sat at a workbench in the yard. Past the first flush of youth but not yet stooped with age, neither fat nor thin, coarse skin with a sharp beak of a nose, he could walk anywhere in England without notice. The drizzle had ceased, and he took advantage of the daylight to stitch a fine seam connecting a thick wooden sole to a leather boot—something the sheriff or one of his noble courtiers might wear.

"Good sir, I come with news for your wife. It's about one of her children left behind at Locksley Abbey." Tuck bowed his head and fingered his prayer beads tucked into his deep sleeves.

"Dom?" The cobbler's wife rushed out the door of their cottage. "What's happened to my Dom?" She wiped her flour-dusted hands on a threadbare apron. It bulged over her swelling belly. A kerchief that matched her simple skirt and kirtle covered her head, but a tendril of dark hair curled around her ear.

Dom had hair that color. And eyes that same shade of deep, dark brown.

"My condolences, mistress. I regret to tell you that young Dominick was killed this morning in an accident."

"No! No, no, no, no. Not my Dom," she wailed and lurched forward.

The cobbler dropped his boot and stood, catching her before she could reach Tuck with outstretched hands curved into claws.

"I gave my boy to you because you said you would keep him safe!"

"My regrets, madam. He was loved and appreciated by all of us. We still have the right to bury him in sacred ground. He was one of us and will be treated with the respect owed to him and to you." Tuck couldn't bring himself to mouth the other platitudes dictated by the Church. "I will leave you to grieve in private." He bowed his head and backed away.

His throat worked at choking back the racking sobs that yanked at his chest.

Grief continued to weigh heavily on Tuck as he made his way north and east of the city to the convent of Our Lady of Sorrows. His breath became ragged, and he grew more tired each time he inhaled. But he had to finish this. When he'd advised Hilde of the loss of her brother, he would beg hospitality. A drink of water and a chance to sit. He found the side road by habit more than conscious will.

Stopping at the top of a little rise, he drew in deep breaths and a longing to fully rest. His heart had given him warning before that he aged. He had to ignore it and press on.

The square and squat building came into view atop the next rise. Isolated, lonely, grim, and ugly, no care had been given to make the convent a feast for the eyes, a promise of the beauty of life and faith, and God's grace. It was a fortress, as much to keep strong-willed women in as marauders out. They had their own well and storage for months of extra food, if planned for and carefully managed. They could feed three villages if famine or plague struck.

He wondered if the nuns left behind had the will and the

knowledge to carry on the work of the Mother Superior in caring for the less fortunate.

Another long trudge up to the closed gates of the convent, and he couldn't lift his left hand to ring the bell. So he pulled on the tight braid of rope with his right. The untuned bronze clanked and clanged, impossible to ignore.

After too many long moments of silence, the pain in his chest eased. Tuck reached again for the bell pull, this time with his left hand, so that he faced the viewing portal fully. Another noisy reverberation. At last he heard footsteps below the ringing in his ears. The sliding wooden panel over a viewing grille opened to reveal a pinched face with a frowning mouth and eyes squinted in wrath.

"How dare you disturb the peace of this sanctuary?" a woman snarled at him.

Taken aback, Tuck jolted out of his lethargy and pulled his authoritarian abbot voice out of hiding. "Sister, I have news from Abbot Mæson. I would speak to Sister Mary Margaret. Now!"

"We have nothing to give in charity to common villeins like you." The panel slammed shut.

Tuck sank to the ground, resting his back against the wall. What had happened here? The same thing as must be occurring all over England. Without leadership, the presence of the Church was withdrawing from their purpose, taking refuge behind high walls and shunning outsiders even when they came with word from an abbot.

Without the trappings of authority, the nun did not recognize him as an abbot, only as a wandering priest.

Was that all his life's work was about: the sumptuous robes and jeweled staff granted him upon his consecration?

No. He was about more, about truly ministering to the people. As soon as this war between King John and Pope Innocent III ended, he would set about righting the many wrongs.

But first he must rest and allow his heart to heal.

A shadow formed between his closed eyes and the blessed sunshine.

Tuck's eyelids fluttered open of their own volition.

"You've a bit o' blue around yer lips," an old woman said. With the westering sun behind her, he could only see an outline and knew she was a plump matron. Her crackling voice gave away her age. She held out a cup and placed it right under his nose so he could smell the warm brew.

"Just a tisane of fairy bell leaves. Three little leaves from the top of the plant, below the flower stalk."

Tuck took the cup from her hands and cradled his aching hands around the husk of dried gourd. "What will it do for me?"

"Steady your heart. Yer needs a cup o' it every morn afore you stir."

"That might be a little difficult. I travel a lot."

"Then fix it a'fore yer sleeps. Works cold or hot, better hot, but always in the morn."

He sipped at the warm liquid and found the taste a bit bitter, but not offensive.

"Drink it up now. Won't do you no good sitting in the cup."

Tuck obeyed. He had a feeling not many dared cross this beldame.

When he'd taken the last few drops, the beldame pried his

fingers off the cup, tucked it in the folds of her kilted skirt, and disappeared within the sun dazzle that still left spots before his eyes.

"May the Lord and his wisdom bless you, lady of the fairy bells."

Hilde paused in gathering herbs to add to tonight's stew. She remained bent over the bush of rue contemplating which of the new leaves she should pinch off, and which to leave so they would grow strong.

Only a few more days until the waxing half-moon rose high in the sky. The bells no longer rang the passage of time, but she knew the precise moment when her twin brother would come and relieve the hours of strict discipline. Dom always came. Without fail. For the full length of this last year since their mother had given her two oldest children to the Church, Dom had defied the rules and punishments to spend a few moments with her two times each month. They talked and laughed and recounted their lives since they'd last seen each other. The restrictive lives of convent and monastery could not separate them.

Neither of them could allow it. They'd always been together, from womb to that horrible day a year ago when Da had died and Mum faced the possibility of their happy family starving to death. She had no choice but to give the eldest of her brood of five to the Church. The cobbler for the castle was recently widowed. He was willing to marry Mum and apprentice her younger children to follow his trade. But he could not take on all five of her offspring. The younger three were too small to go to the Church. So Hilde and her twin had been ripped from their mother's side.

Hilde's happiness for her mother and the other children dimmed the first time she felt Sister Marie Josef's rod across her knuckles and back.

The warm spring air shimmered around her and then darkened. A sharp pain ripped across her belly like a knife thrust. A terrible weight restricted her breaths. Her knees buckled, and she fell facedown in the dirt, her nose filled with the bitter odor of rue.

Sister Mary Margaret rushed to her side, gently enfolding Hilde in her warmth and comfort. "There, there, child, is the sun too hot for you today?"

Hilde nestled against the older woman's lush bosom, pretending that she was back home with Mum, being cradled after stumbling and scraping her knee. She couldn't speak. The pain in her gut expanded to crush her lungs. Gasping for breath, she allowed Sister Mary Margaret to lift her to her feet. Still bent double and clutching her middle. Hilde stumbled beside her guardian nun as she guided her to her cot.

"Rest, my girl. Take a few sips of water. Just a little for now. More later," Sister Mary Margaret whispered to Hilde, clucking like a mother hen.

"Sister," Sister Marie Josef said sternly from the doorway to the dormitory. "There is a visitor at the gate. He asked for you as the senior sister. I tried to turn him away, but he is most insistent and said he had news from Abbot Mæson."

"A visitor? News from the abbot?" Sister Mary Margaret

said, hands fluttering. "Oh, my. This must be important." She made to move past the other nun who stood solidly in the way of an exit.

"He is dressed like a poor wanderer. We have no room or facilities to shelter him. I tried to shoo him away, but he refused to leave until he spoke to you. This is most improper and contrary to the Rule of our Order."

"We owe him common charity. That, too, is as important to the Rule of our Order as isolation and contemplation," Sister Mary Margaret said. The firmness of her tone and her chin defied the taller nun's sternness. She pushed the disciplinarian aside, her footsteps echoing hollowly on the flagstone walkway of the inner cloister.

"Slacking off your chores again?" Sister Marie Josef stomped toward Hilde's cot. She raised her rod high and slammed it down on Hilde's belly.

Hilde screamed. She knew she needed to hide her pain. That was part of being a nun.

"No pain life gives you is greater than the suffering of our Lord. Pain should send you into prayer, not screaming like a child," Sister Marie Josef said on a sneer.

"Think on how that blow echoes through your body and know that it is nothing compared to what will happen to you outside these protective walls. Out *there* you would be sold to the first man who offers you marriage and then he'll rape you every night—rob you of your virtue and your chance to get into heaven every night—until he gets a son on you and you die in childbirth!"

Sister Marie Josef delivered another blow to Hilde's knees.

Thirteen

repare! Elena whispered into Nick's ear. He jerked his head up from his doze. He stood at the head of Dom's bier during the darkest part of the night, hands folded together inside his sleeves, cowl over his head. He'd learned during his earliest years at the abbey how to sleep standing upright, sometimes with his eyes open.

"Prepare for what?" he whispered, wary of disturbing the deep stillness of the Lady Chapel. In normal times the bells would have rung to awaken him at Lauds or Matins. The bells remained silent by order of the Holy Father and King John.

The time is coming when I must ask you to do something very hard.

"As if burying my dearest friend is not hard," he murmured.

Hard enough, but what I must ask you to do will be harder.

Movement at the entrance from the nave across the altar dais silenced his verbal questions.

Your relief has come at last. You have watched your friend through the night. Rest now. I will summon you when the time is right.

The vacancy Elena left in Nick's mind tripped his balance. He reached out to grab the edge of the stone slab where Dom rested, clothed in his least threadbare gray robe, his prayer beads wrapped around his clasped hands.

A hot jolt ran from Nick's fingers up through his arm to his shoulder, finally breaking a knot of tension at his nape. His senses righted, and he assumed his prayerful attitude.

"I see you've learned to sleep standing up," Prefect Andrew said. "A useful skill."

Nick raised his head, startled by the words.

"Never fear, boy. We all do it."

"Sir," Nick bowed his head in respect. Then he came upward with a determined thrust of his chin. In the depth of his sleep he'd thought of something important. "Prefect Andrew, Dom had a sister and a mother. They should be informed of his passing."

"A message went to his mother. She mourns for her son privately. She gave him to the Church. He is ours to mourn publicly and to bury him."

"Sir, his sister was his twin. They were close before . . . before he came here. I believe he visited her on numerous occasions after he came here. She should be told."

"Nicholas, the messenger was turned away by a senior sister. Since the abbess retreated to exile, the sisters can only obey the rules of the Order with the strictest interpretation. Only they know if they told the girl."

"Sir, I'd like to try to talk to her . . ."

"Not your place or your duty. Now go. Your time of wakefulness is over. Seek out your bed for a few hours before the day
begins. You'll want to break your fast before we dig a grave for
your friend. 'Tis a hard thing to bury one so young. Rest as-
sured, he has gone to a better place, free of pain and hunger and
sleepless nights. And worry for his sister's and his mother's wel-
fare. Go now." Prefect Andrew shooed Nick away with a flutter
of his hands. Then he stood where Nick had been stationed
most of the night and ran his fingers through his own prayer
beads while his lips moved silently in the funerary ritual.

Nick had attended plenty of funerals before, beginning with
the makeshift prayers for his parents said by Father Tuck who
had found him digging through the ashes of their hut. But
since then most of the funerals had been old men in the abbey
or barely-known villagers.

Never before had he buried a friend.

At high noon, he stood in his assigned place below the
choir in the church, sorely aware of the vacant spot to his right
where Dom should have stood. He lifted his shoulder and
pushed his elbow outward from long habit. He met only
empty space with no grunt from Dom as he roused from his
latest nap. Then Father Blaine stumbled over the Latin invo-
cation. Nick winced in sympathy. The young man had been
thrust into the priesthood unprepared and years earlier than

intended. Abbot Mæson needed to ensure that a second priest resided in the abbey, alongside Prefect Andrew, before he left for royal-decreed exile. The young priest recited the words by rote, never having presided over a funeral mass before.

"Prefect Andrew should be saying the words, not Father Blaine," Henry grumbled. "We know Andrew can say it right, even if he doesn't sing. Dom deserves better than . . . than a youngster who's never done it before."

"Hush," Nick admonished. He felt the same way but knew better than to speak his thoughts.

Sure enough, Brother Theo's heavy hands landed on their shoulders. He squeezed gently but said nothing.

Nick twisted his neck to better see the face beneath the shadowy cowl. "I know," the man mouthed. "We do the best we can with the tools God gives us. Father Blaine needs the practice." Then he, too, fell silent.

Nick spent the next hour wondering at the monk's gentleness, nay, his *tenderness* toward his students. He put on such stern manners in the scriptorium that Nick only expected the same demeanor in everything he touched.

By the time Nick had eaten in the refectory, said prayers, and climbed into his cot, he realized the strict taskmaster, who presided over the books and the scrolls and their accurate copying, actually cared about all the boys in the dormitory. After an entire night standing watch over his friend, he couldn't sleep. Every time he closed his eyes, he saw only Dom's face, deathly pale, mouth open in a silent scream of terror.

He rolled onto his right side. Henry snored lightly.

With a twist and a *humpf*, Nick turned to his left side. Dom's empty cot remained empty. As did the emotional hole in Nick's belly.

He wondered briefly how Dom's sister must feel . . . if she knew of her twin's death.

He sat on the side of his bed, elbows on knees, face in hands. His fingers rubbed his temples, trying to alleviate the nagging headache forming behind his eyes.

He needed to sneak away and go to the Benedictine convent where Dom's sister resided. He needed to make sure she knew that Dom had passed.

Dared he go now? 'Twas the hour Dom usually crept out to visit his sister, Hilde. Nick needed fresh air and silence to banish the physical pain of his grief before talking to the elusive postulant nun.

As quietly as possible he donned his robe, gathered up his sandals, and slipped out of the dormitory into the cloister. From there, the postern door was only a quick and shadowed walk around the porter's lodge. He'd planned to sit in the garden beside the infirmary, but his feet turned in the opposite direction, to the cemetery between the church and the outer wall.

Beyond earshot of any late-night wandering monks, he slipped on his sandals and made his way along a twisting path to the upright headstones. A lump of disturbed dirt marked Dom's grave. In a week or so, he'd get a flat stone, no higher than the grass, at his head to mark his passing. Until then, he had only a loose mound of soil to indicate where the monastic community had laid him to rest. That pile would gradually flatten beneath the spring drizzle that helped Brother Luke's herbs grow.

Nick thought maybe a clump of herbs or a flowering bush should be planted at his feet since Dom loved working in the fields more than tending to his lessons.

He'd never heard of flowers marking a grave and smiled at the thought. He knew precisely the clump of St. John's wort, a healing plant, in the herb garden that he should transplant. The stuff grew everywhere and would find fertile ground here.

Nick crossed himself and turned his steps toward the shed with garden tools.

A misty figure, vaguely feminine, wavering from one to three silhouettes, stood in the center of the path he should take. She held up a lantern so that it spilled a soft glow. His hand instinctively went to the fold of his sleeve where he kept Elena. The little silver pitcher remained in place.

Not knowing exactly why, Nick knew that he needed to place the pitcher on the grave. He knelt and noticed a little moisture gathered in the bottom of the cup. He tipped it so that a tiny puddle formed. Then he rested the silver piece beside the gathered water in the center of the mound that was now all that was left of his dear friend. Then he rose to complete his chore of transplanting a bit of greenery.

Elena pointed with her glowing lamp back toward Dom's grave.

Nick transferred his attention from the pitcher and the tiny puddle to look for who might menace him.

A cemetery is the ultimate crossroad, Elena said.

Sure enough, a pale echo of Dom stood atop the mound of

loose dirt without disturbing the granules. He looked about in confusion. Then he spotted Nick. His puzzled expression brightened. Dom opened his mouth and formed soundless words.

Nick took a moment while he figured out the shape of the question. "Yes, Dom, you have to go. You have to take the path." He thought those were the right words to whisper into the night.

Dom spoke a silent protest. His mouth shaped a single word, *Hilde.*

"She can't join you yet," Nick replied.

Dom looked as if he'd protest more. *Help her.* The words formed in the back of Nick's mind along with a deep sense of urgency.

"I'll do what I can. I promise. Now it is time for you to find your own path." He stepped aside, not caring that his feet rested upon the flat stone of another grave. A shaft of gentle light flowed outward, seemingly into nothing. It should have stopped at the outer wall. Instead, it continued into more light *through* the wall.

Elena lifted her lamp, its light joining the shaft along the pathway. *Your time has come.*

Reluctantly, Dom set a single step upon the trail. He looked back at Nick, hollow eyes pleading for another choice. His mouth again formed a single word: *Hilde.*

"I'll look in on her, Dom. I promise," Nick said.

Help her!

"I will. Now, please, Dom. Go, be happy. Share a good laugh with St. Peter."

Dom threw back his head as he did when he laughed. His steps lightened and skipped as he nearly danced onward until the light winked out and only the stout wall remained.

Nick choked back a sob. Then he looked up at Elena. She had not faded with her chore complete. "Thank you, my lady. I think. I needed to see him whole once more, not the broken corpse."

"Not all deaths are so easy for the soul. Your friend needed only a slight nudge to set him upon the proper path." Elena became more solid. "Some fight the choice and linger in the half-death of a ghost." She pointed again with her lamp.

Five misty figures wandered around the gravestones, looking right and left, up and down in confusion.

"They weren't ready to go," Nick whispered.

"They left something undone," Brother Theo replied, coming up beside him.

Nick jumped at the sound of the real words, spoken by a living man.

Elena winked out.

"You've said your prayers and seen your friend on his way. You can rest easy now. Time you went back to bed. Dawn comes early this time of year." Brother Theo touched Nick's back and urged him along the solid and moonlit path back to the cloister and the dormitory.

"A moment more, please?" Nick asked.

"A short moment."

As soon as Brother Theo turned his back, Nick ducked to retrieve the little silver pitcher of the three-faced goddess.

"Thank you," he whispered to her as he tucked the vessel back into the fold of his sleeve.

Prepare! A voice echoed through the halls of Faery.

Jane looked up from mending the torn hem of Queen Mab's favorite pink gown, her body still and alert. She'd been promoted from scrubbing floors when Queen Mab noticed that the pile of mending grew and her human slave who had skills with a needle and thread was washing floors. Jane had been mending and embroidering the queen's fine fabrics for . . . a long time before Mab actually became aware of how much nicer her clothes were now. And how many needed mending.

Queen Mab took no notice of the voice that had echoed in Jane's mind. Her Majesty continued to play a mindless game of matching tiles, standing the clay squares on end when she had four of a kind that took them out of play.

Her ladies and courtiers concentrated on the best way to lose the game even when they held winning groups of the designs painted on the tiles.

No one else took notice of the resounding voice either. But it wasn't the deep tolling sounds of doom. No. This one sounded bright and cheerful.

A thrill of anticipation jumped from Jane's heart to her mind, making her a bit breathless.

She felt no sense of wariness or caution in the voice.

"Prepare for what?" she muttered to herself, retuning her

attention to her tiny stitches with gossamer thread and a needle finer than anything she'd seen before her time in Faery.

Soon. This time the voice came to her in a whisper.

Jane knew that the words were meant only for her. The royal court of Faery was excluded from the hope of something special coming.

"What do I need to prepare for?" Jane asked herself and the unusual voice that intruded into this ensorcelled palace beneath the Faery Mound.

Prepare to run. Prepare a weapon.

A numbness around and inside her ears told Jane that the voice had nothing more to say today.

She plied her silver needle carefully while her mind spun with possibilities. What did she have that would threaten or damage Queen Mab? The sovereign was a faery and immortal. Jane had nothing, certainly not a knife or scissors. She had to bite her threads clear of a finishing weave when she completed a mending chore, as she did at home. Though the threads available to her before she'd fallen into a faery trap were much bulkier and sturdier, as befitting farmer's clothing. And her single needle then had been large and clumsy, made from rough iron. She had carried it with her always, woven into a fold of her shift so that she wouldn't lose it.

Here she had a silver needle, stretched so thin it might bend if she looked at it strangely. The faeries supplied her with cobweb-fine threads, but only this one needle. They never touched the silver. Mending was beneath their dignity. And they never quite managed the embroidery.

Jane thought furiously back to the day when Queen Mab

had first told her to mend a rent in a fine silken gown. She'd pointed to the sewing supplies. She had not touched the needle.

She didn't touch the needles because . . . because . . . she couldn't.

One of the tales the courtiers told of a long evening related how the magicians had withdrawn from Faery long, long ago. Queen Mab had insulted an easily-overlooked goddess, of only minor power, because . . . she had been unworthy of Mab's notice. The unnamed goddess had cursed this band of faeries to live underground for as long as Queen Mab lived. The faeries had to rely on their own magic, which touched only themselves, and maybe their human slaves, not ordinary objects brought in from the real world.

Mundane silver repelled Mab, and there had not been a magician with sufficient power to bespell the needles so that a faery could use them for a long, long time.

Jane hummed to herself, satisfied with her conclusions.

She had a weapon. Now she just needed to gather the courage to use it.

Fourteen

repare!

Hilde sat up straight in her bed, clutching her shift close at her throat where the chill night air invaded and raised gooseflesh on her skin.

Her gut still hurt from where Sister Marie Josef had slammed her rod into her. Her chest still felt tight from whatever fit had seized her in the garden.

Just the act of sitting up felt like she'd be ripped in two.

And all of the girls in the dormitory had shunned her since Sister Marie Josef had punished her. The nun had ordered them all not to talk to her, approach her, or offer any kind of solace.

"Who?" Hilde whispered, fully aware of the dozen girls who slept nearby. Dawn crept around the edges of her awareness. One of the novitiates would come soon to wake them all for morning prayers.

A friend, young Hilde. Trust that I am your friend. You must prepare yourself for the one who comes for you.

Hilde blinked rapidly, trying to make sense of the misty form hovering at the foot of her bed.

"Lady, is Dom coming to take me away from here?" The moon phase was not yet right for him to come.

You must prepare for a new phase of your life.

The mist began drifting apart, losing the rough outline of a human form.

"Please." Hilde reached a desperate hand to stay her leaving. "If you are indeed my friend, please tell me . . . tell me . . ." She didn't know what she wanted to know. She just wanted . . . no, she needed a friend. Someone who did not want to hurt her or deny her. Or was afraid of Sister Marie Josef.

"Lady, you could only be our Lady, mother of our Lord Jesus."

The figure coalesced, taking on delicate features and a suggestion of pale hair and skin, with little more color than her flowing moonlit gown. Only there was no moonlight, or even starlight penetrating this dark interior dormitory.

The lady flickered, and her solid form drifted into three.

Hilde blinked, and she became a single outline once more.

I have been called many things. If that title suits you, you may use it.

"I . . . have a sense that I am utterly alone, with only you to accompany me into this new phase of my life."

You will have another at your side soon.

"Another. Dom. My twin brother is the only one who wishes my company."

There is another. But you must be ready. And prepared.

The figure dissolved before Hilde could think of any words that would keep her there.

⁂

Little John embraced his tree and willed his body to merge with the ancient oak. Gradually, his fingers and toes twisted and lengthened into twigs. His arms and legs shifted next, absorbing the bark and inner layers of wood. A sense of peace he rarely knew in his human form spread outward from his torso. Bit by bit, he blended with the other half of his soul. Heaviness lifted from his shoulders and spread upward into the crown of the tree, a momentary dizziness and then . . . he sighed in contentment.

He'd needed this rest for a long time. But worry about Jane had kept him striding among people for too long. He hadn't rested properly since May Day, when Tuck had confirmed that Elena, the key to opening the ensorcelled door into the Faery Mound, had chosen a new student and emerged into the upper world once more.

Without Elena, he knew he could not free Jane. He had to persuade young Nick to part with the silver pitcher long enough for the goddess of crossroads, cemeteries, and sorcery to do her work. Tuck had been too young and inexperienced, too uncertain of who he was and where he belonged the last time the moons aligned, and they could have freed John's love.

Hopefully, Nick could do better.

They still had the full passing of a moon before they could even try.

He closed his eyes and drew upon the strength of the forest to restore him. A robin redbreast had made a nest in his upper branches. He listened to her chirp to her young while they waited for her mate to return with fat and tasty worms to feed the hungry bellies of chicks just coming into their feathers. He smelled the musk of a fox on the hunt for an unwary hare. Then he felt the itch of an aggressive bit of ivy sending out rootlets to anchor itself in his bark. Mentally, he scratched the itch and banished the intruding vine.

Ah, he sighed. No matter the turmoil of mortal souls, the life of the forest continued.

"How fare you, Green Man?" Ardenia asked. She caressed his bark with her moist human hand. Of late, she'd been spending more time outside her spring-fed pond and arguing with Herne less often. And now she comforted the leader of the Wild Folk.

Of all the creatures of the wood, she seemed to be the center, the anchor, the one they all sought to spill their troubles and toils. No wonder the Christians had made her a saint—even if they did change her name from Ardenia to Anne. Not so big a transformation.

The Green Man sucked in the little bit of moisture left from her greeting. The momentary refreshment brought him out of the deep sleep he'd prepared for. He rustled a single branch close to her, inviting her to sit at the junction of the secondary trunk.

"Thank you," she said. "But I do not linger today. I have an appointment with Herne." She smiled, and her touch warmed with pleasurable anticipation. "When I noticed you in residence, I thought I should stop and greet you. You have not sought respite in your tree often, or for long, since May Day."

He rippled his bark beneath her hand in thanks.

"If you do not need me close by, then I shall go about my business and let you rest." She stepped back, her silvery gown glinting in dappled patterns where the light filtered through the shade of his branches. And then she was gone.

Little John let himself relax and shift deeper into his tree.

Before the Green Man could sense the passage of time, an uproar of shouting men, galloping horses, and baying hounds roused him. He gathered his energy, preparing to step free of the tree to see who disturbed the peace of the forest.

New leaves in his crown and outer limbs sought more light and moisture, as much for the need to survive as curiosity. That was the thing about oaks; they needed to see and hear everything. They even occasionally moved around until they got too big and cumbersome and their tap root grew deeper and deeper to support the weight above.

Little John let his eyes nestle within the outthrust leaves. Bit by bit, he followed the shafts of light toward the Royal Road that cut straight through the forest. Dogs led the hunters, smaller dogs with long noses and raised tails bred to scent prey along the ground. They bayed in a high pitch. Then the larger dogs, with coarse brindled fur and wide, strong jaws, belled deep and long. Their long sight followed their prey.

They stayed close to their masters, ready to help take down the boar or deer at the end of the hunt.

Beside the big hounds came the main pack of mounted hunters, wearing leather jerkins and trews. They all carried bows, spears, and swords. Knights and nobles, for no one else could afford a sword or a horse. And then a wink of bright red glinted from the pommel of the sword sheathed at the knee of the lead rider. Only one man in the district boasted such a fine weapon: Sir Philip Marc, Sheriff of Nottingham.

Hunters. A common enough intrusion. Nothing to worry about.

Little John went back to sleep.

Nick looked up from his pages of scribbled notes to check on Brother Luke. The old man had fallen asleep mid-word on a repeated dissertation on the properties of applewood smoke for killing fleas when even fleabane failed to banish them from bedding.

Just talking about the pests made Nick's skin itch. He scratched intently at an imaginary bite on his ankle. Then another itch between his shoulder blades grabbed his attention. He couldn't reach it, so he rubbed it along the edge of Brother Luke's bench. Ah, that helped.

Thankfully, he and the other boys took the time every equinox and solstice to change the rushes inside the mattresses and wash the linens with harsh lye soap and scalding hot water.

He had a faint recollection that the abbey bedding was cleaner than where he had slept in the hut with his parents.

"Brother Luke?" Nick shifted to his knees and touched the old man's elbow. His head dropped as he whuffed a gentle snore.

"Ah, well, you deserve your rest." Nick rolled his parchment and stowed it in its round leather case. His quills, ink vial, and sealing wax went inside his sleeves and scrip.

He debated for a moment if he should help Brother Luke back to his bed or let him sleep in the sun like a contented old cat.

"Nick!" a voice whispered from the top of the wall, right beside the overhanging apple branch. The limb was lush with blossoms beginning to set fruit, so he had a hard time picking out the face within the greenery.

The face appeared slowly, like trying to let the squiggles of a drawing coalesce into a hidden figure in his illumination of a sacred text.

He grinned at the image of Abbot Mæson, or rather Tuck, sitting cross-legged on that branch.

"Leave Brother Luke. He won't go anywhere for hours. And I need you. Now." The former abbot slipped out of view beyond the wall.

Eager with anticipation of a new adventure, Nick jumped up and grabbed the stout branch. In only a few heartbeats he'd joined his tutor and mentor in the orchard.

"Why do you need me?" Nick asked in hushed tones.

Tuck put a gnarled finger to his lips. Then he set out at a sprightly pace, more akin to a prancing Puck than a stately abbot.

Nick followed, eager to help the Wild Folk he already thought of as friends.

❦❦❦❦❦

Tuck hurried forward with new urgency. His cup of morning tisane allowed him to move with haste. He took a deep breath and set a pace that was slow for him, but faster than he could manage a few days ago.

"Come quickly, Nick," he called over his shoulder, only to find Nick beside him.

"I am coming as quickly as I can. Why do you need me with such urgency?"

"I need Elena's wisdom to resolve a conflict."

Nick nodded. "I have a feeling this is but the first of many summonses?"

"Elena chooses a companion when she needs to be out in the world. She chose you for a reason."

Light laughter rippled around the back of Tuck's head.

His shoulders relaxed, and his stride lengthened. Nick matched him stride for stride. Unsurprisingly, he now stood as tall as Tuck. By the end of summer, he'd probably be taller, like the Green Man's kin. He already topped Henry by a whole hand's breadth.

"Nick, there is something you need to know."

"That I have forest blood in me?"

Tuck almost choked on his next words. "You know that Elena always chooses her companions from among those who have at least a little forest blood in them."

"I guessed as much. I do not think I'd be able to see the true nature of the Wild Folk if I didn't share their blood, not even with Elena's help."

Tuck had no answers to that. But his heart swelled with pride. The boy was bright and figured out the way of life more easily than Tuck had. Unusual for one raised in the abbey with limited contact among mortals.

Except that Nick was curious and adventurous. He'd been coming and going as he chose since he was tall enough to reach the apple branch overhanging the back wall of the herb garden. He wondered if the branch drooped lower when Nick and his friends were shorter.

"Who is my ancestor linking me to the forest?" Nick kept pace without deepening his breathing.

Tuck feared he'd have to slow down soon to catch his breath. But they neared the line of trees that marked the boundary of the Royal Forest. Once there, he had tricks to draw strength and breath from the land and the trees.

Then Tuck felt Nick's strong young arm encircle his waist to boost him along.

"When I was young, before I took my first vows, I sired a daughter on a girl from the Woodwose . . ." And so he related the tale of Nick's heritage. Now, in perfect hindsight, he should have recognized Nick's willow-green eyes the moment he saw them. He'd been told his own eyes were that color, as was the girl's.

The boy said not a word, but he didn't change his hurried pace either.

Tuck endured the silence for seemingly endless paces. He

was curious how Nick felt. But he was also grateful he did not need to talk.

"Thank you, grandsire. You and I have had a bond since you first found me. Now I know why. It's more than our shared willow-green eyes." A big grin brightened his countenance, making those green eyes sparkle. "I have family," he whispered. "A real, blood-related family!"

"Aye, boy. Blood calls to blood. You know why your heritage, and mine, must remain secret between us? Those of the abbey will not understand our forest heritage. They will understand our blood ties, but not necessarily accept it."

"Aye, sir. The path forks here. Which direction?"

"Think about it. Feel the tug of anger and fear. Follow your forest instincts."

"Left toward St. Anne's Well."

"Aye, boy. You've the right of it now. Did Elena help you decide?"

"No. I just felt like my left side was heavier."

He is prepared for what comes. Are you, old man?

As long as my heart beats strong and regular, he replied.

Fifteen

"Unhand her!" a masculine voice shouted in the near distance.

Tuck hastened his steps along a path that seemed to open for them but remained invisible to Nick's eyes. He followed his mentor—his great-grandfather—anxiously. He still had to absorb the wonder of having blood ties to anyone. *He had a living great-grandsire*!

Abruptly, they came upon a wide clearing beside a small pool of clear water. It spread out at the base of a waterfall trickling down a rocky hillside. St. Anne's Well. He'd heard the place described often enough but never felt the urge to make the pilgrimage here. The accepted path here traveled a long way by the Royal Road, then a shorter trek along a well-beaten trail across the pond from here. Tuck had brought him by a shorter route that wound through the forest in an almost straight line.

"I claim the lady as my bride. All has been arranged with King John," Sir Philip Marc proclaimed.

Nick didn't like the way the man's eyes narrowed and his mouth smirked.

"King John has no right to decide the lady's fate. He is not her guardian," Tuck said breathlessly. He panted heavily from their rapid trek through the forest. Even with Nick's assistance, he'd moved too quickly for his aging body. The tisane every morning worked well enough for normal activity, but urgency had pushed him to move beyond the limits of the remedy.

"She has no apparent guardian at all; therefore, she falls under the king's jurisdiction, and he has given her to me!"

"Um . . . since when?" Nick whispered to Tuck.

"Since King John said so," the old man replied.

"Why doesn't she just break away and fling herself into the pool?" Nick measured the distance between the lady's feet and the pool. If she was truly a water sprite, then she should become indistinguishable from the flowing water once wet.

"As long as Sir Philip holds her, she cannot break away."

"What happens if she goes with him?" A dire emptiness wiggled around Nick's belly. He sensed something very wrong about this situation, but he couldn't pinpoint his distress.

"She cannot stay dry and away from her pond for more than a day. She will wither and crack into dust," Tuck replied sadly. Then he brightened. "Can you make a distraction? Make him loose his hold so that she can break free?"

Nick looked about him for tools and methods. He couldn't find an apple tree with old fruit to drop on Sir Philip's head. That always distracted Brother Theo. Nor could he find a long stick and a hollow trunk to beat and make loud noises.

If he ran at the sheriff to tackle him, as he would in a wrestling match or village football game, the heavily armed men in the sheriff's hunting party would shoot him, and if they didn't kill him right off, they'd haul him off to jail and then hang him.

While he hesitated, Sir Philip lifted Lady Ardenia onto the back of his saddle. She balanced precariously. She looked toward Tuck and Nick, pleading with her eyes for assistance.

You know what you need to do, Elena whispered.

Nick caressed the little pitcher in his sleeve. "Promise you'll come back to me?"

Silly boy. Of course I will. I have chosen you, and our time of final separation has not yet come. You have too much to learn.

Nick took a deep breath for courage and knelt by the pond. He dipped the pitcher, filling it with water. Then he found a lump of wax with his other scribe's tools in his belt scrip, warmed it with his hands, and stoppered the pitcher. Three quick steps took him to the lady's side. She clutched Sir Philip's leather jerkin desperately to keep from falling off the impatient hunting horse.

Silently, Nick slipped the pitcher into her sleeve. She smiled and winked at him.

He'd had to act quickly, thinking only of the necessary steps to complete the plan. If he faltered at all, he'd not have the courage to release the little silver pitcher to another.

He'd been brought up to think little of possessions. Life in the abbey was contemplation, obedience, poverty, and . . . and charity. Tuck—Abbot Mæson preached the value of charity much more than Father Blaine, or even Prefect Andrew. The little pitcher was a possession, not his to keep.

That it was Elena's chosen home was important. But it was hers. He had no right to it.

I will return to you, Elena told him. Was that a catch in her mental voice? A reluctance to leave him?

He breathed deeply, fearing an emptiness from her absence.

A tiny tingle in the back of his mind let him know that she was still tied to him. For a time yet. She'd let him go when *she* decided it was time.

That time had not yet come.

"Sir Philip, you may keep me as long as you can hold me," Ardenia said, a note of triumph creeping into her voice.

"Then you shall abide in the top of my tallest tower with plentiful guards, my lady. But you will be mine." He kicked his steed into motion and galloped back toward Nottingham.

"That was brave of you," Tuck said, eyes wide in amazement. "An act of charity. You are blessed."

"It needed to be done." But need now left a huge hole in his mind and in his gut, wounding him almost as deeply as the loss of Dom.

I have not deserted you, Elena laughed. *I shall return soon. In the meantime, find Hilde.*

Little John struggled to find himself within the tree. He hadn't been merged with the giant oak long enough to rest properly. Now he was needed by his people, but he couldn't find his hands or feet to start moving outward. He barely had enough mind to know he must.

Blink rapidly. Twitch his nose. Sap in the tree became his blood, flowing inward. Rapidly for a tree. But trees measured time in seasons and generations, not in human days or the arc of the sun. Or even heartbeats.

Heartbeats. He willed his heart to take on the rhythm of the horses pounding along the Royal Road.

Finally, he twitched one bare toe and then another and another. His fingers followed, and he began tearing his way through the tree's heartwood to emerge.

"Easy, John," Tuck whispered. "The lad did what was necessary. Sir Philip has a promise he thinks is his advantage. The lady has a means of escape. And the boy . . ."

"What about the boy?" Little John demanded in a voice that resounded through the forest like thunder. His face pressed into the inner bark, barely reaching the air.

Tuck looked up and frowned. "Do you know how formidable you are in this half state?"

"Yes." His voice boomed, several tones lower than any human body could achieve. "What about the boy?" Warm air caressed Little John's eyes, nose, and lips. He heard four chips of bark land in the moss at his feet. A few moments more. He needed only a few moments more to release himself.

"He filled the Elena pitcher with water from Lady Ardenia's pond, stopped it with sealing wax, and gave it— *willingly*—to the water sprite. She carries a part of her home with her. She can return any time she wants."

"He relinquished the pitcher?"

"Quite willingly, and of his own volition."

"Then he can do it again."

"I believe so."

"He can release Elena to help us open the door to the Faery Mound on Midsummer's Night Eve?"

"One would think so."

"Then I live with hope in my heart and no need to sink myself into this tree." He stepped clear and shook himself free of bark, twigs, and moss. He picked a stray twig from his beard and combed moss back into hair with his fingers.

Find Hilde. Elena's words echoed repeatedly through Nick's head. "How am I supposed to do as Elena commands?" He stood near rooted to the spot where he'd been when he handed the little silver pitcher to Lady Ardenia. His mind and his feet seemed stuck in thick mud.

"Think, lad," Tuck chuckled. "Elena never gives you a task until you are ready for it. It may be hard, but you can do it." The old man wandered off, along with the other Forest Folk. Aimless. They all seemed aimless and unconcerned for the water sprite.

That left only himself to find Hilde, Dom's twin sister.

He closed his eyes a moment and called up one of Prefect Andrew's lessons in logic. "What do I know?" He held up one finger.

"I know that Hilde abides in the convent a league the other side of Nottingham. I have been there, talked with her. She knows me and therefore should trust me." What else?

"I know that Dom left his cot in the dormitory right after

Compline when all the other boys had fallen asleep. And that he returned before Matins. He did this on the night of the quarter moon both waxing and waning, every month without fail."

He studied his feet as he trod the narrow path back toward Locksley Abbey. "Therefore, Hilde must expect a visit from her brother on those two nights and no others. What is the moon phase?" He hadn't thought to check. His life had been regulated by bells for so long, he rarely considered marking the moon, except to note when it was full and likely to betray him if he escaped for his own adventures. That must be why Dom chose the quarter moon for his escapades—barely enough light to keep him on the road, but sufficient to keep him from running into trees or stepping in a mud puddle.

As Nick's steps took him into a modest clearing near the boundary of the Royal Forest, he looked up. Sometimes he could catch a glimpse of the moon during the day. Not today.

He needed help. Was there a book in the scriptorium that charted the moon's passage?

Prepare! The voice of Elena chuckled into Little John's mind.

"Now what?" he snarled, picking himself up off a fallen tree trunk just beginning to show clear spaces within the massive root ball. The tree had been an old friend, gone these three winters and only now giving up the effort to survive. Bracken and other low growing plants had taken root in the crumbling bark and the dirt left among the entwined roots. Out of death comes life. In the forest.

Outside the green shadows Little John could not say the same for his human friends. Dom had been too young and too innocent to die from an accident Little John should have prevented.

How could you have prevented the accident? Elena asked.

"I should have known the axle on the cart was weak and old and ill cared for. I should not have trusted the villagers to . . . to . . . ."

"To know the strengths and weaknesses of a wooden construct that had served them well for many years?" Elena appeared before him, little more substantial than a silver mist, as elegant and graceful as always.

"But . . . but . . ."

"Grieve as you will, silly boy, but do not blame yourself. Your friend was not happy at the abbey. He had no place in the village where he must bind himself to the land or flee. He respected the law too much to ever belong among the Woodwose. Had he the will, he might have lived or moved out of the way."

"No, he did not have the time . . ."

"He heard the axle crack. He knew the danger. He moved to hold up the wheel. You are not to blame. It is not my place or yours to know or judge if he allowed the wheel to fall on top of him. Put aside your guilt and prepare for what is coming." She faded, becoming vague around the edges.

"What is coming?" Little John jumped up, anxiously searching the shadows for an intruder. "Is it Jane?"

Not today but soon. Beware. Elena's voice drifted to a soft whisper of a breeze in the tree canopy.

Sixteen

ilde feigned sleep in her cot. Sister Marie Josef paced the hallway outside the girls' dormitory ready to pounce with her stout stick should any of her young charges venture out—even to use the privy. All around Hilde, the girls breathed evenly, too exhausted from the endless chores and hours on their knees in prayer to do aught but sleep.

The night sky sparkled with distant stars, and the waxing quarter moon rose almost sullenly, unwilling to share her light with the stars. But tonight was the night Dom would come to her. The empty achiness in her belly would go away as soon as she heard the crunch of his footsteps along the graveled path that circled the outside wall of the convent.

Her eyes closed. She imagined Dom's happy countenance when he first caught sight of her through the grille on the postern door.

She startled awake, heart pounding loudly in her ears, at

the sound of bits of gravel hitting the outside wall beside her cot. How had she slept on the night she awaited Dom?

Hastily, she grabbed her thick, gray woolen postulant's habit and hastened along the cloister barefoot and without her wimple. Heedless of the evening chill, she flung herself into the open courtyard and greeted the wind that presaged a storm. Then she had to slow down as her knees nearly collapsed in pain from the punishment rod.

"Dom," she said on a sigh of relief. "When can we run away together? Sister Marie Josef hit me again. I . . . I can barely walk." The last came out on a mournful wail.

"I am sorry," a different voice whispered through the grille. "I am not Dom."

"Who?" She took two careful steps backward, hand to her throat in fear. Had she heard that voice before? Maybe.

"I'm Nick, Dom's friend. I have horrible news."

"No. No!" At the last heartbeat, she remembered to drop her voice to a whisper Sister Marie Josef had notoriously long ears. She heard the faintest of sounds, almost as if she used magic to aid her.

"I dislike being the bearer of sad news. Dom is dead, Hilde. We buried him yesterday. I am so sorry. I grieve for him, and for you. But I guessed the sisters would not tell you even though a . . . a messenger was sent to you."

"No," she sobbed, bending double in renewed pain as she had earlier when she collapsed in the herb garden. The emptiness stemmed from the loss of her twin. Her body knew about her twin's death the moment Dom knew it.

Her chest tightened. Each gasping breath became an agony of effort.

"I am so sorry."

"He died in pain," she gasped.

Silence on the other side of the gate.

"Get me out of here!" she demanded with new resolve.

"I . . . I can't."

"Please, you have to. I no longer need to worry about how Dom would fare on the outside. I need to get away from this awful place," she pleaded with this friend whom Dom had talked about so often. She almost felt as if she knew Nick already; knew his sense of responsibility. She knew he needed to save all those in need. And she needed to breathe fresh air, to not spend hours on her knees in prayers that went nowhere and did nothing. She needed to stay away from Sister Marie Josef, who enjoyed inflicting pain as a way of reinforcing her view of the world. Or relieving her own inner torment.

"If there were a lock on this side of the door, I'd steal the key and just leave," she added.

"Where will you go? If I can find a way to set you free, where would you go? Who would take you in?"

"Dom spoke of a village deep in the forest, hiding from the law. He talked about a dairymaid who had run away from the sheriff and lived with the Wild Folk, the serfs who have fled their landlords, outlaws, and widows, the people the Church says do not exist, but live freely among the trees and streams."

"The Woodwose," Nick said quietly, as if speaking of them

openly would bring the wrath of God and the sheriff down
on him.

Another moment of silence that went on so long Hilde
almost spoke a new argument in her favor—if she didn't leave
soon, Sister Marie Josef would cripple or kill her.

"I think I ken a way to open this door. There is no keyhole
on this side either. There is a way to break the sorcery that
hides the lock. But I can't do it tonight. I need . . . I need a
special tool. I'll be back next week, at the waxing half-moon.
If I'm not here that night, I will be the next. Trust me." His
words faded as the gravel crunched beneath his feet in his slow
retreat from the portal. "I'm sorry that Dom is dead. But I
promised him I'd do what I could to help you. I promise you
the same."

Hilde limped back to bed, new hope in her heart. She'd
have a hard time enduring the hours on her knees tomorrow.
But for the chance of freedom, she would endure.

Nick picked his way along the rutted road that the spring rain
had turned to mud. He longed to sit before the suppertime fire
among the Woodwose. They lived precariously, but they had a
warm fire where the abbey's stone walls always held the chill
and compounded it in winter. His new friends had each other,
bound together by friendship and family—and blood; the same
kind of blood that ran through his veins. The abbey folk might
strive toward brotherhood in their faith, but they did not hug
each other, did not touch in any way. They weren't truly family,

and he was alone. He had no family except distant Tuck, but he might find more kin among the illegal forest dwellers.

Dom had Hilde. His sister and his twin. She would cry and mourn him.

Would anyone ever cry for Nick? Perhaps Father Tuck and, maybe, Little John.

He jerked his thoughts away from his lack of family, dwelling instead on how he'd fulfill his promise to Hilde to help her escape the convent. Not taking care where he placed his feet, he splashed into another puddle that rose above his ankles and mud sprayed up to his knees. A chill ran through his body, moving upward in waves of cold, far above the splash of water. He sought higher ground at the center of the road where a few tufts of grass clung bravely to the less-disturbed mound.

He paused, looking upward toward the faint glimmer of the quarter-moon hiding behind fitful clouds. "Dear Lord, please grant me, your humble if disobedient servant, a respite from this endless wet," he intoned, then remembered to cross himself and conclude the prayer with proper promises of prayer chains with his beads and extra time devoted to his duties.

The comforting rhythm of a plain chant swirled in his mind. He found the words and cadence and sang them under his breath. He missed the tolling of the massive bells calling him to prayer, to meals, to rest. His body remembered the routine of life even without the bells. A bit of weight lifted from his shoulders, and he found the strength to trudge on, going back to his dry, if not especially warm, bed. He might as well start in on those prayer chains while he walked. He reached for his beads in the deep sleeves of his robe. A niggle of disappointment weighed him down again when his fingers found only his beads and not the little silver three-faced pitcher.

A familiar chuckle eased the tight cords of his neck. "Are you back, my lady Elena?" he whispered into the darkness.

Not yet. A little while longer.

"Why do you laugh at me?"

Silly boy, you will figure out what you need to do. Think, but don't think, on the problem.

"Think but don't think? How am I supposed to do that? Either I am thinking about something, or I'm thinking about something else. I should be saying my prayers."

Then say your prayers as you hold your breath. Walking in your sleep will give you little rest.

A peculiar numbness replaced the voice in the back of his head. The lady had withdrawn her favor. Again. He hoped she left him alone because she had nothing more to say, not that she was disappointed in him.

As the moon hid behind a darker cloud, he remembered that he had looked for the lock on the postern door of the nunnery and hadn't seen one. But he'd felt it. He doubted a key would open it, even if he or Hilde could find one. The door had been locked with sorcery.

Sorcery, he whispered. Or had Elena spoken inside his mind again? Either way, the blacksmith who dwelled with the Woodwose couldn't help open a magically-sealed door.

Only Elena could. She was the goddess of crossroads, cemeteries, and sorcery. He and Hilde needed to wait for Elena's return. Enduring the wait was easier for him, he suspected, than for Hilde. Maybe a word to Tuck about the evil sister who thought faith came from the punishment rod could ease Hilde's torment.

His jaw cracked from the pressure of a mighty yawn.

Nick needed sleep. He could barely hold his eyes open or discern where he placed his feet.

He obeyed the lady's instructions and held his breath.

Dawn was just beginning to think about reaching above the horizon when he awoke at the crossroad.

Somewhat refreshed, he rose from his nest of bracken and stretched. Then he patted the stout column of the circled cross and raced the last one hundred yards to the apple tree in the orchard that would give him access to the garden by the infirmary. The physician would find him digging weeds by the back wall when he arose with the first glimmer of daylight.

"How long must I wait?" Herne bellowed. His voice sounded like the roar of a wounded stag challenging the sheriff's hunting dogs.

"For a near-immortal creature of the forest, you have a lot to learn about patience, Uncle," Tuck laughed.

Little John nodded sagely as if he knew how to wait. As Midsummer's Night approached, and the time of the moon phases aligned with Faery, he found it harder and harder to wait. Nigh on fifty human years he'd waited. Now these last few weeks seemed to stretch into eternity.

He knew how Herne suffered while waiting for the return of Ardenia.

The sun had set, the moon had risen and set, sunrise approached. A full night they'd waited. And still they'd discerned no ripple in the smooth waters of the lady's pond. Not even the constant drip of the cascade from the feeding creek disturbed the surface. All the creatures of the wood that depended upon this pond for life had grown silent and still as if waiting with bated breath.

Only Herne disturbed the silence with his frequent roars and constant pacing.

"How much longer?" he asked again, still not muting his tones that bounced and echoed from tree trunk to boulder and back again.

A gentle splash brought him to a frozen halt.

Little John released his breath, allowing his human chest to heave as he renewed and replenished himself.

Slowly a water spout, silvery in the false dawn, rose up from the still waters. The sounds of the creek plunging downward renewed. The forest awakened with chirping insects and the rustling of night creatures seeking their burrows and dens among the underbrush.

Lady Ardenia solidified and stepped from the water, her gown clinging to her body, outlining each curve and pinch of her figure. Quickly the fabric became whole and caressed her skin without clinging, the skirts swinging free as she strode.

"Now, my lords, I will tell you of all that I have seen and done inside Castle Nottingham. The sheriff is much too confident in the strength of his stone walls and stout locks. He had no idea how a watery hand can reach into a keyhole and release a lock, or how quickly that same hand can douse torches so that

weary guards cannot see a thin form flowing along the drain
gutter in the center of the floor all the way down into the dungeons and thence through the labyrinth of caverns where water
trickles outward into a stream that feeds the river and then up
the web of creeks to my pond. 'Twas quite the harrowing journey." She cocked an eyebrow at Herne in mirth. "But now I
need to rest in water. You may sit on the bank, Master Huntsman, and tell me of all that has occurred during my absence."
She stepped backward, retreating to her natural element.

"And what of the Lady Elena?" Little John demanded, no
longer content with only the water sprite's safety.

"You mean the spirit who dwells in the little pitcher?" Ardenia reached inside an invisible fold of her gown and brought out
her empty hand. "I do not know," she said, utterly surprised.

Little John's chin quivered in pain. How could they unlock
the door into Faery without the ancient goddess of crossroads,
cemeteries, and *sorcery*?

Seventeen

comforting heaviness filled the folds of Nick's left sleeve. He waited patiently while the Welsh physician raised his arms in salutation to the sun as its first rays of light shimmered along the damp stones at the top of the wall. The healing monk's voice rose in a clear tenor voice to complete his greeting.

Nick didn't understand the words, voiced in a foreign tongue he'd never heard before. Maybe an older form of Latin, maybe something else.

Ah, Elena sighed. *I have not heard that language in many a long year.*

Welsh? Nick asked her without speaking. He knew the healer hailed from the West Country that had been a thorn in the side of England's borders for as long as there had been a united England.

Older, the mother tongue of all of this land before the Romans defiled our language, our people, and our religion.

Oh.

The monk finished his song of greeting the dawn and drew a deep breath. Then he froze in place, staring at Nick. He shifted his weight to a more relaxed pose.

"You are up early, my boy?"

"I slept fitfully, sir. So I thought to put my wakefulness to good use."

"Commendable. But be careful of the verbena. It needs thinning, not eradication." He turned abruptly and retreated to the infirmary where patients awaited him.

Nick heaved a sigh of relief. And yawned again so deeply that blackness encroached upon his vision and stars glittered behind his eyelids.

But dawn had come, and he'd not get another chance to sleep until after sunset, which was getting later and later each day as they approached the solstice.

He trudged toward the Lady Chapel where all the abbey's inhabitants began to gather. He swallowed his yawns with each step.

The Holy Father had dictated no Masses could be said or sung, no church bells rung, and no sacraments administered except funerary and baptism. That did not mean the brothers and fathers couldn't say prayers, discuss theology, and *practice* singing the Masses.

After a long, long time on his knees, nodding off with only Henry's elbow to keep him upright, while Prefect Andrew meditated aloud about the nature of obedience, and all the inhabitants of the abbey practiced the prayers of the Mass, Nick shuffled behind the other boys on the way to the refectory. Old bread, stale cheese, and a bowl of watery gruel must sustain them all through a morning of chores.

"Your turn to read the lessons for the day," Brother Theo said, prodding Nick with a firm hand upon his back.

"But . . . I'm only a postulant, not even a novitiate," Nick replied, suddenly more awake with the dread of reading aloud.

"You read well enough. And it means fresh baked bread and first cut of cheese from the wheel."

Nick's mouth watered. He hadn't had truly fresh bread since he won the loaf at May Day.

"Since I will not be allowed to eat until after the lessons have finished, does the privilege of reading keep me from singing practice?" He turned hopeful eyes up to his mentor.

"You do not like singing?" Brother Theo stopped abruptly. "Since the loss of Dominic, we need every voice. None can replace his fine, pure notes. But we can hope to overcome the empty spot with volume if not purity. I truly hope that this war between King John and the Holy Father ends soon so that we may go back to our true purpose in worshipping God properly. With song as well as silent prayer."

"I have always enjoyed singing, sir, even if I cannot carry a tune as well as Dom could. But, of late every time I try, my voice sounds like a wounded frog."

"I thought that those with the worst voices enjoyed singing the most. Everyone should enjoy lifting their voices in songs of praise to God."

"My voice sounds more like guttural curses." Nick hung his head in shame.

"Guttural?" Brother Theo tapped his chin. "How old are you, boy?"

Nick had to shrug. "When I was first brought here, Abbott Mæson believed me to be three or four. I was small, so he said I was three. Nine years since then."

"Maybe you were just small for your age, underfed. I must speak with Brother Michael. Only he can excuse you from singing until . . . your voice recovers. Deep baritone, I'd guess." He started forward. "Come along, boy. You may earn an excuse from singing, but you can still speak and read the lessons."

Jane fingered the silver needle between embroidery stitches, judging where the next bit of flower should go to cover a clumsy mend. Her fingertips prickled with the need to rub them along the flowing embroidery. Whoever had done this work before her hadn't cared or known how to fix the torn cloth properly. She wanted to do more than just repair the gown, make it right.

She needed to enhance it. Make it perfect. Her heart tugged her toward an upward spray of flowers.

Queen Mab had drunk more than a little too much mead during the last round of festivities and danced more enthusiastically than usual. She drank to forget that her current favorite courtier, Bracken, had not come to her when called and was not available to dance with her.

He was only the favorite at this moment because he was not there. No one else could compare to him.

Also, because she was drunk and disappointed, she'd tripped on her hem at least once during each dance, and every time she changed partners. The fragile silken fabric that had been torn before did not survive well. But the gown was a favorite, and nothing would do but Jane must mend it properly and the rents must not show.

The needle was as fine as the thread it carried and slid through the weave of the fabric without a trace. Jane's tired fingers resisted the next stitch. She contemplated adding more flowers spraying out from the mends, like bluebells spreading across a meadow. Except her embroidery thread was the same purple as the gown, the same purple as deep twilight on the distant hills. The flowers were only visible when the magical lights shifted and shimmered, revealing the slightly different texture. There one moment and gone in an instant with the sunset. The embroidery made this gown unique among Faerie garb.

Queen Mab would love it.

Therefore, Jane would do no more to enhance the dress. She'd done as asked. If she did more, she risked Mab's displeasure. Reason enough not to try to surprise and delight a fickle queen. She pushed aside the useless feeling of pride in a job well-done.

Satisfied, Jane wove the end of the thread back through a dozen stitches to anchor it. Then she pulled the needle upward, so the thread was taut, and bit it off, leaving no tail.

The needle felt different in her fingers. She ran her finger along the length, seeking an imperfection. There, a tiny bend near the eye. She applied a little pressure to straighten it. Her fingers kept pushing, no resistance. The needle kept bending.

Until it snapped.

It felt like her heart snapped as well and all hope of escape spurted upward through the opening in the ceiling.

She no longer had a weapon to combat her captors.

Nick suppressed his third yawn since he had knelt for Compline prayers. He missed the comfortable weight of Dom's head lolling onto his shoulder. He worried about how to rescue Hilde from the nunnery she hated. And he worried if taking her to the Woodwose village was the right thing to do for her. He'd found safety and sanctuary and . . . and a vocation at Locksley Abbey. Having seen some ugly bits of life outside the sheltering walls, he wondered if Hilde's discomfort at the convent was more about missing Dom than the discipline imposed by the sisters. Perhaps in time . . . .

No. He had promised Dom's shade to release Hilde, and keeping his promise was important. The girl could always go back or to a different convent if she found life on the outside intolerable. Without protection from a family or a husband or a landlord, he had no idea how she might survive, let alone thrive.

He yawned again, wishing Father Blaine would read the lessons with at least as much inflection as a plainsong. Henry was already asleep on the verge of snoring. Nick jabbed him in the gut with his elbow. Henry spluttered and snorted, then opened his eyes wide, realized where and when he was, and resumed a pose of attention.

No one was fooled. The littlest boys dozed with heads dropping in an attitude of prayer. The men and older boys ignored them.

"I'll get them a good rousing game of tag tomorrow afternoon," Nick promised himself and them. They all needed something to break the monotonous routine, something that stretched their bodies and brought laughter to one and all. Father Blaine—not even a novitiate at the time—had done the same for him when he was but six. Why was the man so frowning and . . . timid about breaking the rules now?

Too much responsibility thrust upon him before he was ready. Blaine had not had Elena's gentle laughter and thoughtful tutoring.

Finally, Father Blaine recited the benediction in the same monotone as he read the lessons while making the sign of the cross in the air.

Wearily, Nick got to his feet and herded the youngsters toward their beds. His responsibility, just as Hilde had become his responsibility.

When each of the boys was tucked in with a kiss to the forehead and a bit of a hug, with no help from Henry, Nick flung himself onto his cot, asleep before he could pull up his blanket.

All too soon the Welsh monk from the infirmary woke him with a brisk shake to his shoulders.

"Nicholas," he hissed in an urgent whisper. "Nicholas, wake up."

Nick swam upward through waves and waves of sleep. "Wha . . . what?" He didn't find the courage to open his eyes. "Is it Matins already?" He felt as if he'd only been asleep for a few minutes. Every joint and muscle ached with exhaustion.

"Almost dawn," said the infirmarian.

How could I have slept through the bells? Nick wondered as he struggled to a sitting position, eyes barely opened enough to discern a faint glimmer of pre-dawn at the edges of the small window.

"We grow slack here without the bells to order our day," the physician said. Then he shook himself and captured Nick's gaze with his own. "Nicholas, when did you last see Brother Luke?"

Nick had to think hard. He'd stumbled through yesterday half-asleep without minding where or when he did what. The day before—was it only the day before?—that Tuck had summoned him while Brother Luke dozed in the garden, too tired of life to speak further about his beloved herbs.

"Not yesterday," Nick admitted, ashamed at neglecting his assigned duty to the old man. "I don't remember speaking with him yesterday."

"He's gone now. I thought him beyond the days of wandering without memory. He's so weak, I fear for him. What if he took it into his head to collect new plants in the forest? What if one of the wild creatures killed him? What if . . ."

"I know a place in the water meadow where he might have

gone," Nick said, yawning again. His stomach growled, and his bladder ached. "He spoke often of the abundance of herbs and flowers at the water's edge. May I grab a crust of bread and a mug of new ale before I go look for him?" He didn't remember if he'd eaten last evening or not.

"If you hurry. Clouds are forming to the north, and the wind is blowing up a storm from that direction. It'll likely rain before Prime."

"I won't linger." With more energy than he thought possible, he grabbed his robe and slipped on his sandals as he ran to the privy. Three steps along the cloister he remembered to touch his pocket and make certain Elena still resided there.

I am with you.

"You've been so silent, I wondered," he murmured.

After being on my own for so long, I needed rest.

A chilling thought wiggled into his brain in the thoughtless time while he answered the call of nature. "Am I so tightly bound to you that I needed more rest than usual because you did?"

She replied with a light chuckle. *No, silly boy, you needed more rest than usual because you've been out wandering half the night rather than sleeping as you should. And you are growing. Your body needs more sleep to accept the newness of a bigger size. Now tell me why you've been out and about.*

"If you will tell me how Lady Ardenia saved herself, and you, while in Nottingham Castle."

A fine bargain!

In an instant, he relived the adventure of the water sprite pouring the trickle of pond water on top of her head. With little substance to her limbs, she then slid her hand into the lock and flicked the metal latch so that the guards would be blamed for not locking her in. Moments later she relaxed into a thin stream of water and slid beneath the door to join with the drain runoff at the depressed center of the corridor.

Nick felt in his own hand the smooth transition from liquid to solid, then back to water.

The heavy wooden planks of the door seemed to scratch Nick's back right where it itched the most as he flowed beneath it. He joined with Elena, clinging to the depressions in the stone floor that allowed water from the leaky roofs to drain. He flowed downward with them, ever downward as water is wont to go, into the undercroft and the cellars, then down again into the dungeons and the intricate labyrinth of caves and natural tunnels until they met a stream that traveled out of the city and along the system of creeks and streams, the tiny cup bobbing along invisibly atop the trickle of water and a part of it at the same time. He felt the relentless need to join with . . . with the pond that was the sprite's natural home. Ardenia concentrated so hard on staying fluid and not spreading out to dry, that neither Nick nor the spirit of the water noticed where and when Elena floated.

He knew the sense of exhilaration at the moment of Ardenia's glorious reunion with the spring of water that contained her essence. A shiver of delight passed along Nick's spine, as if he'd just risen from a cleansing bath, barely noticing the bite of cold water on skin.

"I feel much the same every time I wander far and then at

the point of exhaustion I spy the church tower rising above the abbey walls and I have a new spurt of energy to carry my feet home."

Because this is your home. This is where you will always return.

"It's more than the sight of the bell tower. It's the voices. Our brotherhood sings the plainsong all the time. Sometimes they sing it as a prayer, alone or in a group. The brothers sing as they go about their daily chores, practicing to get the intonation just right. I can't imagine the abbey without the soothing cadence of our music. It's the chant that calls me home long before I can see the walls. And I feel foolish trying to match my voice to theirs."

Give it time. The notes and words will settle in your throat before too long.

With that, he sang the benediction very softly to keep his voice from cracking and destroying the smooth recitation.

The sun had risen high enough to paint the underside of the cloud cover shades of rose and gold when Nick left the forecourt of the abbey by the main gate. He shivered in the cold wind the moment he stepped free of the sheltering walls. "I'd much rather be asleep," he muttered, letting his feet drag. He chewed the last of his bread and sipped from his wooden mug. A ball of hard cheese rested comfortably in his scrip at his waist. That was for later, if he didn't find Brother Luke quickly and return in time for a meal in the refectory. Even bland and sometimes bitter turnips sounded good right now.

There are no apples yet to sustain you. I will show you some roots and bulbs you may safely eat down in the water meadow. But only if you tell me what kept you up and wandering while I was away.

Nick breathed deeply and launched into his tale of finding Hilde and her need to run away from her convent.

A door locked by sorcery is no problem for me, Elena admitted. *My worry is about who locked it, why, and who now holds the magical key.*

"Is the sorcery dangerous?" Nick's feet squelched in the sodden grass that wouldn't dry out until high summer. He needed to retreat to solid ground. "More important, I can't see Brother Luke anywhere. Could he have fallen into the shallow pools and drowned?"

I cannot sense him nearby. But I think I know where he has sought refuge. Turn north until you reach the ford, then go west without crossing the stream. You need to hurry.

Nick had never traveled that path. But he trusted Elena more than his own instincts. Once on dry ground with solid footing, he asked again, "Is the sorcerous lock at the nunnery dangerous?"

The sorcery itself does not sound dangerous. But one person inside must control the opening and the closing, someone with a powerful need to remain inside and keep all others out. A convent is a place where they fear sorcery so much they deny its existence. For someone to use it there is considered blasphemy.

"I think I need to tell Abbot Mæson about this." Not Tuck with the horn buds, but the abbot with authority that he hid beneath his rough clothing and broad-brimmed felt hat.

Eighteen

ittle John paused and lifted his head from the plate of eggs and cheese and rough bread the Woodwose gave him every morning. He joined them around the central fire surrounded by makeshift huts. Something was different in his forest. A strange, halting step at the edge. He sniffed and smelled only smoke from the wood fire.

Hastily, he rose from his place to the north of the rocks containing the flames. Once clear of the smells normal to any village—pig, chicken, damp thatch, unwashed bodies, and the privy downstream—he found a trace of someone new. Someone who didn't belong.

Someone who had belonged once, but no more. He let the essence of the man tickle his senses a few heartbeats longer.

"Lyndon?" he asked the air.

None of the current humans was old enough to remember Lyndon. He'd been born to this village when their hovels huddled together at the base of the mound covered with linden trees. They had to move all traces of the village every few years to avoid the sheriff's agents finding them. But Lyndon had heard the enchanting call of the abbey and the prayerful songs they intoned. His soul, like Tuck's, yearned for something greater than the life of an outlaw. He answered the call of faith and took a new name, then after only a few years he'd gone off to someplace called the Holy Land for a Second Crusade.

Little John knew of no land holier than his forest. People had worshipped at sacred springs, standing stones, and at the feet of giant trees for as long as people had lived on the land. Land he'd inherited custody of from his sire, grandsire, and many grandsires before.

He splayed his fingers wide, letting each begin to transform into a twig, his new bark more sensitive to changes in the air than his skin. One by one, he absorbed an awareness of each entity who fell within his duty to the forest. He acknowledged and dismissed as normal each tree, creek, boulder, insect, animal, and person.

One more remained. The essence of the person gave him a direction and showed him the unseen route of the old man. Why had he come back in what for him must be very old age?

Little John strode off toward the fringe of his awareness to confront Lyndon.

A lump of threadbare dark gray wool lay collapsed inside the verge where forest met meadow. It stirred awkwardly. Little John hastened to kneel beside the shapeless mound.

"Ah, Lyndon, you've waited too long to reclaim your heritage," he sighed.

"Please . . ." A gnarled and spotted hand emerged from the vast folds of dark fabric. "I must touch them once more."

Little John knew what the cracked and hesitant words meant. "So, in death, you've forsaken your new faith for the old ways," he grumbled as he lifted the slight weight of the ancient monk into his arms. Lyndon had once been tall and robust. Now he weighed less than a child half his size, little more than skin and bones.

"There is a place for the old and the new," Tuck said, hastening through the underbrush. He raised his right hand, gnarled fingers naturally curling inward below the extended fore and middle fingers. "May the Lord bless you and keep you," he whispered, sketching a cross above Lyndon's lolling head. "May the Lord let His face shine upon you and give you peace." Then the old priest stepped aside, clearing the path to the center of the forest.

Little John bowed his head, acknowledging a prayer that came from the heart no matter which god he addressed.

"I'll follow. Hurry, Little John. He cannot last long now. An hour at most."

"Take me with you," Henry demanded, panting as he ran to catch up with Nick.

"I'm in a hurry," Nick protested. His hand automatically patted his pocket to make certain Elena's pitcher was safely hidden.

"I never get to go anywhere, Nick. How am I supposed to learn how to minister to these people if I don't know them?"

"So you aim for the priesthood rather than a life of isolated contemplation," Nick said. He thought being an itinerant priest was the life he wanted. There was so much to learn and see and do beyond the walls of the abbey. He might want the monastic life someday, when he was as old as Brother Luke. Not yet.

"Henry, if you come with me, you will see some things I cannot explain. You will have to accept and figure things out on your own as we go along."

"Agreed." He folded his hands into his sleeves and ducked his head. But he peered upward at Nick beneath lowered eyelids.

Nick eyed him skeptically. Henry wasn't going anywhere but where Nick walked, so he took his first step away from the crossroad on the path Elena had indicated. He had never encountered any true danger in the forest, only friends, both human and Wild Folk. But all his life, adults had warned him of the evil that lurked in the forest. So had Little John. Outlaws and marauding mercenaries mostly, and they grew fewer each year now that King John resided in England instead of France and tried to impose something resembling order upon his barons. Of the Wild Folk, only faeries with their traps contained any meanness, and he'd spotted a trap quite easily. But he had heard about *other* dangers. Stories grew with each telling. He knew that. But they all started with some glimmer of truth.

Maybe the forest, with its long and deep shadows, had been dangerous once.

"Where are we headed? I didn't think old Brother Luke was strong enough to walk this far," Henry said. He walked in an awkward circle, surveying the trees that closed in on them almost immediately. He stumbled backward over an exposed root.

"Watch where you step. The forest gets dangerous away from the road." Or so the brothers who cowered in the abbey said.

"I won't get lost," Henry said on a pout. "If I step wrong, I'll just call for you and you can rescue me."

"If something awful doesn't eat you before I can find you." Nick paused in place and lifted his head, sniffing in all directions.

"I thought you were friends with all the local creatures." Henry stopped in place as well. His words sounded hesitant rather than bouncy and curious.

"A few. Not all." He turned his attention to his right. He had no idea of the real direction. They'd been walking west. But the trail twisted back on itself and the trees all looked alike, old and covered with moss. In the section of forest he'd visited, around Lady Ardenia's pond at the Woodwose village, the trees grew in a good mix of young, old, and ancient. Every time a massive elder succumbed to age and storm and rot, a dozen seedlings sprang up to replace it, germinating new life from the ruins of the old.

Here, he didn't think any of the trunks, so big around that five grown men linking hands couldn't completely surround one, had fallen since time began. The dead forest giants remained standing, crowding so close together he'd have trouble squeezing between them. And the canopy was so tightly woven of overlapping branches that little if any light penetrated. They walked into perpetual deep twilight.

Groundcover withered and died from lack of light. The trees crowded closer and closer to the path.

He touched the outside of his pocket again, wondering if he had taken the correct path after all.

This is the shortest way to the triad of standing stones. Keep moving quickly, and we will reach the center of the forest in time.

"Is that where Brother Luke will go?"

Yes.

Nick and Henry moved forward warily, pausing frequently to study the path and make sure they followed the real one and not one of the wandering openings to either side—a trap for the unwary.

Had the faeries set those traps? Or something else?

Whenever Nick hesitated and directed a foot off to the side, Elena nudged his mind back to the real path.

Henry crept closer to Nick, frequently clutching at his robe, making a slight connection. Then he'd release his hold and whip his hand back inside his own sleeves.

An icy breeze sniffed around their ankles, sending chills all the way to the roots of Nick's hair.

"Something smells rotten," Henry whispered. "Sort of like the midden on a hot day, but worse."

"I know," Nick replied, suddenly aware of the odor that invaded his nose and penetrated his skin. He didn't feel safe to speak loudly.

You must walk faster! Elena demanded. A sharp, hot prod

to the center of Nick's mind followed her thoughts. *He's dying now!*

The pain lifted from Nick's mind and his pocket fell flat and empty.

Stay on the path. Do not stray. Do not stop until you reach the protection of the standing stones. And she was gone.

"Where is my gown? I must have my gown for dancing to-night!" Queen Mab screeched loudly.

Jane thought her shrill voice must rattle the battlements of Nottingham Castle.

"Here, Your Majesty. I have just completed the repairs." Jane stood and held up the gown so that the Faery Queen could see the invisible mending and elegant embroidery. The embellishment looked incomplete to Jane, but she'd broken the silver needle before she could sew another trail of flowers and vines.

The queen opened her mouth in a joyful "oh" of delight. Then she clamped it shut again and assumed an attitude of offense. "You took too long, and this spray of flowers is off center." She waved a hand in dismissal.

Jane bit her tongue, drawing a drop of blood. Then she relaxed her jaw and nursed the slight wound against the roof of her mouth. Even as a serf in Sir Philip Marc's village, she had not been insulted and humiliated as she was as a slave in Mab's household.

"Well, it will have to do. I have no other gown worthy of

dancing with Bracken. He is such an outrageously funny partner, laughing and turning the most mundane stories into
jokes. Certainly, he will find a way to make your clumsy sewing into sarcastic praise." She looked around at the faeries
milling around the great hall, nodding as she noted each individual and mouthing their names: Rose, Hellebore, Lilac,
Dogwood, and others.

She craned her neck and fluttered her wings to lift free of
the floor by a hand's breadth. "But where is he? Surely he
must know that I have selected him to partner me tonight."

Jane peeked through the maze of flowing fabric that draped
her captors. Lots of vibrant green and soothing pink, but none
of the darker, grayer green Bracken favored, near identical to
his namesake plant. She could only shrug. The young and
bouncy male could be anywhere in the vast underground cave
system. Often the courtiers—except for the five ladies who
attended the queen night and day and never dared sleep or
do anything but shower all their attention on her—sneaked
off to a sleeping chamber to couple or to one of the secret exits
to play tricks on unwary humans without telling anyone.

But Bracken had helped her when she'd fallen on May
Day. He'd smiled and encouraged her and promised that not
all faeries were as mean-spirited as Mab.

Perhaps he'd had enough of the queen and refused to return.

"Your Majesty." Lily, dressed in white that shaded into pink
and pale green, bent into a deep curtsy, the only proper posture when interrupting the queen. "I have not seen Bracken
since we returned from the May Day celebration in the village."
She scuttled back and away from Mab. The enraged queen

raised her hand. Her fingers became bent twigs barren of bark as she curled them into her palm. As she opened her clenched fist, she sent a bespelled bolt of flame after her handmaiden. Lily scooted out of the way. The bolt continued onward, flaring and passing each of the Faery courtiers until it collapsed into dust beneath the opening in the ceiling.

Mab straightened her hunched shoulders and swallowed a look of outrage.

An emptiness invaded Jane, akin to the sadness she'd endured back home when her friend, a girl of her own age, had died in childbed. She couldn't even remember the girl's name or that of the boy who'd married her.

"May Day was only yesterday. He's probably off beguiling some upstart butterfly pixie. He'll return by tonight to renew his powers beneath our Faery Mound. All of the men do." Mab dismissed the speculation that Bracken might be in trouble—on his own without much magic . . .

Yesterday? Jane counted on her fingers the times the light through the chinks in the ceiling had waxed and waned and came up with . . . she ran out of fingers. But the faeries had slept only once and eaten berries and juicy roots and flower pollen only twice. If Bracken had truly been missing for as long as she thought, he'd be starving by now, without enough magic to find his way home.

Then Jane remembered her kitchen garden at home. There was a patch of bean plants that never matured, never set fruit. Had the faeries robbed the blossoms of pollen, never spreading it, but consuming it and thus blighting the patch?

Mab retreated to her wardrobe chamber with her repaired

gown. Her ladies gathered in a whispering knot behind Jane. A few lines of conversation slipped through their guarded secrets.

"No one willingly stays away from our protections for so long," Lily said, a little louder than her companions so that her words cut through the tangle of hissing whispers.

"Something must be terribly wrong," Rose echoed the sentiment.

"The forest is dangerous even for our kind," Daffy-down-dilly said, hand to mouth, smothering any further words.

"With the Church gone away, we are not the only ones free to roam more openly," Lily reminded them.

Jane began to tremble all over. She had to sit down again, but she couldn't find the low stool that had supported her so recently.

The Church gone?

It could not be. How could the world find order and balance and connections to God without the Church? How could people know right from wrong, sin from blessing?

Her foot smacked against a leg of the stool, sending ripples of sharp pain up her leg. She plunked herself down, hard, just as the world seemed to tilt to the left: the sinister side . . . of life.

Nineteen

"I think we should turn back," Henry said. His hand clenched tighter on a fold of Nick's robe.

"Which . . . which way . . . which way is back?" Nick asked, lifting his chin in stubborn defiance of his fear. Maybe if he said it loud enough, Elena would give him a direction. He saw no hint of a break in the sparse undergrowth, nor the depression of a foot or hoof. No glimmer of a way forward appeared to him.

He paused to ask himself what Elena would tell him to do.

Look for landmarks. A triad of saplings? There were none that he remembered for a long time. All the trees looked the same: huge, half-rotten, their gnarled bark twisting into gnomish faces.

A spring? The only sound he could pick out over the rush of wind through the treetops was the sound of his own heartbeat pounding in his ears. But the ground was soggy as if it had not seen the sun in a year or more.

He clenched his teeth and stiffened his spine to keep from trembling before he melted into a puddle of weeping despair and merged with the sodden ground.

"Why did we come this way?" Henry's voice choked on a sob.

"We have to find Brother Luke. I was directed this way as the shortest path to where he has gone to die."

"Directed by whom?" Henry asked. He broke away from his fear to look around for someone—anyone—who might help them out of this hopeless tangle.

"I can't say." Nick lifted one foot to place it directly in front of him. His sandal broke free of the muck with a screech of sucking, cloying, wet.

Something tickled his ankle.

With one foot in the air, he bent lightly to brush away an intruding insect or maybe a fern frond.

A blackberry sent thorns as big as his thumb deep into his vulnerable ankle.

Instinctively, he set his other foot down only to find a dozen thistle plants waving their bristly stems at him. Not the small tame English thistles. These were the huge, menacing Scottish thistles. The ones that nearly had a mind of their own and did not take kindly to intruders.

Meanwhile, the blackberry wound tighter and tighter around his foot, climbing his leg and tugging him down, and down, and down into the drowning mud.

"*Nick!*" Henry called, clasping his arm at wrist and elbow. Small and wiry, Nick's friend braced his feet and held on, yanking Nick back from the yawning hole that spread out from beneath the tangled mass at the base of a gnarled tree stripped free of bark. The knotholes, where ancient branches had broken off, took on the configuration of a face with scrunched eyes, eldritch nose, and a mouth permanently frozen in a gasping and twisted "Oh."

"You are not a friend of the Green Man!" Nick yelled at the roots that opened to reveal a gaping hole between them.

"And you are a friend of his?" The deep, sonorous voice came from every direction and pounded into Nick's mind as well as his ears.

"He calls himself Little John, when he steps free of his tree," Nick said, gaining confidence when the roots and vines paused and loosened their fierce grip. "He helps all those who reside under his authority in the forest."

The deep voice grumbled and mumbled to itself.

"I am no friend of the Green Man. But he does hold mastery over all the trees within his realm."

Henry crossed himself and recited a prayer for preservation from all things heathen.

A tremendous crack echoed around them, much like thunder loosed on a hot August afternoon, only louder, followed by the thrash and crash of a heavy limb breaking away from the tree.

"Duck!" Nick yelled. He reversed his grip on Henry's arms and dragged him backward.

"You may pass for now, only because the Green Man has befriended you. But do not invoke the name of your foreign god again!"

Thistles, blackberries, and roots retreated like someone rolled a tapestry tightly.

The path opened, showing a clear passage past the tree.

"Don't leave me! Help!" a tiny voice cried from the depth of the tree. "I'm trapped and alone. Help me!"

Hilde trod around the cloister behind Sister Marie Josef, head bowed, wimple hiding every tendril of wayward hair, hands tucked into the gray folds of her formal robe. Her knees and back ached from two turns of the hourglass on her knees. Her head ached from the heavy incense the sisters burned in the chapel to ward off the demon of temptation.

None of the other girls had to endure this treatment. They'd all been dismissed to dig in the garden, clean the chicken coops, or whitewash the interior walls. Any of those chores would be preferable to Sister Marie Josef's special attention.

"You met with a boy last night. A boy who was not your brother. The brother is almost forgivable, though you should have broken all ties to him when you entered this holy place," Sister Marie Josef repeated over and over again. "But I have made certain that not you, or any of the other postulants will ever use that door to succumb to the temptation of a man."

Hilde almost believed that the stern sister listened to her dreams and knew she planned to make a break for freedom soon. She need only wait for the waning quarter of the moon.

"Pay attention!" Sister Marie Josef spat her words. "You must constantly meditate on the nature of your sins. Wayward thoughts open a door for evil to invade your soul. Before you know it, you will be forced by demons to leave the safety of our sanctuary and give your body to men. Your soul is only safe here where no one can violate you."

"Yes, Sister," Hilde murmured. A tremble began in her middle, climbing to her throat. Suddenly breathing became difficult, and her knees turned to water.

"A few hours in here should help you focus your thoughts on Holy Mother Mary, forever virgin, impregnated only by the Holy Spirit of God and never any other." Sister Marie Josef grabbed Hilde's arm sharply and thrust her forward into darkness.

Hilde had only a brief glimpse of a half-empty storeroom before the heavy door slammed shut behind her and the sound of the crossbar dropped into place.

Then she heard the scratching of a rat in the back corner behind a crate of withered apples and a sack of grain ready for milling.

"Help!" she screamed as loudly as she could. "Help me! I didn't do anything." What if the sisters forgot her? What if the rats bit her, started eating her before she was fully dead? What if she missed her appointment with Nick who would rescue her?

"Help me," she whispered, heart full of despair.

The sound of her words echoed within her own head.

"Who?" Nick and Henry both stopped and asked. They stared at each other a moment, then both shrugged and turned back toward the malevolent tree.

"We can't just leave him," Nick said on a sigh.

"But we have to get to Brother Luke," Henry said, sounding equally resigned.

"Brother Luke will die in his own good time. Our being there won't help him. He will be among friends."

Henry look skeptical with his head tilted and his eyes half closed.

"I promise, he is among friends." Nick said. Keeping his back to the gnarled and twisted wood and his motions small so the malevolent spirit would not notice, he crossed himself. At the same time, he imagined, Elena and the Green Man standing beside the old man's body, lying in repose beside. . . . There his imagination failed him. He'd never seen standing stones, had no idea of their size, color, or positioning. All he could see in his mind was the tall circled cross standing at the crossroad.

Perhaps that was best. He turned around to face the tree once more. "Who are you?" he called, raising his voice to help it penetrate layers of dirt or bark, or enchantment.

"Halloo! Are you still there? You have to help me. She's coming back any moment now."

Nick and Henry exchanged another telling glance. "His voice is so close and yet so far away, I wonder if the tree's magic is holding him captive," Henry asked. He took a step backward, away from the tree and magic and his own fears.

"Only one way to find out." Nick stepped up to the tree in the region he thought he'd seen a face hiding in the twisted wood. "Sir, we need to ask you if anyone else fell into your trap and you are holding him hostage in some secret chamber."

Henry inched away, keeping his eyes trained on the ground that had recently opened into a black and bottomless pit.

The tree remained dormant and still.

"Help me. I have to get out of here! The ground is draining me, sucking my life and magic out of me."

Nick looked around hastily, seeking the source of that little voice that sounded so desperate.

"Who are you?"

"Shouldn't you ask where he is?" Henry asked, remaining solidly beyond the reach of the tree and its grasping roots.

"Knowing who he is gives us a clue as to why he was captured, and perhaps by whom," Nick insisted.

"Logic means nothing to me," Henry snorted. "Where are you?" He cupped his hands around his mouth.

"I'm here."

"Where is *here*?" Nick joined Henry in squinting to try and focus on tiny imperfections in the tree bark that might hide an entry point.

"Here is here. Where else would she imprison me?"

That didn't make much sense. Henry looked as puzzled as Nick felt. They both shrugged.

"Please, sir, describe your prison," Nick suggested.

"It's a prison—dark, damp, and cold."

Nick shuddered with new chills from the fearful tone of the prisoner.

"Are the walls dirt or dressed stone?" Elena had described Lady Ardenia's tower cell in Nottingham Castle. Dressed stone with large, arched windows that let in a lot of light. He'd heard about the underground dungeons in the castle, also dressed stone within the foundations. The upper levels of the undercroft might have a tiny window opening into the forecourt. No light at all in the lower levels that led to the labyrinth of natural caves beneath the city.

"What kind of walls?" Henry asked. He stepped closer to Nick and raised his voice, much like he did when speaking to Brother Luke, as if yelling very slowly would penetrate his diminished mind.

"They're dirt, with a lot of stray roots keeping them from collapsing."

Nick shifted his gaze to the protruding roots at the base of the tree. With the spirit of the tree withdrawn and no longer masking the ground with darkness, he spotted some gaps. Gingerly he stuck his hand into the largest one, ready to snatch it back out of the hole if the tree should change its mind.

"Hey, you're blocking my light!"

"So how do we get him out?" Henry asked, scratching his head. "We are supposed to help those less fortunate than ourselves. Abbot Mæson preached about that a lot, not so much Father Blaine, but a little from Prefect Andrew—it's as if he obeys the abbot but doesn't quite understand why."

Before Nick could form an answer, a tremendous groan rippled through the ground and it fell away at their feet.

"Noooooo!" Flailing his arms and stumbling, Henry tumbled downward.

Nick grabbed for his feet. His fingers brushed the leather strap of his sandals. Then the ground crumbled beneath him and he fell, too. The mat of dirt and roots snapped back into place, and a hidden latch clicked closed, sealing them in.

Twenty

ittle John stopped his determined march at the verge of the meadow at the exact center of his forest. Ahead of him, three stones stood upright, reaching for the sky, like three fingers thrusting above the crown of Mother Earth in a solemn salute. His head barely reached a third of the way to the rounded peak of the shortest of the stones.

He drew in a deep breath of air freshened by a stiff breeze originating in the North Sea. The cold, enhanced by the mere presence of the three great stones, flooded his lungs with strength and renewed his agility from his fingertips to his toes.

Little John bowed his head and murmured ancient words of respect in a language long forgotten. He didn't know the meaning of the words, only that he must say them before approaching the stones.

"Can you walk this far to the stones?" he asked Lyndon.

The old man's body convulsed with a deep, racking cough, making his back and knees spasm. "I must." Each of his spine knuckles rippled against Little John's hands.

"Three steps. Tradition says that you must approach the last three steps on your own. Crawl if you must." The Green Man took a dozen long strides until he could just brush his fingertips to the stone, as close as he dared bring the dying man in his arms.

Then Little John dropped to one knee. Lyndon's body fell limp. A sob heaved up from the center of his chest. *Too late!*

Not quite. Lyndon spasmed once more and rolled to the ground. His fingers flexed and grabbed the turf. His shoulders heaved, and he drew himself three finger lengths closer. His other arm swung forward, and he repeated the effort. Then he paused to pant.

Elena joined Little John in the vigil. Her transparent form wavered in and out of sight. "It would be very easy for him to give up now before he achieves the final merging." Her voice whispered into Little John's ears as well as his mind.

"This is important to him, despite his years away honoring another god."

"The stones are not god," said Will Scarlett, the bard. He unslung his harp from his back and strummed a mournful chord. His clear voice sang a complementary note, announcing to one and all, mortal or spirit, that Lyndon would be missed, but his time on Earth had come to an end.

Lyndon seemed to revive a morsel of strength as he pulled himself forward one more time.

"The stones represent human need to reach for the divine," Robin Goodfellow added, stepping up to stand at Little John's other side.

One by one, each of the Wild Folk joined to honor one who had been lost to them but returned home to die. The ritual Lyndon attempted would be repeated by each of them in turn, some sooner, some later. To be born in the shadow of the towering stones instilled a need to die among them.

"The stones are our anchor to life and to this land. Only here can we set our souls free by returning the weight of life to the stones," Tuck said, the last to join the circle around the three stones. He lifted his voice in a firm recitation of a plainsong.

Little John didn't understand the language of the song, but he felt the mournful nature behind the words and the cadence.

Lady Ardenia's voice plucked a note from Will Scarlett's harp and embellished it with the slow, almost reluctant flow that sounded like a stream withering in a drought.

Each of the Wild Folk, drawn here by instinct and communal need for sharing Lyndon's last act, added their own voice and song to the melody. Each expressed grief at his passing as well as joy that he was free of pain and the frustration of forgetfulness at last.

A sudden hush fell upon the meadow. The sun rose higher, shortening and defining the shadows cast by the standing stones. With a last surge of strength, the ancient monk heaved himself forward one last finger length and rested his palm against the base of the center stone. A smile crept over him as he stared upward at whatever awaited him on the other side.

Elena stepped forward, a misty outline of her three-faced

self, barely solid enough to hold her shape. She flowed to Lyndon's side and offered her hand to his spirit.

Wavery and losing solidity, Lyndon rose from his body. He touched the goddess' hand briefly and passed into the stone. Light, brighter than sunlight reflecting on water, flashed for an instant. Then the stone faded back to its normal mottled gray.

Elena glowed, too, then faded to nothing. Her obligation complete, she could return to her normal abode in Nick's pocket.

"Where is Nick?" Little John asked. He needed the boy alive and well in only a few weeks' time when the doorway to Faery Underhill could be opened by any sorcerer. "He should be here."

Tuck looked around, startled. "I sent for him. . . ."

Jane looked up from her pile of mending, surprised at the sudden silence surrounding her. The light changed around her, flickering strangely.

Her fingers ached where she'd held her old iron needle for so long. Compared to the slender silver needle, her stitches were now huge and clumsy. This gave the faeries one more reason to sneer at her. But they always had more garments to repair. What good was having sixteen gowns or tunics when they only wore one at a time?

The faeries, one and all, halted their endless games of chance, composition of nonsensical ballads, mock sword fights, and perpetual flirtation. As if summoned by some silent alarm, they dropped all their props and formed a single line behind

Queen Mab. Staring at nothing with blank expressions, they filed through a tiny crack in the cave walls.

Uneven patterns of raw stone piled together from upheavals in the earth and rough erosion from constant trickles of water oozing down them revealed the natural cave. None of the walls or the floors were even or symmetrical. Nothing but unshaped dirt and stone. The air turned cold, and the light coming in through holes in the ceiling faded.

The marble tiles she had scrubbed so endlessly vanished as well.

The illusion of a grand palace fell away as did the masks of youth and beauty on each of the faeries. Their bodies sagged, flabby and weak; long limbs looked like rough branches with twig fingers and toes. Long, elegant streams of hair took on the texture and appearance of dry hay. Only their clothing—mostly mended by Jane—remained bright and colorful, draping gracefully upon withered frames.

Their wings sagged until their delicate tips dragged on the floor, lacking color and definition as well as the near-constant tiny flutters Jane had grown so used to, that she couldn't notice movement until it was gone. The wings looked like autumnal leaves, dry and brittle just before the onset of full winter.

Jane had witnessed this behavior before. The trance affected all the faeries at the same time, but without a pattern that Jane could see.

As one, all the faeries turned sideways and took measured shuffling steps through the crack. Faint yellow light—akin to the color of new buttercups—crept through the opening, intermittently blocked by each passing body. The long shadows falling behind the faeries looked more like their illusory selves than their current dilapidated state.

When the last handmaiden and messenger had passed through the cave wall, Jane gathered her courage, put down her endless mending and followed them, careful to stay far enough behind so they didn't notice her. She'd never had the courage to discover why these fits came over the faeries. But now, now that someone had spoken into her mind, warning her to prepare, she felt she needed to know what overtook them during this mass trance.

Jane touched the white sleeve of Lily. The young handmaiden to the queen had treated her, if not kindly, at least not cruelly. "What is happening?" she asked.

Lily stared forward, like all the others, toward that strange light that grew brighter with each step, and pulsed to the rhythm of a slow and ponderous heartbeat. Lily kept moving toward the light; each step matched the throbbing light.

Jane's fingers had to release her grip on the faery or risk tearing the gossamer fabric of her sleeve. Jane had too much mending already.

Once through the crack, the cave opened into a vast circular room with carved and polished walls that reflected the yellow light in all directions. A series of broad terraces led downward from where they stood. In the center of the room, well below the rim, sat a polished yellow gem that glowed within . . . or maybe only reflected the sunlight now pouring through a circular opening in the roof, so far above Jane that she had no way to judge the distance.

Jane had to cover her eyes with her arm to guard against the glare.

The faeries reached the next to lowest level of the terraces. Now their shoulders touched, but they made no shift of position or posture to indicate they were aware of anything but the stone. As one, they raised their arms until their hands reached for the planes and facets of the glowing rock. None of them touched it. They simply basked in the pulsing glow, bathing in the light.

Slowly at first, then more and more quickly, their twiggy fingers filled out and became normal, as did their arms. Then as the light increased, their bodies, faces, and hair resumed the illusion of youth and beauty, their clothing took on new sparkle. And their wings . . . their wings fluttered up and out, no longer drooping.

With the renewal of their wings, each faery drifted upward, still entranced by the light.

Suddenly, the sun above the chamber shifted, or a cloud moved across it. The light dimmed. Jane's vision cleared of the sun dazzle. Now that she could look directly at the gem, she saw that it was not one huge and glowing crystal, but dozens upon dozens of pieces piled and fused together. Collectively, the facets reflected more light than any single one could.

The faeries shook their heads, casting off the bedazzlement, and they all smiled at each other, slowly returning to the ground.

Their lives had been artificially enhanced and renewed.

Queen Mab was the last to plant her feet on the stone terrace. Her gaze remained fixed upon the stone. She alone took the last step downward and touched the gem. It had lost its glow, seemingly imparting it into the faeries. The queen caressed the clear, yellow, smooth facet, cupping one side of it as a mother cradles her baby's face.

A bright flash, like lightning on a summer night, sprang from the stone into Mab's hand. She jerked her offended limb away, rubbing it against her gown.

Jane smelled burned flesh.

She scuttled back to the main room of the cave, restored to its palace richness in furnishings and decoration. Once more, the floor looked like marble tiles that she would have to scrub as soon as Mab noticed her doing something else. By the time Jane plunked down on her stool—no longer a ragged boulder—the first faery squeezed through the crack in the wall. Jane took careful note of its position before the illusion of tapestry and wooden paneling covered it once more.

That stone was the source of Faery power and magic. They had to return to it to maintain their illusions.

What would happen to Bracken if he did not come home to the stone soon?

Twenty-One

eak light crept through gaps between the roots above Nick. He could almost discern Henry sprawled beside him, like a novitiate prostrating before an altar. Another figure pressed himself up against the earthen walls of their cavern prison.

He looked back, seeking the framework of the trapdoor and its latch and found nothing in this dim light.

"Where are we?" Nick asked the vague man-shape.

"Nowhere you want to be," said the man in the same voice—stronger and less distant—that had summoned them for help.

Nick pulled himself to his feet and tried to touch the ceiling. His fingers just barely brushed the first rootlets dangling through the packed dirt. With a boost, he could grab hold of one and pull himself back up to safety.

"Don't bother trying," the stranger said. "*She* is waiting and will bite your fingers off before you get a purchase."

"Who is she?" Nick tried in vain to remember any tales about a dangerous female living in the forest.

"Mammoch, Goddess of the Hunted. The biggest and meanest wild pig I've ever seen."

Little John had mentioned her when he warned Nick about the dangers of the forest, especially at night. But it was not night. Closer to noon than sunset.

Henry pulled his knees beneath him, shaking his head free of lingering shock from their fall through the forest floor. "*Goddess of the Hunted*," he muttered. "The ancient crone of my village talked about her as if she was a sister. No one else knows the tales, or if they know, they don't talk. The men used to cross themselves and kiss their blessed talismans for protection, then walk away every time they had to pass near the old woman. Said she was a witch. Too afraid of her to report her to the priests."

"Mammoch, I've heard it once from the Woodwose. No one else. I'd remember that name if I ever read about it. And I've read every scroll and book in the scriptorium," Nick said. The hoarded documents rarely said more than a few words about any forest lore other than to dismiss them as remnants of old pagan religions and therefore invalid.

He'd learned more from Will Scarlett who sang as often as he talked.

In the near distance he heard a soft whuffing snort, sort of like one of the village pigs rooting around for things to eat in the dirt.

"By the Starfire, she's coming back!" The faery pressed his

back tighter against the dirt wall of their prison and covered his head with his arms.

"Faery, you are no longer alone," a harsh female voice cackled. "My traps worked. I shall dine well tomorrow." The reek of rancid meat wafted through the roots. She'd already eaten today.

"Why wait until tomorrow?" Nick called out in direct challenge.

"The sweat of fear makes the meat all the sweeter. You need time to ripen."

Nick shifted his gaze from side to side, trying to discern the size and shape of their tormentor. Like the Wild Folk, he guessed that she had to take her human form in order to speak, even if each phrase was punctuated by a grunt.

Then a cloven hoof stepped upon the mat of smaller roots, testing their strength and resiliency. Human fingers but no thumb, crusted with dirt and horny nails, grabbed hold of the mat, and it sagged beneath the full weight of the wild pig. Close to thirty-five stone. Indeed, the biggest of wild pigs, more than the boar he'd seen slung on a pole by the sheriff's beaters. That one was huge—enough meat to feed the entire castle and staff for a week. The kitchen serfs had claimed it to be seventeen stone, and the two-foot-long curved tusks made a substantial trophy to mount on the wall of the great hall.

"Watch the passage of the sun and count the hours. Do not sleep, but cherish your last time alive," Mammoch grunted. Her tusks curved upward from her lower jaw. The silvered tips, shining in the shifting light, came level with her snoutlike nose.

Then she stood up straight, and Nick caught sight of twelve teats, more than enough to suckle a normal litter of piglets.

The shadowy form crouched back onto four legs and sprouted bristling hair that varied from golden brown to silver-streaked black. Grunting and snorting, she wandered off, leaving her prisoners to ripen.

The faery slumped to the ground, burying his face in his knees.

Henry looked like he wanted to do the same.

Nick caught his friend by the cowl of his robe. "We have to get out of here. I don't think she'll be back until dawn."

He drew a deep breath and prepared to whistle, the same birdlike call Will Scarlett had taught him.

His throat clenched; no sound emerged.

He tried again.

Silence. His voice chose not to work, and he could do nothing about it.

"H . . . how do we get out of here?" Henry asked.

Nick couldn't call for help. What would Elena tell Nick to do?

Think, silly boy. Use your head as your God intended.

He didn't need to hear the three-faced goddess to know what she would say.

He hooked his thumbs into his rope belt while he paced the three steps in each direction. Rope belt.

"Henry, how strong are you?" He eyed the shorter boy up and down, shorter and more slender than he, but still solid.

Henry blinked in bewilderment. "As strong as I need to be

plowing, planting, harvesting in our gardens, trimming trees, and hauling off the debris. Why? What are you planning?"

"If we knot our belts together, then I boost you up to clear an opening, could you then haul me up, once you've got solid footing?"

The faery stood up, suddenly interested.

"I'd rather you stand on my shoulders to do the clearing part, and then you haul me up. I'm not liking the idea of being up there and exposed to old Mammoch alone."

"You won't be alone long."

"You're bigger than me. You haul me out." He began unwinding his belt, all six feet of it.

Nick did the same.

"What about me?" the faery asked. He looked down at his own simple tunic and leggings, soft boots, meant for indoors or flying. Not for walking.

"We'll haul you out. It will take both of us. Earthbound, I suspect you are heavier than you look. And you've been down here so long, the ground wants to keep you. Otherwise, you'd have flown out when the pig goddess first trapped you." Nick dismissed him as he studied the woven mat of dirt and rootlets, looking for the section that would be easiest to tear apart.

The faery's wings drooped, and he hung his head. "That is our curse. The Earth is jealous of our wings and binds us tightly. Only our worship of the Starfire frees us."

"There." Henry pointed upward.

Nick squinted his eyes until the pattern of the roofing became clear. No denser than anywhere else. But there was a pattern in the weaving that differed from the edges. Carefully,

he traced the differences until he spied the shape and dimen-
sions of the trap. Was that knotted tangle the latch?

"I see how to do this," Nick grunted as he estimated the
distance he needed to climb and where. "How do you get me
up there?"

"Just like we did when stealing apples on branches too
weak to climb onto," Henry said kneeling down and patting
his shoulders.

Nick slung his legs over his friend's shoulders. Henry
tugged on Nick's knees so that he sat on his friend's narrow
shoulders.

"Take off your sandals. It will be easier on us both when
you stand up." Henry admonished. "I'll tie them to the end of
the rope."

Nick complied. Henry gripped his knees fiercely and nodded
for Nick to settle. Then Nick placed his palms flat on the wall
to give Henry a bit of leverage. The slighter boy grunted and
lurched upward. He staggered until he found his balance and
Nick could release his scrabbling at the wall to reach upward.

The tough skin of the roots scraped Nick's hands, reluctant
to let go of their neighbors.

Gritting his teeth against the minor pains and burns, Nick
yanked and tore at the roots with the same fierceness he tack-
led words in strange languages and obscure meanings. He never
slid over a problem by making a tiny notation in the margin
that the word was Greek and therefore untranslatable. He always figured it out and Brother Theo appreciated that he didn't
interrupt the flow of work in the scriptorium to stop and ask
one of the few scholars who knew the ancient language.

He tugged repeatedly at a particularly tangled clump of ground vines. They did not budge, not even a tiny wiggle of movement. He investigated the intertwining roots and twisted greenery with his fingers. Mote by mote, grains of dirt hit his face. Then . . . then he encountered something more solid. The frame of the trapdoor!

"If I can't break the frame, I'll have to move around it." He moved his hands to the right and found looseness again in the mat.

"Just do it. You're getting heavy," Henry protested.

Nick attacked the dirt with more vigor. Before long, he had made a hole as wide as his shoulders. Then it was a not-so-simple maneuver to get his feet onto Henry's shoulders to haul himself onto solid ground. His palms were raw from grabbing at slight handholds until he stood upright, head, shoulders, and chest well above the roof of the cave. He braced himself on the more solid framework, then wiggled and twisted, pulling himself forward until he could get one knee up, then the other.

He paused to breathe deeply.

"Are you free?" Henry called.

"Yes," Nick panted.

"Then get me out before the pig comes back!"

"Coming." Nick sat on solid ground, well back from the crumbling edge of the hole that had trapped them before. He tied one end of the rope around his waist and a goodly-sized knot on the other end and dropped it through the hole.

In moments, Henry scrambled upward as quickly as he climbed the ivy on the outside wall of the dormitory. Nick had never trusted the plants not to betray his breaking of the rules by sneaking in and out that way.

"What about me?" the faery yelled.

Nick and Henry looked at each other.

"Rescuing him is how we got into trouble," Nick said, as he dropped the knotted end of the rope back in the hole. "Help me pull."

Henry grabbed the rope and started pulling as soon as they felt the weight of the last prisoner.

Bringing him up was harder than their own escape. Sweating and panting, they finally spotted the man's green hair emerging through the opening. Then his pale face and grimy clothes. At last half his body lay sprawled on the chancy root mat.

Nick began looping the rope together.

"I'm not free yet," the faery whined. His wings appeared to be the same faded green as his clothing, the color of old bracken ferns.

"Then crawl. You can't expect us to do everything for you."

He looked honestly bewildered, his long nose nearly meet-ing his sharp chin, and his pointed ears twitching among strands of brittle hair that looked like dried moss. "Queen Mab says that's what humans are for, to bend their knees to us and hasten to satisfy our every whim."

"Queen Mab isn't here, Bracken." Nick chose the name on a whim, because the faery's coloring and clothing reminded Nick of one of the specimen plants in Brother Luke's garden. The faery didn't even notice, too eager to be free.

Henry yanked the rope free of the faery's hands and untied their sandals.

"She's been wrong before, not that I'd ever say that to her face."

"Is that the excuse she gives to claim the right to trap people and take them back to the Faery Mound as your slaves?"

"Yes."

"We aren't slaves, nor are we serfs!" Henry shouted angrily. "We joined the abbey and our vows to God set us free!"

"Huh?"

Nick wound his belt around his waist so that it held his robe high enough he didn't trip on the hem. Henry did the same, needing to pull up the lengths of heavy wool higher than Nick.

Then they pelted off down the track in the direction they'd intended to go some hours before.

Twenty-Two

ilde leaned against the door to the storeroom, pounding feebly on the stout wooden panels. "Help me. Somebody, please help me," she wailed, though it came out as little more than a whisper through her tired and raw throat.

Her hands were raw from pounding on the door; her fingernails ripped to the quick from trying to pick away the mortar between stone blocks. Anything to escape.

She rested her forehead against the door, eyes closed and palms flat against the wood. A tiny sound caressed her ears. She opened her eyes wide, as if vision might augment her hearing. The sound did not repeat, but she realized that her eyes must have adjusted to the feeble light.

Hours had passed. How long had she been trapped inside this tiny space? She was surprised she could still breathe. Now she could pick out shapes. Lumpy sacks had been piled into neat stacks.

Her stomach growled with hunger and the pressure below built steadily without a chamber pot or privy available.

Was the humiliation of using a corner to relieve herself any worse than being trapped in here by a vindictive nun?

Not for the first time, she wished the Mother Abbess would return. Sister Marie Josef seemed calmer and less likely to take out her anger against the outside world on the girls when the Mother Abbess maintained her authority over all the sisters and the orphans and girls pledged to the Church by their parents.

But the Mother Abbess was gone, and by the king's decree, no one could take her place to keep a balance of discipline and mercy.

Her bladder would wait no longer. Maybe if she cleared a space behind the sacks of grain against the outside wall, then covered the spot again, no one would know. If anyone ever released her.

Crossing her legs, she gingerly bent to slide the first sack of grain aside. The weight of it nearly undid her resolve to hold it all in. But she persevered and soon had three sacks, almost as heavy as herself, cleared away from the wall.

And there lay her salvation. A small arched opening where the floor joined the wall, designed for drainage in wet weather, and the only source of light. The roof must not be tight on this wing to need a drain. But the arched opening also provided an entry for mice and rats.

She shuddered at the thought of sharing this room for so long with vermin. At least they'd been polite and not made their presence known.

Another poor choice was to use this room for storage of

grain and tuber vegetables. They'd *invited* rodents to come in. It should have been used as a *garderobe*.

Whoever had built the convent had been more concerned with solid walls that could not be breached than proper drainage and seam-free roofs.

She bent to examine the size of the opening, forgetting about other pressing matters for the nonce. One look showed her that the ground was only a few feet below and led to the herb garden. She didn't see anyone working the long rows of greenery; plants she'd made tidy with her own hard work.

Maybe the builders thought that short distance between the ground and the opening would deter vermin. Not likely.

They'd also made the hole big enough that if she twisted and stretched just *so*, she might fit. Good thing that Sister Marie Josef preferred to starve the girls rather than let them grow plump enough to attract a husband.

First things first. Her escape route would be a tight squeeze and put undue pressure on her bladder. She scrambled to the far corner, hiked up her robe, and squatted.

Relief let her drop her hunched shoulders to a more natural level. When her thighs began to shake, she stood and righted herself. Time to manage her escape.

Spreading her fingers on both hands, Hilde measured the height and breadth of the opening. Should she go head first? If she did that, then once her shoulders cleared the opening, she could easily slide the rest of her through, but end up facefirst in the dirt below. Arms, head, shoulders . . .

A scraping sound at the door brought her upright with a jolt.

Someone outside lifted the bar that locked her in.

She was done pleading for help and appearing weak. She remembered Dom fighting off older and stronger boys who tormented their younger brother because he was weak of mind and dragged one leg. She'd not appear weak again. Sister Marie Josef might not direct all of her venom toward Hilde if Hilde fought back.

"Still waiting for rescue by some man, I see," Sister Marie Josef said as she threw back the door so hard it banged and bounced against the outside wall. She held the crossbar as if preparing for battle with a quarter staff. "Have you learned the error of your ways yet?" Sister Marie Josef asked.

Hilde met her question with stony silence.

Then the sister wrinkled her nose. "Uncivilized wanton! You should stay in here with your own stink a while longer."

"No," Hilde replied, rushing forward. She grabbed the crossbar and pushed the older woman hard until she stumbled against the stacked grain bags. She plunged forward, onto the covered walkway before she turned and spoke again. "I'll go live in the wild before I succumb to your twisted view of discipline. I'd rather live as a beldame for the rest of my life than subject myself to your punishments for imagined sins."

"You deserve to be humiliated and die at the hands of a man, no better than a wild beast. Both you and your defiler!" Sister Marie Josef shouted. Her face turned bright red and spittle dribbled from her mouth in anger.

Hilde didn't care if she fell into a fit. She turned abruptly and marched three steps back toward the dormitory only to bump into Sister Mary Margaret. They both recoiled, flailing for balance again.

"What troubles you, child?" the senior sister asked, hands reaching to soothe and straighten Hilde's hair where it escaped her no-longer-tight braids.

"She troubles me." Hilde pointed back to the storeroom as Sister Marie Josef staggered through the door, still clutching the crossbar.

"Oh." Sister Mary Margaret's face fell into folds of disappointment. Age wrinkles deepened around her eyes and down from her mouth. "I thought we agreed that you may no longer use that place to discipline the girls."

"They need . . ."

"You think we need torture?" Hilde screamed. "You are so afraid of yourself you have to make us cower at your power. No more. I'm leaving. Right now."

"Then you go with no more than your shift!" Sister Marie Josef's hand reached to tear the heavy woolen robe from Hilde. Her fingers arched and clutched like the talons of a lord's hunting hawk.

"No." Sister Mary Margaret stepped between them. "Mother Abbess thought this place would bring you peace, Sister Marie Josef. I know you were ill-used by your father and it destroyed the balance of joy and despair in your mind. But you can no longer use that as an excuse to make the girls hurt as much as you do. You need time to yourself, on your knees in prayer."

"You have no authority . . ." Sister Marie Josef protested.

Sister Mary Margaret stopped her words with an upheld hand. "Mother Abbess left me in charge until she returns from exile when this war between our king and the Holy Father ends. I know we are supposed to make these decisions together, with all the sisters in Chapter Meeting. But you have gone too far. You will go to the Lady Chapel now and pray for forgiveness." She pointed toward the little church at the corner of the square cloister. "And you will not speak to or touch any of the girls again, until a priest comes to hear your confession and sees you repentant and worthy of forgiveness."

Clenching her hands into fists, Sister Marie Josef turned and marched to the church, cutting across the normally peaceful flower garden at the center rather than folding her hands into her sleeves and walking along the stone-paved shelter of the walkway.

"I apologize to you, Hilde, because *she* never will. I am certain the punishment meted out to you was undeserving of your misbehavior."

"'Twas not misbehavior. 'Twas her anger that needed satisfaction in punishing anyone for not being a victim."

"Please, find it in your heart to forgive her. To forgive us. She sought safety here. But she never found peace. Her mother blamed her for her father's misdeeds. Sister Marie Josef believed her mother's accusations and continues to try to shift the guilt from her own shoulders to you girls."

Hilde shook her head. "I do not trust this place. I'm leaving."

"You have no place to go, child."

"I'd rather live with the Woodwose than endure one more night here."

"No!" Sister Mary Margaret gasped, clutching her throat and her chest. "They trespass on the king's preserve. Runaway serfs. Outlaws! They and their village are so far outside the law that they will hang one and all if they are captured."

Hilde shrugged her shoulders. "I'll take my chances. Life in the forest seems safer than in here."

Little John sighed with a tear in his eye as the other Forest Folk lined up to touch each of the three large stones in turn. After receiving blessing from the triad, they separated to touch a much smaller stone at the far side of the fire pit at the center of the sacred space. A brief prayer, a deep breath, and they drifted away in ones or twos or small family groups. Only Tuck and Little John's sons remained to share these last few moments of mourning. Lyndon had passed, his left hand flat against the base of the tallest standing stone.

"I need my tree," Little John said. He nodded to Derwyn, the eldest, the one most likely to succeed him. "Please stay and take care of what needs to be done."

His son nodded acknowledgment. He was not yet comfortable with human speech. But he'd learn.

"One more chore, then you may sleep until Midsummer when it will be time to free Jane," Tuck said, touching Little John's arm in a truly human gesture of comfort.

"Do we bury him, or do you?" Little John asked. He surveyed the outer circle, seeking a gap. He found a small one between two well-worn stones marking the burials of two of the folk so long passed no one remembered whose bones lay beneath the boulders. Yet Little John, the Green Man and Lord of the Forest, remembered. The knowledge had been passed to him by his father, along with many other things. Both of those graves belonged to humans, one a runaway serf, the other a thief missing a hand for his crimes. Both had been welcomed when the Romans ruled sections of this land. "The Romans never truly ruled the people of our land. We nodded compliance then did as we chose, as those two did," he said.

"Brother Luke shed his attachment to the Church and returned here to die. His soul has merged with the stones, as have so many others. He may rest here in the circle, as he chose, remembered as Lyndon." Tuck bowed his head and made the sign of the cross, then he, too, made the rounds, touching the triad of standing stones, then the marker where the Huntsmen were entombed, one atop the other, all in the same place, no one individual remembered as anything more or less than *The* Huntsman of his generation.

Little John nodded. The duty of digging a grave fell to him. Derwyn could help, but Little John needed to plant his old friend.

A thrashing through the undergrowth diverted his attention away from his sad chore. He centered his awareness on the noise. Three sets of feet trod the ground, in a hurry. More like two and a half.

Nick was easy to identify. He'd already made enough of an

impression on the forest for the land and plants to remember him. The second felt akin to him. Another abbey boy. But the third?

He sniffed the air and found nothing familiar surrounding the third person. Defensively, he stepped outside the circle, unwilling to defile the sacred space with violence if it came to that.

"Who comes?" he bellowed.

Nick burst into sight, running hard, constantly looking over his shoulder. Behind him, a slighter, fairer boy followed, falling a little bit behind with each step.

"Sanctuary!" Nick gasped, panting heavily and looking pale beneath his normally robust complexion. His willow-green eyes had lost the brilliant shine of curiosity in favor of panic.

"I grant you safety within my realm," Little John replied with the ritual words.

"Thank you," Nick and the other boy said at the same time as they skidded to a halt just before the boundary of the circle. They both bent over, hands on their knees while they gasped for breath.

Little John barely looked at them, all his attention on the third set of halting steps.

And then he saw wavery movement within the undergrowth. His back stiffened and the hair at his nape stood on end.

"Why do you trespass, faery?" he bellowed again, widening his stance and balling his hands into fists.

"Please, Lord of the Greenwood, I, too, beg sanctuary." The faery with drooping wings fluttered and stuttered to a halt just behind the two boys. He stood taller than Nick by a head, yet appeared slighter as if he had no flesh on his bones. Everything about him made him look more akin to the ferns than humans, from the shape of his wings to the texture of his hair.

"Why should I grant shelter and safety to my sworn enemy?"

"What?"

"You can't tell me that you don't know that you and your kind trapped my Jane, my one true lady love, and took her back underground as your slave!"

"Jane?"

Little John stared at the faery, speechless. "What one of you knows, all of you know," he finally spat out. "I will trade you for Jane."

"Would your Jane be human rather than dryad? I only ask because, you being the Green Man, Lord of the Forest, one would expect you to mate with your own kind," the faery said. He looked around rapidly, startling at every sound.

"I did long ago, and as is the way of the dryads, she left me for another. But aye, Jane is human."

"Pren be me mam," Derwyn said, his voice a dry and cracking whisper.

"I believe you seek the one Mab calls Jonquil? Um . . . I think she may be Queen Mab's newest pet. We call her Jonquil, a name more suited to one of us. In Faery, we have made her beautiful and graceful. In the outer world, she was plain, even by human standards, and what kind of name is 'Jane?' It says and means nothing." He was babbling now, clearly nervous. "She's much too sweet to be the queen's slave."

Beneath the spurts of noise coming from the faery's mouth,

the forest grew silent. Birds stopped chirping. Little John looked to Will Scarlett as he fluttered to the ground and shifted to his human form. The bard shrugged. The insects landed and stilled their wing rubbings. Winds ceased dragging storm clouds toward them.

"Please, Master Little John," Nick looked up at him. "Mammoch imprisoned all three of us. She follows our trail, seeking to make a meal of us."

The usual sound of wild pigs rooting in the dirt for roots and grubs grew louder. The rancid odor that accompanied their kind intensified.

Little John and Mammoch avoided each other. He granted her the illusion of being independent of Forest Law. She granted him the illusion of retaining rule over all the forest denizens.

"We call this faery 'Bracken' because that's the color of his wings," Nick said on a quieter note.

"I didn't tell you my . . . ." The faery cut off his words as he stared at the boy in shock, only now realizing that Nick had called him that at the pit.

Little John suppressed a chuckle. Apparently, observant Nick had guessed the faery's true name and now they all had a degree of power over him.

"I should give you to Mammoch," Little John snorted at Bracken.

"Please, sir, I beg sanctuary. I was not part of the trap that captured your lady. If I knew how to free her from Queen Mab, I would help you in that quest. She is kind to us when she has no cause to be. I would return the favor. Please grant me protection from Mammoch."

"Do you, Bracken of Faery Underhill, vow by all that you hold sacred that you will aid my quest to retrieve my lady in whatever way I deem necessary?"

"Yes, yes, yes. I so vow. Though I know not how you will do it. The only door that those not born of Faery can use is locked by sorcery. Even Mab cannot exit or enter the Faery Mound by that passage."

"There are other routes in and out of your underground cave, but no one else can use them, even if they found them," Tuck added. He chewed his lip as he thought. "Little John, I am inclined to take this faery's word and bind him by the sacredness of this circle. By your decree, once he passes beyond this boundary stone," he pointed to the boulder at their feet, "he may not leave again without your permission."

"So be it," Little John proclaimed, and his voice reverberated among the stones, setting their magic into place.

"But . . . but I need to return to the Mound. I need to renew my strength at the Starfire. Without it, I cannot fly," Bracken protested.

"But you will live. That is all I need. We will return you to the Mound when the moons align on Midsummer Night. Enter this circle and live, or stay outside and become Mammoch's next meal. Your choice."

Reluctantly, the green faery took two steps forward, placing him just inside the circle.

With an audible snap the boundary stones sent a spell around the perimeter, connecting them with an invisible barrier Bracken could not cross.

"We have not used this space as a prison or as a sanctuary

for many long years. I hope not to need it again for many, many more," Little John grunted. The hope in his heart that he'd nurtured for nigh on fifty years, hope that Jane would return to him, burst forth in tiny blossoms. He had one more ally. He almost dared believe in a future with Jane.

Twenty-Three

ick backed up from the boundary of the circle. He didn't want to risk Mammoch's wicked tusks goring him. He imagined her keeping all four hoofs outside the boulders and still reaching her snout inward, almost a man's full length. Obeying Forest Law and defying it at the same time.

"Let the Green Man deal with the Goddess of the Hunted," Tuck said, squeezing Nick's shoulder reassuringly.

A sudden heaviness in his sleeve pocket told Nick that Elena had returned to her silver pitcher. He patted it more out of habit than needing to know her whereabouts.

"Why have I never heard of this being from anyone except the Wild Folk?" Nick asked, noting that Henry hung close to Tuck's left shoulder.

"Few people want to talk about her lest speaking her name brings her out," Henry offered.

"Exactly right. You know more than you let on in classes at the abbey," Tuck replied.

Henry looked at him questioningly.

Nick decided to let Henry figure out where he had met the abbot in disguise. (Or was the abbot a disguise for the man from the wild?)

The snorting of Mammoch as she paced the circumference of the circle demanded most of his attention. As he followed her around, paced by Little John, Nick surveyed the open ground. The three standing stones arrested his attention. Each of the pale gray stones stood at least twice the height of a tall man. The center one, tallest of all. The other two stood slightly angled so that their smooth dressed faces looked at both the other two stones. A cold fire pit guarded a wide gap between the smaller of the three giants. One had to pass around or even through the fire to enter the region of stone shadows . . . to worship?

Acknowledging the power and presence of the stones prickled Nick's skin uncomfortably. He'd heard that before the Romans brought the true Church to England, the inhabitants worshipped many different gods in many different ways. This was the first time he'd encountered standing stones, though he'd read about them.

"The Wild Folk do not worship the stones themselves," Tuck said, as if reading Nick's thoughts. "They use the stones to closely define a sacred space within the sacred space defined by the boundary stones. They serve a similar function to the rood screen between the main altar and the Lady Chapel."

Nick stopped when he identified Brother Luke at the base

of the tallest stone, hand still pressed flat against the chiseled face. His wide-open eyes staring at death and the absolute stillness of the rest of the body told Nick that the old man had died.

"The physician sent us to find Brother Luke and return him to the abbey for burial," he whispered, awed and respectful of the death.

"When you return to the abbey, you must tell the brothers that you could not find Brother Luke."

"Not exactly a lie. We did not find him alive."

"True. And since you are here, I think you should help Little John bury our old friend, where he chose to die, as so many of our folk have done."

Nick turned around in a tight circle searching for signs of other burials.

"Each of the boundary stones is a burial marker."

"Oh."

Henry kept shaking his head. "This is not real. I am not here. I am dreaming."

"You have permission to keep believing that, boy," Tuck said. "But since you have trouble embracing the evidence your eyes and your emotions give you, then you will not return here. You will not be able to find this place even if you try."

"That's fine with me. I've had a lifetime of adventure today. This is not just a lark through the apple orchard to see if we can get away with stealing some fruit. I want to believe it is all a nightmare." Henry stumbled over to an odd stone neither among the boundary or the standing giants and bent his knees as if to sit.

Little John abandoned his monitoring of Mammoch to

grab Henry's cowl and keep him upright. "You may not des-
ecrate the final resting place of the last Earl of Locksley! He
was a greater friend to us than many a lord since his death."

"Sorry, sir. I didn't know." Henry hung his head and
backed away. "I'll happily leave as soon as you banish yon
monster pig. If you'll point me toward the Royal Road, I'll
find my way back to the abbey on my own. And I'll never
leave there again."

"Mammoch!" Little John called.

The Goddess of the Hunted paused in her circuit of the
open space and lifted her massive head to face the Lord of
the Forest. Still in pig form, she snorted derisively but could
not speak.

"You will not feed today on anyone here. It is time for you
to return to your wallow."

Bracken clung to Little John's shadow, his wings drooping
and his face looking more wizened by the moment.

Mammoch swung around to face the Green Man and
reared up on her hind legs. Her twelve teats looked engorged
and her belly full.

"No wonder she's so hungry," Henry gasped. "She's
breeding."

"Pigs breed a lot and often," Tuck added. "Unchecked,
they can overrun all the available land. They upset the balance
of life. They need to be hunted to keep them from becoming
so numerous that they tear up the ground cover, destroying
new growth . . . ." The old man shuddered.

"So I need to check her predatory instincts here and now,"
Little John said, almost sadly. With one long step, he cleared

the boundary and faced the Goddess of the Hunted. They stood nearly eye to eye and equaled each other in mass.

But Mammoch had those wicked tusks capable of gutting a man from neck to gullet.

Nick wanted to turn away. He couldn't bear to watch his friend taken down in a gory mess.

He had no experience with those who dared defy the Green Man. Which of these forest giants had the advantage?

Little John's arms extended, becoming woody and covered with tough bark. His fingers stretched and stretched again as they became grasping twigs. His bushy beard dried into brittle moss. The giant pig dropped to all fours and backed up two small steps, putting just enough room between herself and the enraged Lord of the Forest. She backed away warily. Little John grew taller and taller until he blocked out the sun. His arms stretched as his fingers extended from twigs into clasping vines.

Nick expected the Green Man to become rooted to the ground, his thick bark the only defense against those wicked tusks. Not so. The half tree/half man took one giant stride forward, resting one massive foot on the pig's back.

"Choose, Mammoch, mother of pigs, Goddess of the Hunted. Choose death at this moment or to run away and hide until humans come for you and your young with their dogs and spears and arrows with flint heads the size of one of their hands."

"You can't kill me . . . I am as immortal as you," she grunted in a series of moans and snorts that somehow Nick understood.

"I am extremely long-lived, like any tree left alone to grow without facing the mortal dangers of fire and ax, but I am not immortal. And neither are you. You, in turn, will be killed—if not by hunters, then by one of your own get when you grow old, tired, weak, and beyond bearing young. I, too, will be replaced when my tree home succumbs to age and begins to rot from within. Then my son Derwyn will step into his tree and make it the tallest and largest in all the forest. That is the natural and balanced cycle of life. Until our demise, by treaty established long ago, long before the humans came to our land, you are subject to me, the lord of all I survey. Do I crush you now or send others to hunt you—which you might or might not survive?"

"I bow to your mastery. For now. But remember, the Faery Mound exists outside your law. The faeries were never part of the original pact or any established since. You give shelter to one of them. They do not have to return the favor." She scuttled backward, out from under the angry foot crashing down where she had been. A moment later, she galloped off through the undergrowth, making her own trail.

Little John shrank back to his normal size and form as he shook his fist at the retreating pig.

Nick expected the Green Man to be triumphant. Instead, his hands shook, and his skin paled from rough bark to palest inner core oak exposed to sunlight too long. Sweat dripped from his face, and his posture sagged.

He and Henry looked to Tuck for an explanation.

But the old man showed the same symptoms. Both forest denizens dropped to the ground and buried their faces in their knees, arms wrapped around their legs, pulling them into self-contained balls. The other tall man, Derwyn, stood protectively between them.

Henry knelt beside Tuck, hugging him tightly. Nick did the same for Little John.

"What ails you?" Nick asked the big man.

Tuck recovered first. In a shaky voice he said, "We are all a part of this land. Any time the balance is upset, or a dispute among us becomes violent, we all feel it. We all become part of it. That is why we work hard to get along. We have our own etiquette to facilitate this. Politeness overrules dislike and distrust."

Nick's mind jerked forward and back. Some of his unanswered questions found solutions. "Father Tuck, is that why you did not go into exile, as commanded by both our king and the Holy Father? You are tied to the land with more rigid bonds than serfdom."

Tuck nodded, his throat working as he sought the stability to speak further. "The Wild Folk move about freely within the forest. Here, we are strong. Out there," he gestured vaguely toward Nottingham. "Out there, our strength is limited, our steps heavy, our lives shortened. I spent two years in Paris studying with some of the great theologians of our time. My friends and benefactors had to send me home, ill and weak from a wasting disease, not expected to survive."

"Will that happen to me if I go abroad to study?"

Tuck shook his head. "You are far removed from your forest blood. More mortal than I. I expect you may move through the world as you wish and as politics allow." His voice sounded firmer as he wiped sweat off his brow with his sleeve. It did not return. Not so, Little John. "I am three or four generations removed from the Wild. I am more human than Huntsman, else I could not have left England at all." Tuck rested a bit more. "Though if you ever sail away from these shores, you will not rest comfortably until you return."

"Serfs are tied to the land," Henry reminded them all.

"Serfs are only tied to the land by human laws, not by the blood that courses through their veins," Nick said. "To leave the land makes them outlaws. To defy the owners of the land makes them outlaws. No wonder the number of Woodwose grows every year."

"Living in a Royal Forest is the closest thing to protection they have." Tuck looked away, gaze roaming the forest verge beyond this clearing. "Legally, even the Sheriff of Nottingham cannot trespass on this preserve without the king's permission except to travel the Royal Road. The next time King John visits Nottingham, he must renew that permission. Which he will most likely do, since the sheriff bought his title. If Sir Philip Marc defies the king for any reason, even to rebel against tyranny, he forfeits all of the benefits of the office, including his own purchase price. The king is above the law and can change it as he needs, even to redefine rebellion."

"King John's biggest crime is that he stays in England and enforces his own laws so that the barons, the sheriffs, and others of their ilk cannot do as they choose, making up laws to suit their immediate needs," Nick mused.

"Ah, you have been reading, boy. And thinking. I'll make a leader out of you yet." Now mostly recovered, Tuck struggled to his feet, with a supporting arm from Henry. "Time for you to go home, Nick and Henry. Little John and I must bury Brother Luke and mourn him in our own way."

"I don't think Little John is ready to move yet. I'll stay and help you dig the grave," Nick replied. "Henry, you'd best stay until we're finished. Then we'll walk home together."

"You'll stay the night with the Woodwose," Little John said, his voice tight with fatigue and pain. "There is a storm brewing. You'll need shelter by sunset or risk a fatal chill. And without a guiding light . . ." He shook his head sadly. "I'll not have you losing your way again. The forest is not always a friendly place. Even if I sent Derwyn here with you as far as the last copse, he cannot protect you against everything. He does not yet have my authority. You need to stay. Best to get you to the Woodwose before the storm. We will attend to the burial."

Nick nodded, acknowledging finally that rampaging god-lings and Wild Folk were not the only dangers in the woods.

Twenty-Four

 light drizzle created a fine film of moisture on Hilde's gray wool robe. She raised the cowl to cover her hair and tugged it lower on her forehead. Her bundle of personal linen and a packet of bread, dried meat, and cheese rested heavily across her shoulders. She'd been on the road only a little over an hour and already she longed for the sound of another voice, the outline of a building on the horizon, *something* to indicate she was not alone on this muddy road to nowhere.

Sister Mary Margaret had pointed to the main road six hundred paces beyond the convent that should lead her to Nottingham and then to the Abbey of Locksley. She'd seen no one since.

Dom's friend Nick had made the journey from his abbey to her convent and back again in one night. She wondered if she'd make half the journey before nightfall. She had no lantern or torch, or even a candle stub to light her way once all lingering traces of daylight had disappeared. Even the moon would not show itself through the clouds. She supposed she could curl up under a tree at the side of the road and sleep until morning.

But that ran the risk of predators from the forest and outlaws and . . . rampaging mercenaries finding her.

"How can I defend myself?" she asked. No one was about to answer her.

Maybe she needed to address her plea as a prayer. Every lesson she'd had at the convent told her that God was always watching over the faithful.

She found a relatively dry patch of ground beneath a copse of saplings and knelt. With palms pressed together and hands raised level with her nose, she looked up to the sky and began reciting the *paternoster* the way she always did. The familiar words settled her mind and soothed her body twitches. They also helped her ignore the discomfort of rough dirt and twigs pressing against her knees. No worse than the flagstone floor of the chapel.

Before she could form a proper prayer for help and guidance in her mind, the diminishing twilight of the heavy cloud cover told her she needed shelter. The convent hadn't prepared her for surviving a wet night in the open. Her life in the village before the convent had. She and Dom had often sneaked out on a hot summer night and built a rough lean-to, so they could watch the stars wheel overhead, or listen to the rain bringing life to the thirsty fields. They'd whisper local gossip to each other and giggle over the improbability of one maid walking out with one man while secretly meeting a trader when he passed through on his rounds. Dom talked of his dream of owning a few cows someday and breeding them with different bulls to get a stronger herd with more milk.

Hilde didn't have dreams for her future. Looking ahead only brought her to sad conclusions. Her life looked no different from her mother's: endless toil during the day. Enduring her husband's grunting affection at night, and spitting out child after child. Bearing children was often a death sentence, more painful and dreadful than a hangman's noose.

Why look forward when she saw only despair? Better to live each moment as if it were her last.

And then the convent had made her life more miserable and she looked forward to Dom's visits every two weeks on the nights of the quarter-moon. For those few moments while whispering to him through the grille of the postern gate, she could almost imagine them lying out in the fields watching the stars.

Now she was out on her own, with no cottage or family to take her in. And no Dom to protect or guide her.

Panic wiggled its way up from her belly to her throat. Her breath came in short, sharp gasps, painfully tight in her chest. She needed to scream. She needed to run.

She needed to think. That's what Dom would have told her to do.

She'd said she'd rather live as a beldame than in the convent. What did that mean? She thought back to her life in the village. They had a beldame attached to the community. An ancient crone who lived on her own, her single room wattle-and-daub hut carefully removed from the cluster of homes by twenty yards. Part of them, but not. The villagers took pains to make sure she never caught their gaze and turned it against them. They also made sure she had food and fresh thatch so she would not curse them. The old woman's nieces spoke of three stillborn children and then a husband taking his own life. Certain signs that she employed black magic. Her knowledge of plants—which of them cured, which killed, which brought on a woman's labor, which took the child away before anyone was aware of its coming—were also viewed as witchcraft. But most telling of all, she never wore a carved wooden charm on a thong around her neck. The wandering priest who came by once a year to sanctify weddings, baptize children, and say funeral prayers for the dead also blessed the charms each year, renewing their sacred protection.

Hilde fished inside her robe and drew out her own charm, a flat disk with some squiggly lines etched into the polished wood. Those lines supposedly represented the Virgin Mary. If she squinted her eyes just so, she could make out the circle of a halo and the impression of two eyes and a smiling mouth. Everyone in the village wore the same design on their charms, all carved by the same man long ago and passed down to new generations.

She wasn't supposed to keep the charm after entering the convent. The sisters all wore a metal crucifix. The charms were deemed primitive superstition. But Hilde had kept hers, as had Dom, as a token of remembering happier times together, when Da had still lived, and Mama could feed her large family.

In that moment, Hilde knew that the solitary life of a beldame was not what she wanted for herself. She wanted the closeness of family and friends in a village. She just had to find one.

Fat raindrops plopped onto her nose as she turned her face to the heavens, finally knowing what to pray for.

Faith meant enduring a little pain now and again. She let the rain fall on her exposed face while she said what needed saying. The blessed virgin had come to her in a vision. That must mean she would listen to a respectful plea.

"Holy Mary, mother of our Lord Jesus, please help me find a safe home in the forest. Help me become worthy of a loving man and a brood of children. Grant me the courage and knowledge to help my new village survive through the perils of this life. Amen." She crossed herself, then rose from her knees to search for shelter for the night.

There! A twisted and gnarled oak of ancient years sent thick branches out and then up from its trunk just about level with the top of her head. Without thinking, she hitched up the thick wool of her robe and climbed into a nook between tightly crossed branches. Resting her back against the trunk, she feasted on half her bread and cheese. "Dom, where are you?" she whispered into the night. "I need you here to help me find my way."

A soft rustle of the breeze in the tree's canopy brushed her cheek, like a finger caressing her face. It felt so much like Dom's touch!

Her tears fell, unchecked by shame or guilt or fear of

discovery. For tonight, she was alone. So very much alone. And empty inside for loss of her twin.

"This isn't a proper funeral, I know," Tuck said, face raised to the heavens and the constant fine rain.

The clouds thickened as he spoke.

In disapproval?

No, he didn't think God responded so quickly to the words of a humble itinerant priest.

While Little John and Derwyn bent their backs to the task of digging a grave for Brother Luke—it was a good thing that Little John had finally named his heir and included him in the work of managing the forest—Tuck wandered off to a little clearing within earshot of the creek. The sound of the free-flowing water soothed and refreshed him. He fished an oiled leather pouch from an elderly maple tree with a hollow just above his head. Silently, he withdrew his priestly tools, kissing the cross embroidered on the point of his stola and draping it over his neck. Then he pulled out a simple wooden cross standing upright on a flat base. A wooden bowl sufficed for a chalice, and he carried stout ale in a water skin on a thong attached to his belt. Not sacred wine. But one must make do with what one had while living in the wild. He poured a small measure into the bowl, nearly losing himself in the red-dish glints in the liquid as it scintillated in the rays of watery sunlight. Dried grapes from the abbey arbor had gone into the barley for this brewing. Had he had a flash of foresight last autumn during the harvest that he'd need this particular batch to replace communion wine?

His knees protested as he knelt to the ground beside a flat rock. He had only a scrap of linen from an old shirt to use as an altar cloth. He whipped it out of the pouch and let it flutter open before letting it rest. It was just big enough to accept the cross, the bowl, and a single bite of bread.

With a deep swallow to loosen his throat, he sang the mournful chant to commemorate the dead. The Latin words had meant something to him once, the promise of a lightened soul seeking the Lord in heaven. Today, he sang them by rote, thinking about his old friend Brother Luke and all the healing knowledge the old man had brought to the abbey and the village.

The chant came to an end. Tuck dropped his forehead to the makeshift altar and sobbed. "I'm going to miss you, old friend."

His knees stabbed him with shooting pains that ran up into his hips and down to his heels.

Tuck drew another deep breath, promising himself he'd rise in a few moments. He wouldn't sleep well tonight; he might as well use his aging body as an excuse.

Then he took up the bread and recited the words, blessing it, turning it into the holy host of the Eucharist. It tasted fresh, a miracle of the Mass. Likewise, he sang the necessary words over the ale, then took a single gulp.

He let his tears add their own sorrowful blessing as he spoke the Benedictus and washed the bowl and linen in the creek and secreted them once again in the aged maple tree.

He lifted his face to the dripping skies, drinking in the

refreshing air and the peace of the Mass that always lingered. He blew a kiss in the direction of the standing stones. "Good-bye, old friend. You lived long and well. May you find peace and fulfillment."

His lungs drew in a deep breath. He exhaled fully, and his senses came back to life, no longer crushed by grief.

"I can never allow myself to forget that I am a priest for life. This is the one thing King John cannot steal from me." He bowed to the altar and backed away respectfully.

Twenty-Five

"This isn't the way I remember life in a village," Henry said as he and Nick took places in line to share supper from the huge cauldron resting atop a wood fire at the center of the clearing.

"How so?" Nick asked. He bowed slightly to the elderly woman who handed him a hunk of bread on a wooden slab. She smiled at him, showing large gaps in her teeth. Her breath smelled sour, but he said nothing. He'd noticed that Brother Luke and other elderly monks had a similar odor of decay about them.

"These people are all together, sharing their meal. One feasts, they all feast. One starves, they all starve. Doesn't seem right."

"I have no memory of a village or family. This seems very right to me. Similar to the way we live at the abbey."

"But that's the abbey. At home, it's each family fends for

itself. That way if someone commits a crime—like poaching the hare they feast upon—the rest of us can't be blamed for it." Henry seemed to shrink within himself, as if fearing contamination.

"These people are all outlaws, runaway serfs, petty criminals. Just living here in a Royal Forest they are breaking the law. Banding together helps them all survive," Tuck reminded them. He seemed brighter, less burdened by loss than when he left the circle of standing stones. Carefully, he ladled a heaping portion of stew—mostly venison with only a few withered turnips—onto his own bit of bread. "Here, we live off the bounty of the land. Can't afford to stay in one place long enough to grow much. We trade with the abbey village for flour and beer and such. Before the interdict, the abbey provided as many supplies to both villages as we could afford. Now our contact with people outside the abbey walls has become limited."

Henry eyed the old man with cocked head and squinted eyes. "I know I know you . . ."

"Don't think too hard. It will come to you when you need to know and not before," Nick whispered.

"I fear that without direction, Father Blaine and Prefect Andrew will isolate the abbey even further from the needs of the village. We are supposed to withdraw from the world for a life of contemplation *and* charitable works. We should spend much of our time in prayer and the work of supporting the abbey. But we cannot ignore the needs of people . . ." Tuck muttered into his beard. He wandered to a stump at the edge of the firelight, still grumbling to himself regardless of listeners.

"Abbot Mæson?" Henry whispered, nudging his elbow into Nick's ribs.

Nick juggled his trencher and cup awkwardly until he regained his balance from the sharp blow. "Took you long enough," he said in disapproval. Henry could really be annoying at times. The elbow to the ribs was totally uncalled-for. It wasn't as if Nick was nodding off during prayers at Matins.

"What's he doing here? I thought he was supposed to go to Rome or Paris, like the other abbots and bishops and such."

"By staying in England, where he feels he belongs, he's an outlaw. That means he has to live here with the other outlaws." Nick suspected Tuck was also keeping track of life and villagers and politics in Nottinghamshire. When this war between King John and the Holy Father ended, Tuck would be the one the peacemakers must consult.

Nick crossed his legs and lowered himself to sit at Tuck's right. Henry placed himself on the other side of Nick, as if reluctant to associate with the abbot in disguise, but still close enough to hear any wisdom passed down.

All too soon, Nick finished his plate of food. He wanted more. Even with short rations during Lent, the abbey offered him more sustenance than this.

"There is no more food tonight," Tuck whispered. He, too, looked longingly at the empty cauldron.

As if to make the gathering forget their partially satisfied bellies, Will Scarlett stood and tuned his mandolin. He strutted around the circle, bobbing his head, and making the red feather in his cap wiggle like the tail of a bird about to sing. He began a mournful ballad in memory of Brother Luke, or Lyndon as the Woodwose knew him. His clear tenor voice surpassed even Henry's in sweetness and projection of emotion.

Nick wiped away a tear from the corner of his eye before it triggered a flood. "I'm going to miss Brother Luke. He told wonderful tales of adventure in foreign places and the healing plants that grew there. He knew so much more than I could ever learn."

"Don't underestimate yourself, Nick," Tuck said. "Brother Luke knew his healing herbs, but he understood little of politics and diplomacy and how to communicate with people about anything other than his plants. You may not know as much as he did on that one subject, but you already know more about history and languages and the strategies of war from your reading. I expect you to grow into a much higher place than scribe at a small and unimportant abbey."

Heat rose from Nick's belly to his cheeks. "But I . . ."

"Enough. You have been taught to be humble, and you are. But sometimes we need to take pride in ourselves so that we push through a problem and help others do the same. You'll learn to balance your gifts along with the needs of others. Now listen. Will Scarlett is about to use his talents to bring the villagers out of their grief and begin focusing on life once more."

With that, the bard strummed a new chord on his instrument, set his feather to bobbing faster, and merrily danced a jig step in time with his new—and bawdier—tune about how often the sheriff's arrows flew astray.

The Green Man slept. Pale reflections of an evening of music and song and dance slipped into his dreams. His mind joined the gathering, but always as an observer outside the circle that crept closer and closer to the fire as the spring evening chilled and rain worked its way through the tree canopy to penetrate to the skin without warmth. He cherished a new fullness in his heart from watching his son begin to integrate with the villagers. He'd need to know them as friends and helpers when the time came. . . . Little John considered handing the boy the reins of power as soon as he freed Jane and began a new life—a mortal life—with her.

His spirit basked in the warmth of friendship and the fire while his body took comfort in sleep and renewal within his tree. He drew nourishment and water from the earth.

With a niggle of concern, he watched as Tuck kept up the two boys from the abbey well past the tugging of the moon against his soul. It set behind the clouds; he knew it without seeing it. The trio sat talking of this and that, things important and not. Their words did not reach the Green Man in his slumber, only the drooping of tired eyelids and sagging of weary bodies.

At last, as the monks at the abbey softly chanted Matins, when the bells should have rung midnight, the boys and Tuck curled up on the ground beneath a makeshift lean-to beside the fire, asleep the instant their eyes closed.

The Green Man withdrew from the world. Not even his dreams told him of Mammoch's rampage through the village attached to the abbey as she attempted to climb a tree where a girl cried in her sleep.

Nor did he hear the distant thunder conjured by Queen Mab when she realized that her current favorite courtier had not returned with her entourage after May Day.

But even within the depths of his long-overdue sleep, the Green Man sensed a tiny insect burrowing through his bark in search of any sign of decay or rot within his aging wood. Quickly, he sent a flood of sap to surround and drown the intruder. Sleep was a good time to repair and patch the hole the bug had made. When he awoke, he'd check to make certain the patch grew into solid wood to become an integral part of him, and not just a bandage atop a festering wound . . . if his human mind remembered. . . .

Nick stretched. He pushed his arms over his head to lengthen his spine while each bone popped out and back into place. Then he shook himself to loosen the muscles he'd tightened while curled in on himself to stay warm while sleeping. A warm pressure against his back reminded him that he shared this rough shelter with others. Quietly, he tried to get his knees under him so he could leverage himself up. The joints protested the shift from a tight bend up against his chest to straight. His feet tangled in the length of his robe as he tried to keep from kicking and punching to get his limbs moving. He didn't want to wake Tuck sleeping beside him or Henry on the innermost spot of the lean-to.

Curled up with his two companions, the woven mat of branches, and the glowing fire, plus the thick gray wool of his robe, he'd stayed warm enough through the short night. But now the sun kissed the horizon and the fire had burned down to glowing embers. He had to reach forward to find any warmth lingering within the fire ring.

Morning dew dampened his robe. Last night's light rain hadn't penetrated the thick wool still redolent of the natural oils that kept a sheep warm and dry.

The thick, dark clouds of a menacing thunderstorm had moved north, taking the cold wind and heavy downpour with it.

Time for him to be up and about, even if Brother Theo wasn't waiting for him in the scriptorium. Slowly, he got his knees under him, then rolled to his feet while he surveyed the village. Henry still slept curled in a tight ball. Tuck . . . wasn't in sight. A moment ago he'd been pressed up against Nick's back within their crude shelter. He must have slipped away while Nick stretched and thought about rising.

A bubble of panic rose to his throat. "Tuck?" he whispered, trying not to waken anyone who needed to sleep longer.

Nothing changed.

Where could the old man have gone? The guilt of failed responsibility gnawed at Nick's gut. Knowing that Tuck was truly Abbot Mæson and needed to return to the abbey as soon as King John lifted his exile made him anxious to ensure his mentor's well-being.

A rustle of movement drew his attention to the verge of the clearing. Green on green in that shift of ground cover and low-hanging branches. No help at all. Most of the Woodwose wore cloth dyed with green leaves, nuts, and berries and fixed with iron salts discarded by the blacksmith. Whatever was handy. They blended into their surroundings well. If they stood still, he doubted he could find them until they wanted to be seen. Even Tuck had adopted the trick of fading into the forest and becoming no more visible than any other collection of branches and twigs just like his Huntsman relatives.

The blob of mixed greens resolved into the bent and gnarled form of Robin Goodfellow. The short being twisted his hose and scratched, then righted his tunic.

Nick realized the man had completed his morning ritual, and his own needs pressed hard in his abdomen.

"Back thataway." Robin cocked his thumb over his shoulder. "Make sure you stay downstream and not directly into the creek. Let Mother Earth absorb your waste and cleanse it before it poisons the fish. Besides, Lady Ardenia don't like us fouling her stream." He reared his head back and laughed mightily. "Go ahead. No need for shyness. I'll wait for ye here. Tuck, who speaks for the Green Man whilst he sleeps, says I'm to guide you two to the road this way." He pointed in the opposite direction of the makeshift latrine.

Nick nudged Henry awake with his toe. Henry lifted his tousled fair head and blinked sleepily.

"Is it dawn already?" he asked petulantly.

"Aye, and then some," Robin replied. "Shift yer arse and get moving. You'll be missed and have a heap of explaining to do when you get home."

"Food?" Henry asked as he rolled to his knees and inched his way upward, stretching every joint along the way.

"Jerked venison and a bit of porridge will have to do you. Now move. The sun awaits no man."

Before long, the three of them wove their way through the underbrush toward . . . Nick didn't know for sure which direction they followed. The thick trees and wandering streams obscured the sun and changed the angle of the light every dozen or so steps. Maybe they wandered in circles.

Maybe this was yet another trap set by the Wild Folk to keep outsiders so confused they could not tell the sheriff their location.

Nick's feet hurt, as if the forest objected to each step he took and stabbed him. His sandals rubbed tightly around his ankles and heels and flopped loosely around his toes. Henry also walked as if his feet hurt, shifting from the outside edge to the inside and not resting either foot on the ground any longer than necessary.

"On May Day, Sir Philip Marc called you 'Locksley,'" Nick said when their walk did not look like it would end soon. He needed to occupy his mind so that he didn't think so hard about his hurts.

"A long story not worth your time," Robin grunted.

For an instant, the form of the tall archer in Lincoln green overrode the short gnomish figure.

Nick blinked, and blinked again, and the two personalities

remained. He had to look away so that the double image didn't make him dizzy. Not once since he began carrying Elena's pitcher had he glimpsed both sides of the Wild Folk for so long. He patted his sleeve to make sure the little goddess remained with him. The comforting lump fit neatly into his cupped hand as if she had moved her container to caress his touch.

"We have time," Nick reminded Robin. "Please lighten this journey with your tale."

The gnome sighed, and his human form sank back into his shorter self. "You've a right to know some of it at least since Elena chose you as her companion."

"Does your story have something to do with the abandoned castle on the far hill?"

"Aye. 'Twas my home in my misbegotten youth."

"And . . ."

"And I was the younger son, sent to study with the monks in yon abbey. My role was supposed to be clerk and adviser to my older brother, and maybe even serve the king."

"So you learned to read and write and add up a few numbers."

"That and more. I learned of lands far away and sloe-eyed enchantresses. I longed to feel desert winds on my face and smell exotic spices in the markets. So, when Pope Eugenius called for Crusaders, I took the Cross."

He bowed his head, and his right hand twitched as if the old habit of making the sign of the cross reasserted itself.

"That was a long time ago," Nick replied, remembering Brother Luke's tales of his own holy journey.

"Aye."

"And yet you were not among the Wild Folk sixty years ago."

"Like Lyndon, your Brother Luke, I got lost on the way home. I hired out as a mercenary for a time. Then I spent too many years studying the people of Greece and Italy. I lingered too long in the high mountains and lost myself in the vineyards of France while I waited for the right time to return home." His voice trailed off into distant memory. The archer replaced the gnome completely. Robin of Locksley retained the unlined face and clear eye of a man in his prime.

Henry gawked as he, too, could now see the transformation.

"And?"

"And one day I woke up and knew I had to return to England. Only I had been gone so long, nigh on ten years. In that time both my father and older brother had died, leaving no heirs. King Henry that was had declared me dead and the family title and honors forfeit. He decided not to bestow them on a favorite. The castle was abandoned, burned; many of the stones went into new buildings in Nottingham."

"How did you end up . . . as one of the Wild Folk?" Henry asked. He edged closer to the archer, fingers twitching against his thigh as he so often did when counting the rhythm of a plainsong.

Nick wondered if his friend had been inspired by Will Scarlett and now composed a ballad in his head.

"And how does Sir Philp Marc know you as the long-lost heir?" Nick asked.

"The sheriff thinks me the grandson of the long-lost heir. As for the rest? A warlock's curse. He'd taken up residence in the castle ruins and didn't like my attempts to claim my patrimony." The archer became the gnome once more, mouth tightly closed, and his long, warty nose touched his chin.

"What of the warlock now?"

"Long dead. Look over there, the light is brighter. We approach the road north of Locksley Abbey." Robin pointed forward and to their right.

"Hush!" Nick whispered as a new sound reached him. He knew from experience the grunted exclamations as Mammoch rooted in a circle around her prey.

Twenty-Six

" ow dare he desert me in my time of need?" Queen Mab screeched. Lightning crackled around her fingertips. Her hair was red today, to match her mood. She'd chosen her yellowish white gown to make her look like the fire she conjured.

The color combinations did not complement each other.

Jane continued plying her clumsy iron needle, not nearly as fine as the silver one she'd broken, but just as poisonous to the faeries. She cowered on her stool, keeping her head down and her stitches neat. Anything to avoid the queen's attention and, therefore, the blame for Bracken's absence.

One of the courtiers stepped forward uttering soothing words. "He hasn't abandoned you," she said quietly, bowing and scraping, keeping her head down and never meeting the queen's gaze. "We believe he was kidnapped by one of the forest monsters or possibly one of the Wild Folk when he went to check his traps."

The lady beckoned a young male forward. Someone new to the queen's favor. He bowed deeply and offered his arm to Mab.

The queen batted her eyelashes and blushed. She took his arm with a practiced hesitancy, then she led the boy toward her private chamber.

Jane released her pent-up breath. She had time to put down her needle and close her eyes.

The vast hall grew quiet. Moments later, or was it hours? Or even days? Jane was startled awake by a susurration of sound. Faery wings had begun fluttering again.

Mab emerged from her chamber still clinging to the young courtier's arm. He hid repeated yawns behind his hand. Mab's hair had calmed to blond and she had changed her gown to a soothing green bit of froth that floated around her when she set her wings to flight. "Music! I must have music for dancing," she proclaimed.

Strummed strings sent a sprightly tune wafting into every crevice of the cavern. Couples joined and began flitting through the patterns of a dance.

A male with wings shaped like a bright yellow butterfly's and clothes to match, approached his queen, a sad smile on his face. "Your Majesty, I fear that Bracken may have fallen into a trap created by one of the lesser gods of the Wild Folk. Something predatory." He bowed his head as if he mourned a lost friend, but he continued to peer at his queen through slanted eyes that did not engage her gaze. His feet drifted restlessly, as if ready to set into the next dance, or flee her wrath, whichever mood she exhibited next.

A wary one, Jane thought. *Rightfully so.*

Mab did not respond.

He edged backward, finger-length by finger-length.

"How dare you speak kindly of the traitor!" Queen Mab slapped the butterfly faery across the cheek with a crack like thunder. Her rings, turned inward, gouged his face, leaving a gaping wound behind—much like the sky when split by lightning—that ran from the corner of the male's eye to his mouth.

He clapped a hand to his face, then gasped as yellow blood seeped through his fingers. He withdrew his hand and stared at the seeping mess. His knees wilted. He tried to remain upright and failed, his eyes rolling upward in faint.

All of the court danced away from him and from their queen, circling and weaving in and out of the pattern.

Jane had not seen that kind of violence since coming here. She wasn't even certain that faeries could bleed, let alone bleed the same color as their skin and clothes.

Slowly, she set aside her mending and rose from her stool.

You don't see me, she whispered, hoping that the queen's attention remained fixed upon her fallen courtier. With slow, even steps she walked to the spring that drizzled down the far wall and gathered into a stone basin. Overturned and upright cups lay scattered around the cool refreshment, as well as soft towels for cleaning sticky fingers or mud-stained clothing that a spell could not banish. She soaked one of the towels and turned to face the sneering queen.

Mab's hair turned red again, as did her gown, no longer floaty but heavy and dragging the ground. Her fingers continued to flare with lightning and her face withered into the visage of an ancient crone.

"Majesty, may I help him?" Jane asked, careful to keep her face lowered and her shoulders hunched in deference.

"If the sight of a traitor's blood bothers you so much." Mab spat at the shoes of her closest lady-in-waiting.

The handmaiden curled her lip in disgust. She shook her foot to dislodge the gob and failed. Surreptitiously, she kicked off her shoes and melted into the dancing courtiers, staying a foot off the ground and pulling her feet up beneath her hem to hide their naked state.

"Take him elsewhere. I do not wish to see him for a while. And if Bracken dares return, do not allow him through the portal. He's been gone long enough to be tainted by humans. He will smell of their mortality." Mab flicked her hands dismissively.

Jane forced herself to remain still and show no sign of shock. *I am mortal still, aren't I?*

Otherwise she'd never be able to return home to her John.

Carefully, she went to the fallen butterfly faery and pressed the cool, wet cloth to his cheek.

His eyes fluttered open and took in Jane's placid countenance. His face and lower jaw worked as if he needed to speak.

Jane held one finger to her lips. She noted the barest flicker of acknowledgment in his eyes.

Still pressing the towel firmly against his face with one hand, Jane helped him to his feet and led him in the opposite direction from where Queen Mab had exited.

When they were in a separate chamber barely big enough to contain them both, she asked, "Can I ever be mortal again?"

The butterfly faery shook his head. "I'm sorry. She will never let you go. Even if she did, I don't think you will ever be but as you are."

Hilde's nose twitched with a rancid odor that made her think of the pigs running wild at home in the village. She tried to roll over and ignore the smell. It was her and Dom's job to round up the animals before they ran feral and out of reach of the villagers. Once a pig found freedom in the Royal Forest, ordinary serfs could not hunt them.

Dom had a way with animals. They listened to his soft crooning voice and calmed, recognizing him as safe. None of them ran from Dom.

Hilde could capture the pig as well as her twin could, but she didn't do it often. Dom just did it better, and without thinking. She had to work at staying calm and extending it to the animal. She preferred catching chickens and rabbits that couldn't kill her.

The smell persisted. But the sound of pig hooves on the turf or slamming through the groundcover hadn't disturbed her.

With her first movement, she had a sense of falling and immediately righted herself.

How did she get into this tree?

Memory slammed into her. Tears stung in her eyes once

more. Dom was gone. Never again would she run with him in search of the big sow that would provide many a suckling for meat, enough to feed the whole family for months to come.

But the stench of pig still irritated her nose.

Why didn't she hear the snorting and whuffing noises of a pig rooting through the underbrush for food?

Cautiously, she looked right and left as far as her neck would turn. Her chin brushed the damp neckline of her robe that she'd drawn up over her head to ward off some of the chill.

The odor and the sound of a pig rooting around the base of her tree continued.

With a deep breath for courage, she shifted slightly to her right, keeping as much of her as possible in the crook of the massive oak branch. Her eyes shied away from the massive sow below her. The sharp tusks curled upward, level with her snout. A boar's teeth would curl upward to his ears. The smaller female teeth were still long enough to rip her in two.

Her throat closed in panic just as she was about to swallow. That sent her coughing loudly and repeatedly, painfully dragging in new air between each panicky spasm. A knife stabbing her between the shoulder blades couldn't hurt worse.

The pig looked up. If a beast that large could smile, this one did, mouth gaping, tusks waggling up and down.

Hilde's coughing eased, and she swallowed the last of them, fighting to find some moisture, any moisture, in her mouth. At last she swallowed easily and cleanly, her throat working properly once again.

Then slowly, amazingly, unbelievably, the sow stretched and thinned, limbs growing longer but retaining their wickedly sharp hooves. And she stood up, half human and half pig.

Hilde gripped whatever bark her fingers could latch onto.

"Mine," the pig woman snarled, her mouth—still with those murderous tusks—mere inches below Hilde's protective branch.

"Mammoch, give off!" A man wearing a green tunic brighter than the surrounding groundcover ran out of the trees, a longbow strung, and an arrow nocked. "The Green Man, Lord of the Forest ordered you away from his friends."

Miraculously, behind the man ran Dom's friend Nick and another boy of similar age. They fetched up a bare arm's length away.

The pig woman turned awkwardly from her upright position to face the newcomer. "She hides not among the Sacred Stones. She lives not in the Woodwose village. Therefore, she is fair game. Mine!"

"Not while I can release this arrow with a flint broadhead that will penetrate your tough hide all the way to your shriveled little heart," the archer replied.

Hilde dared shift her gaze from to the boys to the pig, Mammoch, the man had named her. The boys looked as pale and frozen in place as she felt.

Mammoch, she knew that name. Chills coursed through her of the lurid tale to frighten children into staying in bed once the sun set. The nightmare made manifest.

Mammoch dropped to all fours and shifted from almost

human to full wild sow. She turned and charged the archer, tusks gleaming, little eyes eager with anticipation.

Stay! Elena commanded Nick. *Face her down. She shies away from a direct challenge.*

Nick gulped and kept his feet in place. He looked toward Hilde where she cowered in the nook of the tree rather than look into the murderous red eyes of Mammoch.

The instant he looked away, Mammoch changed direction, shifting ever so slightly to pass Robin and rip out Nick's guts.

Robin loosed an arrow. The taut bowstring sang. The arrow sped faster than Nick's eye could follow. The broad head embedded itself into the sow's spine.

Nick heard the thunk and scrape as the arrow made contact with bone.

Mammoch slowed, but still she plunged forward.

Nick backed up instinctively, not quite running backward. A hand's breadth and then an arm's length of distance gaped between him and the Goddess of the Hunted.

The pig slowed, stumbled. Blood spurted from her back. Her hind feet pedaled faster than her front as her body rolled to the side, her snout thrashing, seeking meat for her tusks to impale.

Nick took another step backward. "Will . . . will she die?" He didn't want to watch life leak from her eyes. He couldn't look away.

Chills racked his body from toe to brow and back again. His once warm robe now felt damp and no longer protective.

"Doubtful," Robin replied. Deftly, he placed one foot against Mammoch's spine. She screamed. He ignored her and yanked the arrow free with both hands on the shaft. It came away with a squelching sound, coated in blood. He let the gore drip to the ground as he inspected the flint for damage.

Mammoch sagged into unconsciousness.

"She is not mortal as you and I are. I could only kill her if my arrow struck her directly in her heart."

"How long?" Hilde scrambled down from her nest among the interwoven branches of her tree. She pressed her back against the trunk, ready to flee or climb, whichever seemed more prudent.

Robin shrugged. "Long enough for us to get away, if we hurry." He turned in a full circle, shading his eyes from the rippling patterns of light and shadow, then pointed ahead and to their right. "The road is there. Best you lot get on home."

"What about Hilde?" Nick asked. "If she is here and not in her convent, then she has no home to go to."

"We can't take her back to the abbey, or even the village," Henry said. His eyes remained fixed on the girl.

"You promised to find shelter for me among the Wood-wose," Hilde said, lifting her chin.

In that moment with her dark hair curling across her fore-head from beneath her cowl, she looked so much like Dom that Nick had to gasp.

He reminded himself that he'd promised his friend, as well

as the little goddess, to help Hilde. Only then did Dom allow Elena to escort his spirit into the light. Nick had watched him depart this world without regret. But only if Nick helped Hilde.

A blink, and then another, and he saw the softer features of Hilde's face, the same way Dom had looked a year ago when **he'd first come to the** abbey, before he'd begun to mature with a dark fuzz on his upper lip.

He rubbed his own face, surprised at the thick but soft fuzz forming.

Robin and Nick both looked at Mammoch, who still worked her legs as if running rather than lying on her side.

"You don't have enough time to take the girl to the village and then get back to the safety of the road. Mammoch is going to be one mighty angry sow when she gets her feet under her, and with Little John asleep in his tree . . ." Robin said.

"Can you escort Hilde to the village?" Nick asked.

Hilde sidled around to the side of her tree, trying to ease away from the handsome archer.

"You can trust him," Nick said.

Henry was already shifting toward the road. His need to return to the abbey and safety showed in his twitching hands, anxious eyes, and steady progress away from the forest.

"My lady, I vow by my knightly honor to protect you and leave you unharmed." Robin bowed deeply, right arm across his middle. He still clutched the dripping arrow in his left hand.

Hilde's gaze darted toward Nick.

"Believe him, Hilde. He is an honorable man and abides by his promises. But you must go quickly."

Mammoch heaved as she tried to regain her feet.

Still hesitant in step and carefully walking around Mammoch, Hilde separated herself from the tree. "There is a trick Dom used to do with the animals at home," she said quietly. A hum began in the back of her throat.

Nick's heartbeat slowed toward normal. Henry paused in his flight. Robin stood straighter and watched the girl with wary eyes as she knelt in front of the pig and grabbed a tusk in each hand, forcing Mammoch to look her in the eye.

The hum grew stronger. The sow's feet moved more slowly.

"Stay here and rest while you heal," Hilde chanted. Her humming took on the cadence of a lullaby.

Nick fought to keep his eyes open.

Henry sighed, and his knees bent as if ready to drop to the ground for a nap.

Only Robin remained upright and unaffected by the girl's tune. Then he shook himself all over, replaced his arrow in its quiver, and unstrung his longbow.

"Come, my lady. We must go." He turned on his heel, seeking an almost invisible path along an old game trail.

Hilde stood from her crouch, keeping her gaze locked on Mammoch. "Are you certain I can trust him? I was taught . . . Never mind. If you say I should go with him, I will."

"Go with him. He has promised your safety. I believe him. If he does anything to frighten you, he must answer to the Green Man."

She raised her eyebrows almost to her hairline. Nick nodded, hoping she'd accept his affirmation. Then she kilted up the long skirts of her robe and followed the archer, who retained his human form.

Nick saw nothing of the gnome beneath his guise.

Because he started his adventure as a human. The gnome is an added enchantment, Elena informed him.

Twenty-Seven

ane stayed with the now-exiled butterfly faery, renewing the cold water to press against his wounded cheek.

The beautiful man sat on the floor slumped in on himself with his back to the doorway. "This is never going to heal. I will be scarred forever!" he wailed. Tears leaked from his eyes.

"I did not know faeries could cry," Jane said.

Butterfly man placed one hand against his face, mouth agape in surprise. He pulled his palm away and stared at the moisture trickling down his fingers. "I didn't think we could either. It is such a . . . a human response."

Strangely, his youthful appearance did not slip as Mab's did. Perhaps he wasn't truly as ancient as the queen. Or had the queen's innate evil poisoned her appearance?

Or perhaps he was not fully a faery.

Jane looked at the wet towel. It had taken on a yellowish

tinge—similar to his skin and clothing color. Did the wound bleed? Another thing she had never seen among her captors. Not a drop of blood ever blemished their skin——probably because their tears, like their blood, blended so well with their skin. She had pricked her fingers and bled numerous times while mending their clothing. Though she'd not had a single monthly bleed since coming here. Bleeding fingers must mean she was at least partially human still.

Perhaps once she escaped she would revert to what she was before.

And she planned to escape. She just hadn't figured out how yet.

"Butterfly, do the faeries keep any healing herbs or special cooking ingredients?" Her mind ran through her knowledge of common plants that both flavored food and helped the body heal.

"Why would we do that? We never ail, and our magic turns whatever our minions gather into whatever tastes we want to eat at that moment."

"I have eaten meals that look like filling porridge and stews with bits of chicken . . ."

"Illusions, my child. We survive on illusions."

"Then why can't you cast an illusion over that gouge so no one sees the scar?"

"Because the wound was inflicted by our queen. Her spells are not subject to illusion."

"Meaning all of your people can see through the illusion."

He looked confused. "She gave it to me. It must remain."

WALK THE WILD WITH ME 259

"I can make it hurt less if I can gather some willow bark."

"That is forbidden! If the queen gave me pain, I must endure it. Otherwise, I diminish her authority over me and all the others!" He fluttered his wings and rose to his feet.

"But . . ."

Butterfly flew upward and then dashed toward the door and slumped back onto the floor.

"Why do you remain here with me, the lowly slave, when you could mingle with your friends?"

"Queen Mab has exiled me. Never again—until she changes her mind—will I be able to enter the same room as my sovereign. I have no friends. Never again will I be allowed to join my fellows in the great hall. No more will I laugh at the unchanging jokes and games that fill endless hours of idleness."

Unchanging.

Jane pressed her back against the wall of this small chamber and sank to the floor. Sitting with her legs crossed, she stared into the distance of her mind, thinking about how to upset the routine in order to force change.

Brother Theo looked up at the afternoon sky through the wide windows of the scriptorium. "Another hour of good light through the windows," he said, turning back to his own desk and bending his head to copy a faded and worn scroll.

Nick suppressed a sigh, taking a moment to raise his arms and arch his back. He welcomed the warmer weather of the season. At the same time he was forced to spend longer hours hunched over his station applying decorative designs to initial letters of the manuscripts.

He loosed a long breath as he stretched. Brother Theo looked up sharply and frowned. "Discipline, young Nicholas. You must learn to discipline your body," he intoned.

With a last fleeting glance at the sun shining down on the gardens, he returned to his work.

He'd been home a day. One day and already he longed for another adventure. He'd heard nothing from Father Tuck or any of the Wild Folk. The familiar routine of the abbey absorbed him easily, almost as if he'd not faced Mammoch, a pit trap, and a rogue tree trying to swallow him.

But thoughts of Mammoch made him think about Hilde. He'd promised his friend that he'd ensure her well-being.

Tightness in his belly told him something important awaited him. He needed to be ready. Tonight after supper, while it was still light enough to travel, he'd sneak out and find her.

The next manuscript he needed to illuminate with curls and swirls that dissolved into leafy vistas looked empty, plain, boring. He needed to add something. Something that might tell him what was coming.

Another scowl from Brother Theo made him jerk his quill away from the drawing before he connected lines to show Mammoch, Goddess of the Hunted, prowling through the greenery, and Hilde hiding in a giant oak.

"We will recite a funeral mass for Brother Luke tonight," Brother Theo said. "I can see by the shape of some of those plants in your drawings that you miss your time compiling his knowledge of healing herbs. Perhaps when you have properly mourned his passing, you can move onto other things without his plants intruding into everything you do."

"Brother Luke has only been gone a day. He might . . ." Though Nick knew the elderly monk had died and been buried in the forest, he needed to pretend he hadn't found him.

"I have heard from a reliable source that Brother Luke has passed. Considering how weak and ill he was, I am not surprised. Brother Luke ranged far and often as a younger man. I thought he'd found peace and grown beyond his restlessness here in the abbey. I can only presume that in death he succumbed to the never-ending urge to be elsewhere, never satisfied with any one place."

Father Tuck must be the reliable source.

Nick swallowed a smile. Not everyone was ignorant of the abbot's hiding place.

"Knowing how frail and weak he was, I guess I have to accept that Brother Luke is truly dead, then. A single night alone in the wild is a long time for one in his condition," Nick replied. The image of Mammoch still tugged at his quill. He needed to draw her and her chosen prey to give her reality. He stared out the window at the stone walls that confined him, protected him, limited him.

Any image of the giant wild sow also brought thoughts of Hilde. He needed to know how she fared in the village with the Woodwose. He needed to see her again, to know that she was happy away from the security of her convent.

"Go work in Brother Luke's garden for a time. I can see

that you are useless here until you cure yourself of mourning him. Consider that, in keeping his plants thriving, you honor his memory." Brother Theo removed the quill from Nick's clutch and dusted the wet ink on the parchment with sand.

"Thank you, Brother." Nick stood and bowed his head, folding his hands into his wide sleeves.

He walked sedately toward the infirmary and the adjacent garden, as any proper monk would. As soon as he was free of observation, he lengthened his stride and aimed for the apple tree overhanging the wall.

If he ran all the way to the village and back, he'd return in time for Sext near sundown.

"You don't have a well," Hilde said looking at the brace of leather buckets connected by a wooden yoke. If she listened closely, she could hear the nearest creek chuckling along its bed two hundred paces toward the sunset.

"We rarely stay in one place long enough to dig a well. And if we did, it would betray our presence to the sheriff," replied the old man. Tuck. Robin, the courtly archer, had introduced him when she first arrived.

Something about his kindly manner prompted her to trust him. He made her feel welcome. Too many of the Woodwose watched her as closely as Sister Marie Josef, as if they waited for her to trespass so they could reject her, forbid her the refuge of the village.

"Carry the buckets, and I'll show you a safe place to collect water," Tuck said, pointing at the contraption. He slung another brace of buckets across his own scrawny shoulders. He looked far too ancient and frail to carry heavy water as far as he must.

Hilde shrugged. Why had she expected a life of ease, only working when she felt like it? Life here was little different than at the convent. Here, however, she had no walls. She could walk away whenever she liked. If she had a place to go.

She did not have Sister Marie Josef's hate and need to punish the world instead of herself.

When she thought about it, the Woodwose were merely suspicious as they would be of any stranger. She hadn't earned their trust yet. Helping Tuck carry water would help her build that fragile acceptance.

"We all work so that we may all enjoy the fruits of our labors," Tuck said, watching her shoulder the yoke.

"You sound like Sister Mary Margaret," she said quietly.

He heard her anyway. "Why, thank you. I admire the good sister for her gentleness and her piety. She manages the convent admirably in the Mother Abbess' absence."

"You know the sisters?" Intrigued, Hilde followed him along the faint trail, matching his spritely pace.

"I have dealt with them many times." He bit the insides of his cheeks as if he was trying to suppress laughter.

"Sister Marie Josef doesn't deal with men. I think she hates all men."

"Yes. The sister has enough anger for a dozen women."

"Yes," Hilde agreed.

"I suspect you were on the receiving end of her disciplinary rod."

"Yes." Hilde squirmed under the cumbersome yoke. She didn't want to talk about her time at the convent. She'd been unhappy there since the day her mother announced that Hilde and her twin must separate and trust the Church to take care of them henceforth.

She and Dom had not been separated since birth, within minutes of each other according to village lore.

And now Dom had died.

Would he still be alive if they'd run away to the forest together without having to endure separate lives for over a year?

"This is what we use as a well," Tuck said, pointing to a half circular inlet in the stream.

Hilde could see the depth of the quiet water by the ripples of tiny fish hiding in the shadows of overhanging ferns.

Tuck gestured for her to fill her buckets first. She laid each one on its side as far out in the stream as she could safely reach. She drew them back, spilling only a little water on the hem of her robe. Sister Marie Josef would have slapped her cane across Hilde's shoulders for sloppiness.

Tuck tugged off his soft boots and waded into the creek, sighing in relief as the water soothed his feet.

Hilde stared at him, amazed.

"This is the forest, child. Here we live wild. Strict rules and regulations don't work out here." From the center of the inlet, with water lapping at his knees, Tuck filled his own buckets and sloshed up to the bank. He looked askance at his boots discarded nearby. "I'll come back for them." He led the way back to the forest, barefoot and whistling a spritely tune Hilde remembered from youthful village fetes.

She found herself singing along, the first true song that had crossed her lips since she entered the convent. Sister Marie Josef did not approve of singing, even the plainsong of a Mass, and especially the tuneless humming Hilde could use to calm animals. That kind of music came too close to magic for the sister's taste.

Hilde was convinced that Sister Marie Josef had willed the lock on the postern gate into invisibility without knowing she used magic herself. What depths of depravity would that knowledge drive her to?

Back in the village, Tuck accepted the help of one of the strong young men who lifted the yoke off of the old man's shoulders. Tuck sighed in relief and rotated his joints.

Hilde put her own buckets on the ground beside Tuck's without help. But then she wasn't anywhere near as old or frail as the man with the same green eyes as Nick.

As she ducked out from under the yoke, a series of bird calls circled the village. The women working around the cauldron suspended over the central fire paused and looked up. Then, without seeming to move, they drifted silently away.

"Hoi! It's me. Nick." His voice announced him before he was visible from the compound.

How had the villagers known that someone came?

A sharp whistle followed Nick into the center of the circle

of huts. A lookout, of course. She hadn't seen anyone, but she didn't know the villagers well enough to know who was missing or how far they ranged in the endless quest for food.

"Hilde, how fare you?" Nick asked, without pausing to acknowledge the other villagers. He strode forward at a steady rate, but his chest heaved, drawing in deep breaths, as if he had run the entire way here.

Hilde felt her face grinning wide enough to stretch her cheeks at sight of the familiar face who had a connection to Dom. She reached a hand to him, disregarding any sense of propriety.

Tuck scowled at her and moved in front of Nick, preventing him from reaching her.

"We did not expect you, young man," Tuck said.

"I . . . I had the opportunity to slip away and decided I have an obligation to verify Hilde's safety and well-being," he panted.

"You don't trust us?"

Nick blushed.

Hilde felt the need to giggle. She placed fingers in front of her mouth to keep it back.

"Of course, I trust you. That's why I sent her here. But . . . but . . ."

"But you are a boy and she is a girl. I know." Tuck said on a sigh. "I should have expected something like this. Where is Henry?"

"On his knees, cowering in the Lady Chapel. He vows never to venture outside the abbey walls again," Nick said. He sounded sad.

"You have temporarily lost a companion in adventure. Not a dear friend." Gnomish Robin Goodfellow slapped Nick on the back, nearly knocking him into a stumble.

Nick's eyes found Hilde again. His gaze was so intense she returned his blush and sought something, anything to say, that would break the tension building between them. "Well, if you intend to share our supper, then perhaps you could carry the buckets of water over to the cauldron."

Twenty-Eight

here is something I must do.

The thought broke through the Green Man's dreams, forcing him to rouse.

He couldn't yet bring himself to open his vision to the world around him. Sleep tugged at his mind, demanding more.

There is something you *must do.* The shrill, feminine voice stabbed at his mind.

His eyes opened, and he looked around him through old knotholes formed by discarded branches, openings in his bark.

Movement. Dim outlines of people going about daily tasks. A sniff identified them all, including someone new and someone familiar who didn't belong here.

He closed his eyes again and concentrated on scent and listening. Voices separated into individuals. Soon the cadence and the pitch coalesced into a person speaking. Then the words began to make sense.

"Huntsmen 'aven't returned. Haf to make do with a single squirrel in t' stew."

"Found some turnips gone wild from 't village. Give some crunch to t' stew."

"New cabbage leaves!"

"Blacksmit' fixed a new 'andle on t' ladle."

Ordinary conversation. Everyday matters. The important things to his people.

He opened his eyes again and concentrated on the newcomer. His first glance startled him.

A ghost. Thick dark hair. Shapeless black cowl. Broad face with keen dark eyes. And an aura of anger. Dom, the boy from the abbey who had died, come back to haunt the people who had welcomed him and showed him kindness.

But no. Not Dom. He knew that Elena had escorted the boy *beyond*, where he could find peace.

He made the effort to peer more closely. A feminine flick of the wrist. A slighter breadth of shoulder. And more importantly, a slightly different cut to the cowl. Sturdy gray wool, thick and raw enough to shed moisture. Expensive wool by village standards, though crude in the monastic community. Imported from the Mother House in France. Nowhere else did people have access to dyes that retained the colors and did not fade rust from iron salts.

This must be Hilde, Dom's twin, run away from her convent. That would make the other outsider Nick. No matter how much time he spent here, among the Woodwose, he would always remain a stranger looking in. Little John could not picture the boy as separate from the abbey, just as something of the abbey clung to Tuck, a part of both worlds, and yet separate from both.

Nick walked through the village with an air of familiarity, as if he'd spent a lot of time here in the weeks while Little John slept.

"Time to wake up, old man," Robin said, leaning casually against the Green Man's tree. The tightness in his muscles belied his relaxed pose.

Little John sniffed again, alert to whatever kept Robin as tightly strung as his bow.

"The girl reminds me of my Marian. She was about the same age when I went off Crusading, in search of fortune so I could come home a rich hero and marry her, without title or lands. I stayed away long enough so that she had a chance to grow up. Then one more month became one more year, and another, until I'd been gone ten and everything changed." He dropped his head sadly.

Little John shook himself free of bark and pith and sap. A deep breath of air through his lungs, not seeping in through new leaves, and he was able to step free of his bower.

"How long have I slept?" he asked, stretching his arms over his head and twisting at the waist to loosen his muscles.

"Almost too long," Robin replied. He yawned with his hand over his mouth. "The moon rises a full two hours after sunset," he whispered behind his hand.

"We need to be knocking on the door of our destination at the moment the moon is one hand's breadth above the horizon," Little John said, excitement rising in his belly like a hunger that could never be sated.

"The boy is ready," Robin said. "Tuck has been talking to him about Elena and how if he stays with the Woodwose to woo Hilde, he must give up the goddess. Tonight will be a test of his commitment. He must give her up for a few hours to see if he can do it for the rest of his life."

"Which way will he go when tonight's adventure, for good or ill, is over?"

"I cannot tell. He is much enamored of Hilde, as only a boy on the verge of manhood can be in love."

Little John said nothing in reply. But he watched Nick carefully, focusing just beyond his left ear. The energy of life emanating from him did not yet merge with the villagers. He doubted it ever would, even if he stayed.

A mood of lighthearted gaiety filled the Woodwose village. Nick watched as people gathered up foods they could transport, a blanket or other covering against an eventual chill, and donned their cleanest and most sound garb. They prepared for a festival.

As the sun passed the zenith, people danced off toward the standing stones in pairs and small groups. Many carried kindling and small logs to add to a bonfire.

He watched Hilde gather new redberries. She bent over each low-growing vine, pulling only the ripest of the new crop, leaving plenty of green bits of fruit to ripen for the days to come. She'd settled in at the village well enough to provide this lovely addition to the festival feast.

Resolutely, Nick gathered an armful of firewood and got ready to follow.

If he paused and listened carefully to the life of the forest, he thought he might feel the magnetic pull of the stones, even from this distance.

"No." Tuck grabbed hold of Nick's arm, forcing him to drop the firewood. The children, no more than six or eight years old, darted in and made off with the precious burden of his kindling.

"I would like to share a village ritual so that I might feel a part of their community." Nick did his best to find a logical reason for joining the exodus and hid his disappointment. At times like this, loneliness weighed him down. He didn't even know how these people would celebrate one of the major events of the year, the night of the shortest length of darkness.

And he would so much like to feel a part of the lives of these people.

At the abbey, the brothers and students would spend much of the lingering twilight in prayer and listening to Bible readings.

"Not this year, Nick. There will be wild dancing around the bonfire at the center of the stones. There will be feasting on wild boar—not Mammoch," he added at Nick's frown. "And mutton. Tough old animals that have wandered away from the flock. The people will welcome the moon and the sun in pagan rites."

Nick hung his head. "We of the Church and the Light cannot combat pagan rites unless we understand them."

"I know. Maybe next year. Tonight, you are needed

elsewhere—for something very important." Tuck caught his gaze with his own and directed him to look toward the west side of the clearing rather than north toward the stones.

Little John paced nervously back and forth by the entry to a path. Will Scarlett examined his lute, tuned the strings, and plucked an annoying chord. Then he stuck the instrument into his pack and pulled out a flute. It, too, released an experimental trill, discordant to the lute. Without bothering with the concealment of the pack, Will passed his hand across the long reedlike instrument, and it shifted into a small harp.

Robin shot an arrow into the air, watching it waver and fall, judging the distance and the breeze. Then he scowled, licked his finger, and held it up to determine the direction of the air movement. An eyeblink later he shrank into his gnome figure and shook his head.

In his stag form, Herne the Huntsman pawed anxiously at the ground.

"What?" Nick asked in wonder. He'd never seen the entire group gathered and succumbing to the same somber mood.

"We travel far in a short amount of time," Tuck answered.

"For what purpose?" He knew, of course. He'd overheard enough discussion between Tuck and Little John to understand the purpose of tonight's journey. He just didn't know why he had to come along.

Nick's sandals didn't fit right today. A frequent occurrence as he seemed to outgrow them every week or two. He doubted he could walk far with any speed or comfort. So he wanted to stay tonight, Midsummer Night's Eve, to spend time with Hilde.

"Tonight, the moons of both Earth and Faery align," Tuck replied.

"Oh."

"I am going with you," Hilde said. She stood with her hands on her hips and feet planted wide, just like Dom did when he decided to be stubborn. It didn't happen often, but Nick's friend, so pliable most of the time, knew how to get his own way when he needed to. The only time he needed to avoid midnight chores and prayers were the nights he planned to visit his beloved sister.

"This is no mission for one as young as you." Robin stepped away from the knot of travelers discussing their plans. He placed his hands on her shoulders gently and engaged her gaze.

"Don't do that to me, Robin Goodfellow!" She turned her head away and looked at the ground rather than at Nick, Tuck, or Little John. "I've seen the way you entrance villagers and monks to share food and tools with you. They do it, then have no memory of doing it. I'm going with you."

"Why, Hilde?" Nick asked. He knew better than to argue with her. Arguments never worked on Dom either.

"I know how to send the guards by the entrance to Faery to sleep."

"Like you did with Mammoch?" Nick asked. "Will that trick work on a faery?"

"I don't know. But you watched me gather the first of the wild redberries. I've packed them in leaves to keep them fresh. Those leaves are special. Human or fae, the guards will sleep."

"I don't know," Little John said. "Do faeries even eat human food?"

"Doubtful," Tuck replied, chewing his lip. "But the aroma of the berries in her pockets is making me want to sleep."

"Then give me the berries," Little John said. He crouched and began drawing a map in the dirt with twigs and rocks as landmarks.

"No. I go, or you fend for yourself." Hilde turned her back on the men and made as if to follow the villagers toward the standing stones.

"Sir." Nick tugged on Tuck's sleeve to gain his attention. "If the faeries don't eat human food, then we'll need her to put them to sleep in her own way."

Tuck sank into a moment of deep contemplation. "Nick is right, Little John. You have no power or influence over the faeries as long as they are inside their Mound. We need the girl."

"Besides, after years of enslavement, Jane may not trust us. We could be just another faery illusion. She's more likely to trust another woman; believe that we are human and real," Robin said.

Nick took Hilde's arm and brought her the three steps back to the group.

Inside Nick's mind he heard Elena chuckle. *You are learning, silly boy. Observe others to sense what they truly need. Hilde needs to be a part of your adventures as her brother never did. Jane needs to learn trust again. To trust herself as much as your friends. She has lived with illusion too long.*

"If I'm going to deal with faeries, I guess this will be an impediment." Hilde lifted a leather thong with a wooden disk dangling from it over her head.

Tuck grabbed the disk, enclosing it in his hand. "How long

have you had this?" He closed his eyes tightly, as if he could read the carving by thought alone.

"Always," Hilde replied. "Mum gave it to me when I was but a babe. Dom had one, too, identical." She grabbed it away from the old man. "I think we teethed on them."

"What is it?" Nick asked, stepping closer to see the carved talisman. He'd seen others like it worn by villagers and Henry. But not on Dom.

"This is what stands between common folk and the Wild Folk," Tuck said sadly.

"An itinerant priest came to our village once a year. We weren't within an easy walk of a church or monastery. He blessed our charms each year. It hasn't had a blessing since I left home. Sister Mary Margaret said I didn't need it anymore, that my prayers within the convent would protect me from forest evils better than this homemade thing." She ran her thumb over the carvings, knotted chains of some sort, then placed it in her pocket, along with the berries.

"A very old practice. Not common anymore," Tuck said. His fingers twitched as if he needed to reach out and hold the disk a bit longer. "The blessing is actually a rough spell. Your priest may have had a bit of magic in him, but untutored, barely noted. He acted on instinct rather than knowledge. The spell would wear thin in time. All it did was prevent you from seeing the true Wild Folk beneath the human guise. Unseen, unknown. Protection for you from wild magic. Protection for us from persecution."

"Is it of any use now?" Hilde asked.

"Only as much as you give it," Tuck replied. "Common

folk do not expect to see the Wild Folk, so they don't, wearing a recently blessed charm or not."

"We have a long way to go in a short amount of time," Robin Goodfellow said, starting along a path Little John had paced before. It seemed to open wider and clearer with each of his steps.

"We have little time on this shortest night of the year," Little John proclaimed, looking along the path with eyes focused on a far distant point. Without another word, he scooped up Nick and set him on his right shoulder. Hilde went onto his broad left shoulder. Tuck jumped aboard Herne, appearing as a magnificent twelve-point stag. They galloped off. John looked askance at Robin and shook his head. "You have your own magic, Robin Goodfellow. Get there as you can."

Then the forest giant set off with long strides that ate up a league in just a few steps.

Nick gasped at the speed, wondering if his soul could keep up with the swift movement of his body.

Twenty-Nine

ittle John watched the moon. A faint silver glimmering on the horizon appeared too soon. The Faery Mound remained a small lump in the far distance. He was running out of time.

Jane was running out of time.

Movement fluttered around his left ear. He raised his fist to bat away whatever insect dared bother him.

"Hey!" Hilde cried as her two hands wrapped around his fist.

"Oh, sorry," he apologized. "Must have been your skirts waving in the wind."

But when he thought about it, she wore heavy gray wool. Her robe wouldn't lift in the slight wind of their passage across the valley between the lines of hills.

"It's me, trying to get your attention," the faery Bracken said. He moved forward on long bouncy strides, letting his wings lengthen his step.

"What do you need? I thought I left you in the sacred circle," John replied.

"You need my help to get inside the Faery Mound."

"No, I don't. I have a plan and people to help me implement it."

"Whatever your plan, you cannot anticipate all of Queen Mab's traps. You won't get beyond the first corridor."

"Why would you help us against your own people?" Nick asked from John's other shoulder.

"Because I have listened to the trees gossip with the wind. Queen Mab has condemned me to exile, with no possibility of reprieve. I . . . no faery can survive long outside the Mound. We must return to the Starfire or we fade away to nothing. We become . . . we lose substance and exist as only a memory or an extra chill in the breeze."

"Starfire? You mentioned that when we were in the pit," Nick mused.

Little John decided he needed to listen to this conversation. He snagged one of his fingers into the back of the winged man's shirt and hoisted him along with the others. Tuck, Will Scarlett, and Robin Goodfellow would come in their own time, with their own traveling magic.

"We do not speak of it outside the Mound. It is forbidden."

"You are forbidden inside the Mound," Nick reminded him.

Bracken took a deep breath and looked around for eavesdroppers. Then he settled his glance on the ground. "There is a great yellow stone—many stones fused together actually—that fell from the sky at the beginning of time. We combined the stones to make them more powerful, then built the Mound around them with an opening to the stars. Every time new stones fall to the ground, we gather them and add them to the original. They stick together and become one as if they were all a part of each other before they fell and need to join together again. The stone is now huge. From time to time the noon sun shines through the opening and sets the stone afire with light. We bathe in the shooting strands of Starfire and it renews us."

"What happens if the Starfire loses its potency?" Hilde asked.

"It can't. It is eternal. As long as the sun rises and sets, the Starfire sustains faeries."

"How big?" Little John asked. His chest heaved with strain at carrying the extra burden of his passengers. His speed suffered, and the distance seemed to increase with each step.

"As tall as that tree." Bracken pointed to a sapling not much taller than Robin the Archer. "And as broad as that boulder."

"About as big as me," Little John said. He wondered how rugged the stone, or stones, might be. Would it fragment into the many tinier stones and lose its power?

"I guess," Bracken said. "I have heard that it is fragile, a crystal, or perhaps a gem. If you strike it just right with an iron tool, it will shatter into its smaller parts. No faery can handle iron without burning up, so the stone will remain forever."

Little John sensed movement above him, Hilde and Nick shifting positions to look at each other.

"What are you thinking, children?" he asked them.

"We can handle iron," Nick spoke for both of them.

"Do we need to destroy the faeries?" Little John asked. He

paused a moment to breathe deeply, as much to replenish his body as to think.

"If it becomes a choice between rescuing Jane or letting the faeries live?" Nick asked.

His voice held undertones of Tuck when he waxed philosophical. But he also heard hints of Elena in the phrasing of the question.

Little John had no defense against the two. "Jane must come first. Whatever we must do to rescue my lady love. She has been a slave to faeries and their illusions too long."

"If you destroy Queen Mab, the rest of the faeries will be able to take a bit of the Starfire with them and leave the Mound," Bracken mused. "Kill our evil queen, and you will free my people along with your lady, Little John."

"Agreed," Robin added coming abreast of them. He wore his gnome guise tonight so he could access Forest magic, taking long bouncing steps to match the Green Man. "Would that I could rescue my own love," Robin muttered to himself.

But Little John heard his lament.

"We will find her," Little John reassured him. "We will help you break the curse."

A trilling note from a bird flying overhead, undoubtedly Will Scarlett, echoed the sentiment.

Then, as if conjured by his own longing, the Faery Mound loomed ahead of them, no more than half a mile distant.

The horizon cut the moon in two, half showing big and bright, half still hiding beneath the edge of the land.

A few more long steps and Little John bent double so Hilde and Nick could disembark.

"Where's the door?" Nick asked, looking at the folds of the steep hill for an imperfection or opening in the turf.

Little John looked more closely at the greenery pouring down over a rock wall. He reached out with his forest senses to caress and mold these plants into his domain.

Nothing. They did not react to his mastery. It was as if they did not truly exist or had no reason to acknowledge his existence.

"You are part of my dominion!" he commanded with voice and magic.

"Elena says to look through her eyes and not your own," Tuck said. He reached out and tried to push the vines and ferns aside. They did not move. Then he jerked back his hand, sucking on red burn marks across his palm and fingers.

"Help me, Elena," Little John pleaded, opening himself to her presence. One blink, then two more in rapid succession. The plants faded, became transparent. He saw through the illusion to an arched wooden door banded with iron. The portal was almost as tall and broad as himself. But the metal bands crisscrossed stout wooden planks so tightly he could touch the wood with only one fingertip. And that was uncomfortably warm.

"This door was put in place by mortal men and ensorcelled to keep the faeries in, and people out," Tuck said in disgust.

"What good does it do if there are other portals known to the faeries so that they come and go at will?" Nick asked.

"Because the wizards and sheriffs of old only saw this one portal, they presumed it was the only one," Robin replied. He stretched and grew back into his human guise. His hand came within inches of the iron before he jerked it away. "Sorry. My curse rides close enough to the surface that I, too, am poisoned by iron." He bowed his head and backed away.

They looked to Bracken, his wings drooping, and his knees sagging. "This portal was designed to keep me and my kind away from humans. I cannot penetrate it."

"And the other openings?" Little John demanded. He balled his fist, not certain if he wanted to hit the frail faery, or just give him a good shake until his pointy little teeth rattled and his uptilted eyes crossed.

"Only Queen Mab can see them from the outside. And they were designed for faeries with wings to fly in and out; they are placed in the roof of the mound. To enter from the outside means a fall to the death for humans. Thrice the height of the tallest tree in the forest."

Little John and Tuck turned to look at Nick and Hilde.

Hilde shook her head and bowed her head. "I have encountered a door ensorcelled to never open and had no luck in finding a way to remove the magic."

Nick shrugged and approached the door. He ran his hands over the breadth of it. "I can't find a lock by sight or touch."

Little John nearly wept. The moon rose higher, a full hand's width above the horizon. He had to get through this portal now—or once again he would lose his chance to rescue Jane.

Jane left the wounded faery sulking in the small chamber. He kept the cold cloth pressed against his cheek, as much to absorb his tears as to soothe the wound. She had no trouble passing through the door. *She* had not been exiled by Queen Mab. In the great hall, a buzz of noise, like a swarm of enraged honeybees, greeted her.

All around her, faeries bounced and flew, high and low, across the vast distance and close at hand. They moved so swiftly, in convoluted patterns, she had trouble tracking the path of any one of them. Colors blinked from drab to vibrant and back again. They looked more like insects flitting in and out of moonbeams than the creatures she had come to know for however long she'd been enslaved by them.

"What is happening?" She couldn't remember seeing this level of . . . of panic among them.

Deliberately, she turned her gaze to the crack in the far wall that led to the Starfire stone. The illusion was still in place, so she had to squint and peer at it from different angles to see more than just a line in the dressed stone blocks and beautiful tapestries—which she now knew to also be illusions. The opening glowed faintly, as if the sunlight touching the stone radiated far beyond the twists and turns of the entrance.

Alarmed, she checked the openings in the ceiling. Thick darkness covered them.

But wait! A bit of silver, like a full moon reflecting on a still pond, glimmered around the edges. This was different. Something new.

She needed a break in the routine to aid in her escape. This might be a natural time for her to simply walk out.

Cautiously, she made her way to her stool and the neverending pile of mending. She pretended to sift through the lovely fabrics magically dyed unusual colors as if looking for the next task. Instead, she sought one swath of gold gauze shot with silver threads. She'd embedded her broken silver needle into the weave. Now she needed the clumsier iron needle as well. Either could be a weapon against the fae.

"Are you looking for this?" Queen Mab stood in front of her, holding up a square of sturdy brown wool with the iron needle tucked through the threads.

"Why, yes, Your Majesty. I need it to finish the torn hem on the golden gown," Jane replied demurely.

"Liar!" the Faery Queen screeched. "On this most important night of the century, you need this for only one thing. It is the only tool in all of Faery that can shatter the Starfire. Your lover already beats at our door to try to rescue you. You need this to destroy me. But I shall destroy you first."

The queen snaked out a skeletal hand, barely covered in flesh, and tangled her twiggy fingers into Jane's hair. All trace of illusion vanished in the wake of Mab's anger.

With a painful jerk and twist, they rose into the air. The queen's powerful wings took them high, higher, higher.

Jane clawed at Mab's hands, trying to break the scalp-wrenching pain of being dragged by her hair. Upward, ever upward. Dizziness swamped her as the ground, solid and safe, retreated beneath them.

And still her head screamed with pain. Her stomach lurched with unease.

Harder than ever before, she tried to make the illusion of limp wings on her back become real. Anything to break the queen's grip on her hair.

Jane's imaginary wings sagged. Useless.

Thirty

ittle John's desperation leaked into Nick. He tried again to find some imperfection in the ironbound door. Something, anything, that might indicate a way to open it.

The blacksmith who'd fashioned the intricate ironwork and fixed it into the door had been an excellent craftsman, blending wood and metal seamlessly flush against each other. The pattern of the sinuous bands of iron reminded him of the circled cross at the crossroads. The sorcerer who'd sealed the faeries inside had also known his business. Not a speck of rust marred or weakened the surface, despite the passage of time. Hundreds of years? Thousands?

"Silly boys, why not let the goddess of sorcery open an ensorcelled doorway?" Elena asked on a chuckle. *"Nick, may I leave your protection for a bit?"*

"Yes, my lady. Do as you must." Nick felt the lurch and sudden lightening of the near-constant weight in his sleeve.

An emptiness opened in his gut and at his nape. He bit his lip to ease the sudden ache and stepped away from the door. He bowed respectfully to the column of mist that took on the vague shape of a lady clad in the draperies akin to an idealized Roman figure.

"I've learned to trust you, my lady. Now I must learn to trust myself and not call you back until you are ready."

"I never had the courage to grant her free rein," Tuck murmured. "I was too afraid of losing her completely and forever." He hung his head in shame. In that moment of vulnerability his visage showed more of his real age than Nick had ever seen of the seemingly ageless man possessed of many lifetimes of wisdom.

Elena coalesced into a solid personality. "This is so much easier with all of you to help." Elena brought her hands together and bowed to each member of the little troupe. "Now, Master Bard," she called, lifting her face to the sky. "I have need of a strong marching cadence. The sorcerer was of a military bent and used strong rhythms to create the seal."

An overly large red bird wearing a miniature red cocked hat dropped from the sky, growing and stretching into the form of Will Scarlett even as his wings spread to become arms and his feet grabbed the ground for balance. He produced a small skin drum, about the size of Nick's head, from his pack and began a catchy beat that made Nick's feet itch to march.

Hilde bunched her skirts to lift them above her feet as she shuffled in place, smiling.

Only Tuck's hands on her and Nick's shoulders settled them. "Best not to become too enthralled by magical music.

You would become its captive and dance away until you died of exhaustion or starvation," the old man said. He shifted his weight from foot to foot as well.

Nick sobered and ceased moving his feet.

Elena lifted her face again, eyes closed. Moonlight bathed her in silver glory. She glowed from within as well as without. Her lips moved in silent incantation.

Misty bits flew away from her, circling and twisting around her no longer substantial body. Her silver gown floated, stirred by a celestial wind that Nick could neither see nor feel.

"Archer, prepare your bow."

Were those words or merely a sigh on the evening breeze?

Robin raised his bow and drew back the string, arrow nocked and ready.

"More."

The muscles and cords in Robin's neck stood out with the strain of pulling the string to his ear and a bit more. Elena became an ill-defined vapor once more, turned darker, became almost solid as she formed herself into a flint-barbed shaft, then wove herself into and around the real arrow already aligned with the bow.

"Now," Elena commanded. Robin released the string. It snapped forward propelling the arrow with supernatural force. Elena dove into and through the door, her chiming laughter overriding the military rhythm coming from the drum. Will Scarlett froze in place, hand above the resounding stretched hide.

Nick couldn't tell if the bard lifted his hand away from the last beat or prepared to strike the next.

A loud creak drew the gazes of all of them toward the door.

Slowly, groaning with each half inch of movement, it opened outward, hinges protesting and hillside resisting.

Elena drifted through the narrow opening, still more mist than person. "You'll have to do the rest, now that I've finished the hard work." She sounded winded, much less lively and amused than before.

"You are welcome to rest within your pitcher, lady goddess," Nick said.

Thank you, she whispered into his mind. A faint passage of cool air caressed his cheek and a familiar pressure at the base of his neck told him she resided where she needed to be, ready to rouse from slumber if he required guidance, grateful for the rest if not.

Little John shoved and heaved at the door, careful to keep his bare hands away from the ironwork, until it opened wide enough to admit his own massive body.

Bracken and Hilde ran forward, squeezing past the door before any of the others could take a single step.

Will Scarlett and Robin moved cautiously. Will transformed his drum into a small harp, fingers poised over the strings for whatever chord he might need. Robin nocked another arrow, bowstring partially taut.

"Wait!" Nick protested. He elbowed aside Will and Robin, staying hard on Hilde's heels, and stopped short.

"Nice guards, gentle guards," Hilde crooned to the tall muscular faeries, each carrying a bronze sword as long as she was tall.

"Illusion," Bracken whispered to her. "Don't trust your eyes for anything." He pressed a dry and withered leaf of devil's milk into her hand.

She stared at it. She knew the flowers would ward off spells and curses, sending them back to the hex caster. But the leaves? She had to trust the faery who risked everything to help them tonight.

Even if the three guards were not as strong as they looked, they had barbs and knife-sharp edges on their thistle-shaped wings and unwelcoming glints in their squinty eyes. She gulped and wished Dom was there instead of her, or at least whispering advice and reassurance into her ear.

If only the faeries were small and gentle like rabbits or chickens that she could calm into acceptance of their imminent death. Though rabbits could kick and chickens scratch if she wasn't quick enough with her songs. She had to accept her talent for what it was, magic. Not just tricks. Magic.

And if she had magic, then she belonged with the Wood-wose who lived with magic and magical creatures all around them day after day.

Already the guards looked a little cross-eyed and blinked rapidly as if they couldn't concentrate on the intruders.

Nick skidded to a halt behind her. "The berries. Offer them the berries," he said, panting and gulping air as if he'd run a great distance.

Gathering her courage, she withdrew three small leaf-wrapped packets from the pocket within her sleeves. "Lovely berries. Fresh berries. First of the season," she continued her lilting chant. "All for you. Guards need to keep up their strength." She'd liberally mixed the berries with dried and ground cocklebur to induce sleep.

"Take them. A special offering from one who loves and admires the faeries. You have nothing to fear from me," she sang in the same special cadence as she had hummed Mammoch to sleep.

The first of the guards reached out a hand to take one of the open packets. His hand did not reach far enough, as if he ran out of energy or resolve.

Hilde stepped forward and held her breath. Too close. Too close to dart away if they should grab her. She forced herself to maintain eye contact with her prey, humming her calming litany all the while.

She pushed the first packet into his outstretched hand. He raised it to his mouth and gobbled the half dozen berries. Before he had time to react, Bracken whisked the other two packets into the hands of the remaining guards. They, too, gobbled the food.

Immediately, their eyes rolled up, and they slumped to the floor snoring. The illusion of strength and height faded until they were no larger than Hilde herself. Their swords were merely long blades of river grass—they still had sharp edges that could slice unwary fingers. And their wicked-looking wings became gray-and-brown butterfly appendages with soft, round edges.

Nick hugged her shoulders. "Thank you," he said.

She leaned into him, grateful for his gentle support when

her knees turned to water in relief at the success of her bold scheme.

"Lead on," Little John gestured for Bracken to proceed into the main cave.

They traversed a narrow and twisted cavern, bare walls, broken by seams of crystal that reflected the faint moonlight just enough to keep them from stumbling into the walls or over imperfections in the floor.

"This all looks strange," Bracken said turning and staring all around. "I know everything Underhill is illusion. I know that the tapestries and lighting are not real, have never been real. But I've grown so used to them, I forget how plain and ugly this place is."

Even as he spoke, his wings took on more green color and strength, snapping outward in crisp imitation of new ferns growing abundantly and vibrantly on the hillside.

The passageway grew narrower as it wound deeper within the Mound. Little John's shoulders brushed the dirt walls, scraping at his leather jerkin and linen shirt. He turned sideways and took smaller, more cautious steps.

The light grew dimmer and the air cooler with each step. His instincts made his eyes droop and his blood flow sluggishly, as they would before a long winter's sleep . . . .

A wall of noise from panicky voices and untuned string instruments slammed into Little John. His steps faltered. But his eyes opened, and his mind grew alert.

Ahead of him, the cave expanded into a vast cavern. His party of rescuers spread out into a semicircle, leaving space for him in the middle with his back to their escape route.

Screeching voices and pounding drums warned that the hill had been breached. Strangers approached.

All eyes lifted toward a blaze at the center, a tower of swirling air and flame that rose ever higher toward one of the hidden exits at the summit of the hill.

Little John's feet wiggled and dug into the floor of the cave trying to form roots. His heart pounded loudly in his ears. Fear stabbed at his limbs and his heart.

"No." He knew his mouth worked, but he could hear nothing other than the cacophony of distressed faeries all around him. Dirt and sticks and rocks that might also have been furniture swirled into the churning storm. At its center hovered two figures, writhing in the unnatural wind. One was Jane.

Not again. He would not lose his Jane again. There had to be a way to extract her from the clutch of the mad Faery Queen who held Jane's long braid of hair.

"Shoot her!" Jane yelled, clutching her head close to the queen's twiggy grasp. "Archer, shoot her now!"

"No!" Little John broke through his numbness. "Robin, by all that you hold holy, if you shoot, Jane will fall to her death."

"Shoot the Starfire instead," Bracken said, pointing to a glowing crack in the wall on the far side of the cavern.

Robin swiveled his head between the lightning at the center of the cavern and the source of Faery power.

"Either way, she falls," Robin said to Little John.

Bracken grabbed an arrow from Robin's quiver and dashed toward the glowing crack that now pulsed and drew the attention of all the faeries. Two dozen of them flew in hot pursuit of the renegade Bracken.

Will Scarlett strummed a chord on his harp that matched the vibration of the throbbing light. He sang something soothing and yet irate, trying to capture and make sense of the wild noise.

Elena streamed out of Nick's sleeve, pulsing as she hovered in front of Little John. "Think with your head and not your heart, silly boy. Master Archer, I have need of your bow once more."

Little John shook his head to clear his mind of looping thoughts of watching his beloved die crumpled on the cave floor, broken and bleeding.

"Have you forgotten how to play catch?" Elena giggled as she swirled into a glowing strand of light fitting neatly against Robin's bowstring as he drew it taut.

Little John looked up, following the swirling progress of the column of fire and air. He couldn't judge how the storm would dump Jane and the Faery Queen.

Far above him, Jane twisted and flipped, trying . . . he couldn't tell what she did, only that the strain of the queen's grasp on her hair drew her features upward in a tight grimace as her hands fought the twiggy fingers.

And then . . . "Do what you must, as I do what I must. But I will not live as her slave any longer," Jane screamed. One hand twined inside her trailing skirts and came up bearing a minute strand of something that glinted in the uncertain light.

A needle. A silver needle that Jane could wield, but a faery could not.

Queen Mab's eyes went wide in horror. She screeched and loosened her grip.

Jane reversed her hold so that she dug her fingers from her left hand into Mab's wrist and followed with a hard jab from her right. The needle penetrated faery skin and drew smoke.

Mab screamed in pain, completely dropping her hold on Jane.

At the same moment, Robin loosed Elena through the crack in the far wall. Blinding yellow light exploded from the crack, filling the cavern, leaving no shadows, no place to hide. Then the thunder of cracking rock nearly deafened Little John. His natural urge to retreat into a tree, any tree, twisted his mind.

He couldn't think. Couldn't see. Couldn't hear.

And Jane writhed in the tower of wind, dropping closer to the ground with each pounding heartbeat.

"I'm free!" Jane exclaimed as she fell through the twisting storm of spiraling air and dust.

Little John swallowed the lump of fear in his throat and dashed across the vast room trying desperately to stay beneath his love.

Thirty-One

ollow, Elena called to Nick as she took on the form of a pulsing arrow of light. Robin had moved to stand directly in front of the source of the throbbing glow.

The intensity of the light made him wince and squint. He wanted to put his hand in front of his eyes as a shield but was afraid he'd miss something vital.

Dazed and uncertain, he grabbed Hilde's hand and dragged her to the crack in the far wall. He figured that whatever Elena planned, she'd need him close by when she finished.

The arrow zinged past his ear straight into the narrow opening.

"What?" Hilde asked. She looked around, trying to take in all the little spots of action.

Nick's gaze followed Elena. He tugged Hilde's hand to draw her attention.

As he hurried to follow the little goddess, Nick watched the marble tile floors crumble to dust and the elaborate tapestries of wild hunting scenes fade and shred. The energy required of the Faery Queen to maintain the illusions now went into the violent twisting storm of dirt, debris, and flashes of dry lightning.

He and Hilde needed to be far away from that vortex before the entire world of Faery imploded, trapping the only two mortals in the collapse. He had an idea, but he didn't have Elena in his pocket to save even himself.

At the crack, the pulsing yellow light of a benign noonday sun took on the hues of a fiery dawn, and then darker into true blazing flames, the kind that wiped out huge swaths of forests after a hot and dry summer, sparked by lightning.

He had only the comforting dull light of Elena's arrow to lead them on. Unlike a true arrow, she did not fly straight, but conformed to the twists and turns of the passageway until it opened into a new cavern.

As vast as the great hall where the faeries lived, this one was set up like an old Roman amphitheater he'd seen in drawings. Broad shelves of rock led downward into a deep bowl. At the center of the depression rested a huge, uncut yellow gem. Crystal glinted through strands of raw rock encasing the stone. Was it topaz? He'd never seen one, only read about them.

Bracken flitted about the stone, low and high and on all sides, chipping at the sharper edges of yellow with his flint broadhead arrow. Tiny flakes and stones drifted to the ground, lying inert and dull away from the parent stone. Then Bracken swooped down and gathered up three of the largest pieces, secreting them inside his tunic.

"I'll not be broken along with the rest of Mab's idiots," he chortled. "I will no longer have to come to the Starfire because I'll carry it with me."

His restored wings took on a new vibrancy as he flew upward, ever upward, far beyond the pointed tip of the Starfire stone and through a tiny opening to the night sky. The brightness of the Midsummer moon blotted out his silhouette.

"What just happened?" Hilde asked.

"I don't know. But Elena has paused in her approach." The arrow of light, dulled in contrast to the glowing heart of Faery, circled the stone, losing speed and power with each passage.

"Hurry, my lady goddess. We are running out of time, and you are running out of power."

With his words, the cave walls shook, and new cracks opened in the floor.

Nick braced himself with one hand on the wall and the other still clutching Hilde's.

Elena apparently made a decision and lined herself up with her chosen target on the stone, then raced forward.

Nick felt her close her eyes and heard her silent prayer to all the powers of universe.

The arrow penetrated the stone.

Nothing happened.

Nick despaired at losing his companion. His belly and his mind felt empty. His head seemed to lift from his body. His eyes couldn't keep up with it.

Clenching his eyes closed, he waited for a seeming eternity.

Just as he knew he couldn't hide from the truth any longer, a heaviness plunked into his sleeve.

Hold your breath. Your life depends upon you not breathing!

Nick obeyed.

But he had to watch as much as possible.

The fabric of the air within the cavern ripped apart in blinding bolts. Then the stone rocked on its base. Tiny movements that grew and arced into larger sways.

Dozens of faeries darted in. Each gathered a fragment of stone and fled upward, out of the Faery Mound and into the wild.

"I can't stand any longer," Hilde wailed. She tried to pull her slippery, sweating hand free of Nick's as she dropped to her knees.

Don't let go of her!

Was that Tuck's voice or Elena's?

Nick wasn't sure which, but he knew he couldn't speak and continue to hold his breath. Easier to follow Hilde to the floor, ducking a fallen piece of the ceiling, and clutching her tighter.

Oh, please let me pass out now!

The floor opened along a seam of lesser rock that crumbled. Splinters of the stone exploded outward, driving shafts into the solid rock of the cave.

Another piece of the roof dropped.

Hilde screamed in pain.

Still, Nick clung to her hand and kept his breath within himself.

The edges of Nick's vision darkened, followed by blinding sparkles. Then . . . nothing.

Jane welcomed the release of Mab's clutching grasp of her head. Her scalp continued to prickle with pinpoints of pain.

At the same time, air whooshed up around her, flaming hot and icy cold in splotches. She almost welcomed the crumpling of her body against the jagged rocks on the floor that had been furniture and a smooth dance floor only moments before.

But Little John, her magnificent giant of a man, scuttled about, arms extended, trying to stay beneath her. She had hope of survival, if only long enough to relish his embrace once more.

The earth, cracking and quaking, broke through the screams of the faeries escaping through any portal they could find. Three of them jammed together, blocking one exit as they all tried to fit through the too-small opening at the same time.

A wild wind grabbed hold and threw her sideways then jerked her back. Below her, John had trouble keeping up with her. The air needed her to linger and play a bit, delaying her fall.

Yellow fire streamed out of the crack that led to the inner cavern. Pieces of the yellow jewel defied logic and constriction, ejecting into the main cavern.

One shaft, as long as Jane was tall, aimed above her, seeking . . . seeking bits of itself to join with.

Mab screamed and tried to fly higher and faster than the missile aiming for her heart.

Six other faeries blocked her way as they scrambled to escape the maelstrom within the cave.

The piece of Starfire sped up with the fleeing queen until
it tore through her.

Mab fell, a withered old hag made of twigs and moss. A
splinter of a broken yellow jewel pierced her heart and dragged
her down faster than Jane. The bitter old queen broke apart
and scattered across the floor.

Jane couldn't help but laugh, choking on the dust and debris filling the twisting storm that held her captive.

And then . . . then the entire cavern, all of the Faery
Mound exploded. She dropped into the momentary stillness.

Jane closed her eyes, expecting physical pain to fill her as
she died, finally free of the mental anguish she'd endured for
so long.

"I've got you, my love," Little John whispered to her even
as his arms tightened around her body. "But we have to get
out of here. Now!"

Jane opened her eyes to the continuing devastation of her
prison. Little John leaped with the long strides of a forest giant
come to life. Three steps to cross the hall. Shorter steps ate up
the twisted passageway to the outside.

And then she gulped fresh night air and watched the moon
begin its drop toward morning.

She clung tightly to Little John's neck and breathed in the
fresh scent of new green life that defined him.

He paused in his mile-eating stride to kiss her gently.

Her heart woke and rejoiced.

Thirty-Two

"W here are we?" Hilde asked, blinking rapidly at the rising sun. A light dew sparkled on the tips of grass blades, and the air warmed rapidly. By the time her eyes had adjusted to the changing light, she made out three roads meeting and veering off into new directions. She sat in the island of wild greenery still holding Nick's hand and saw Tuck sprawled prone on the other side of him.

"The crossroads?" Nick said, stretching his arms and legs. Then he discovered his hand still entwined with Hilde's, and he grinned.

She jerked her hand free of his, uncertain what she was supposed to do about this growing bond between them.

He partially sat up, bracing himself on his elbows and fore-arms, and looked in all directions. Then he patted his volumi-nous sleeves, as he often did.

"The crossroads," he affirmed.

Hilde looked behind them and realized they sat in the shadow of a huge stone cross with an inscribed circle connecting the cross arms.

"It didn't used to hurt so much," Tuck groaned, lifted his head a tad, and dropped it back down, face in the grass.

"How did you get here?" Nick asked coming alert and up to a sitting position.

"How did any of us get here?" Hilde added. She wanted to trace the knotted design on the cross and examine the tiny flowered plants growing at its base. "And where is here?"

"It's magic," Tuck said as he rolled onto his back and studied the few white and puffy clouds in the sky as it brightened to a deep and soothing blue. "Nick carries the statue of the pagan goddess Elena. She allows him to save himself by holding his breath until he passes out. When he awakes, he is always here."

"That pitcher thing?" Hilde stared at the small distortion in his crumpled and filthy robe.

He looked at her with an eyebrow raised in query.

"I've watched you commune with it."

He relaxed and lay back, arms crossed behind his head.

"Tuck carried her for a while," he said. "Is that why you are here?"

"Only insofar as I heard her command you to follow her into the inner cavern. She had to have a purpose for that, for she never does anything without a reason. So I followed also, and the moment things started flying apart, I grabbed hold of your robe and held on for dear life. Good thing I did. I believe the Faery Mound is no more." Slowly, he sat up, testing each joint and muscle as he moved. He groaned twice before he managed enough leverage to set his back correctly.

Hilde wanted to aid him, but a stern look from Nick kept her in place.

"I used to rejoice at being mostly human," Tuck said when he finally achieved a sitting position. "I thought it brought me closer to God. But I've learned through the years that God loves all of us: Woodwose, Wild Folk, and human, whether noble or serf. It is my life's work to minister to them all. But growing old is painful." He groaned again, pressing both hands against his lower back.

"Do you need to return to the abbey and the physician's potions?" Nick asked. He turned and rose to his knees, concern drawing his mouth into a deep frown. "He and I will keep your presence secret so the sheriff and king don't find out that you aren't in Paris or Rome."

"Or Athens or Cairo." Tuck quirked a mischievous smile. Then he groaned and clutched his head. "Not yet, boy. Not yet. The temptation to remain at the abbey and risk discovery is too much. My work outside the cloister is not finished. It won't be until after the war between King John and Pope Innocent concludes." The sun highlighted his profile as he turned his head to the east to bask in the warmth of the new day.

She knew that face . . . .

"You aren't just a venerable member of the Woodwose, are you?" Hilde asked. Something resembling truth niggled at her mind.

"For now I am."

"But, before, you held a position of authority that Sister Mary Margaret respected."

"Aye, child. I did. I've tried to keep the abbey and the convent balanced and functional without the heavy hand of the senior clergy. It's difficult to keep the peace when everyone, and I mean *everyone*, thinks they have inherited the right to speak for me, deserving or not. As one of Sister Marie Josef's victims, you should realize that."

Hilde hung her head. "I believe that her mind became unbalanced before she sought safety in the convent."

Tuck nodded. "Convents have always offered refuge and sanctuary to those crippled by life outside those stout walls. Some people are beyond our ability to heal. For them, it is best we keep them safe from the outside world, and keep the outside world safe from them." He sighed and scrambled to his feet, appearing much younger than he had a few moments ago.

Hilde needed to know more about the old man before she could figure out how to help him.

"Once you found your way out of the convent, I knew you'd be an asset to the Woodwose. Finding the right place for people is part of maintaining the balance of life, of village and castle, of Church and everyday life." He looked at each of the three roads, as if deciding which would take him where he needed to go.

"Nick, it is time for you to choose. Will you return Elena to her niche in the crypt to wait for another student to teach, and then join the Woodwose? Or will you return yourself to the abbey and make penance to Prefect Andrew for your absence?"

Nick drew the tiny, three-faced pitcher from his pocket and stared at it long and hard.

"For now, I think my place is at the abbey. I have much to learn. And I will be safe there until I can choose." He tore his gaze away from the silver talisman of an ancient people and a nearly forgotten religion and looked up at Hilde. "I'm sorry, Hilde. Part of me wants to stay with you, protect you as Dom could not. Another part of me knows that I am one of the few people who can keep Prefect Andrew and Father Blaine in balance. Perhaps later, you will help me choose which path is right for me and for all the people in and around the forest."

"Later, then." Hilde offered a hand up to him. "I do not know which road to take today. So I will walk the wild with the others until I can learn where I truly belong."

"We have choices," Nick whispered to himself. Then aloud he proclaimed, "We have choices! What we do with this life is our choice."

You are no longer a silly boy. Just a boy with much to learn.